HENRIETTA CI
INQUE.

VERNON LODER was a pseudonym for John George Haslette Vahey (1881-1938), an Anglo-Irish writer who also wrote as Henrietta Clandon, John Haslette, Anthony Lang, John Mowbray, Walter Proudfoot and George Varney. He was born in Belfast and educated at Ulster, Foyle College, and Hanover. Four years after he graduated college he was apprenticed to an architect and later tried his hand at accounting before turning to fiction writing full time.

According to the copy of Loder's *Two Dead* (1934): "He once wrote a novel in twenty days on a boarding-house table, and had it serialised in U.S.A. and England under another name . . . He works very quickly and thinks two hours a day in the morning quite enough for any one. He composes direct on a machine and does not re-write." While perhaps this is an exaggeration, Vahey was highly prolific, author of at least forty-four novels between 1926 and 1938.

Vahey's series characters were Inspector Brews, Chief Inspector R.J. "Terry" Chace, Donald Cairn (as Loder) and William Power, Penny & Vincent Mercer (as Henrietta Clandon).

With a solid reputation for witty characterisation and "the effortless telling of a good story" (*Observer*), Vahey's popularity was later summed up in the *Sunday Mercury*: "We have no better writer of thrill mystery in England."

Henrietta Clandon Mysteries
Available from Dean Street Press

Inquest
Good by Stealth
This Delicate Murder
Power on the Scent

HENRIETTA CLANDON

INQUEST

With an introduction by Curtis Evans

DEAN STREET PRESS

Published by Dean Street Press 2020

Copyright © 1933 Henrietta Clandon

Introduction Copyright © 2020 Curtis Evans

All Rights Reserved

First published in 1933 by Geoffrey Bles

Cover by DSP

ISBN 978 1 913054 89 2

www.deanstreetpress.co.uk

STRING PUZZLES BY THE COZY FIRESIDE

The Mysteries of Henrietta Clandon

> Who is "Henrietta Clandon"? We don't know—we wish we did!" Anyhow, "she" has written one of the best murder novels we have read in a long time.
>
> --*newspaper advertisement by Geoffrey Bles, publisher of the Henrietta Clandon detective novels*

TODAY we know, as the coy "she" above hinted, that Golden Age mystery writer Henrietta Clandon, author of seven detective novels between 1933 and 1938, was in fact a man: John George Haslette Vahey (1881-1938). Women mystery writers adopting the guise of masculine or sexually ambiguous pseudonyms was a common enough practice during the Golden Age of detective fiction, as it had been with their Victorian and Edwardian sisters. Margery Allingham wrote a trio of mysteries as Maxwell March, Americans Dorothy Blair and Evelyn Page five as Roger Scarlett and Lucy Beatrice Malleson over three score as Anthony Gilbert, while the names Ngaio Marsh, Moray Dalton, E.C.R. Lorac and E.X. Ferrars--the latter three respectively pseudonyms of Katherine Mary Dalton Renoir, Edith Caroline Rivett and Morna Doris MacTaggart, aka Elizabeth Ferrars--left readers in doubt as to the authors' actual genders and male book reviewers often referring, in their early years, to the excellent books by Messrs. Marsh, Dalton, Lorac and Ferrars. When in doubt, assume it is male, so the thinking then seemed to go. (More recently the late scholar and mystery fan Jacques Barzun referred to Moray Dalton as a "neglected man" while another, Jared Lobdell, speculated that "Moray Dalton" might have been yet another pseudonym of prolific British Golden Age mystery writer Cecil John Charles Street.)

It was commonly believed, in those days, that men were more credible to readers as writers of detective fiction. It also was presumed that readers of detective fiction were predominantly male as well. "[T]he detective story... is primarily a man's novel," emphatically declared a woman, American Marjorie Nicolson, then serving as dean of the English department at Smith College, in "The Professor and the Detective," an essay originally published in the *Atlantic Monthly* in 1929. "Many women dislike it heartily, or at best accept it as a device to while away hours on the train. And while we do all honor to the three or four women who have written surpassingly good detective stories of the purest type, we must grant candidly that the great bulk of our detective stories today are being written by men."

This was an attitude which began decidedly to change, however, with the rise of Britain's so-called four Queens of Crime in the 1930s: Agatha Christie (first mystery novel published in 1920), Dorothy L. Sayers (1923), Margery Allingham (1928) and Ngaio Marsh (1934), not to mention a slew of additional talented British women detective writers, such as the aforementioned Anthony Gilbert and others like Patricia Wentworth, Moray Dalton, Gladys Mitchell, Annie Haynes, E.C.R. Lorac, Joan Cowdroy, Molly Thynne, Helen Simpson, Ianthe Jerrold, Elizabeth Gill, Josephine Bell, Mary Fitt, Dorothy Bowers, Harriet Rutland and, coming along a bit later in the 1940s, Christianna Brand and Elizabeth Ferrars. (In the United States there were, aside from Roger Scarlett, an admittedly minor player in the world of Golden Age detective fiction, the hugely popular Mary Roberts Rinehart and Mignon Eberhart and their many followers.) By the late Thirties and early Forties readers and reviewers alike had concluded that classic detective fiction was a form of fiction at which women excelled as much as, if not more then, the male of the species. It was, indeed, the men who might have been well advised to watch their backs, for fear of fatal feminine thrusts from wicked-bladed letter openers or jewel-encrusted hatpins.

It is this altered environment which led to the appearance, with the novel *Inquest* in 1933, of another purported woman

INQUEST

crime writer, one who was emphatically a lady in tone, if not in fact: Henrietta Clandon. In the hands of Dorothy L. Sayers and, I would argue, Agatha Christie, with such novels as *Strong Poison, Have His Carcase, The Murder of Roger of Ackroyd* and *The Murder at the Vicarage*, there had arisen so-called "manners mystery" murder fiction, filled not just with corpses, crimes and clues, but witty and sardonic observation of people and social mores. (Male authors Anthony Berkeley/Francis Iles and C.H.B. Kitchin were also signal contributors in this regard.) Margery Allingham would follow suit in 1934 with the marvelous *Death of a Ghost*, accompanied by Ngaio Marsh's debut novel *A Man Lay Dead*, but Henrietta Clandon actually had already anticipated the two younger Crime Queens with a fully developed manners mystery in 1933.

When he created Henrietta Clandon, John Haslette Vahey was no new hand at mystery mongering. Born on March 5, 1881 in Strandtown, a district of Belfast, Northern Ireland, Vahey was the middle son of Herbert Vahey, a superintendent of Inland Revenue (i.e., tax collector), and his wife Jane Lowry Vahey, a daughter of a wealthy Belfast watchmaker and jeweler. Like his contemporary, author and crime writer E.R. Punshon, "Jack" Vahey, as he was known, after walking away from careers in business around the turn of the century (in Vahey's case insurance and accountancy), had started writing fiction professionally. Vahey published his first novel in 1909, while residing at a Bournemouth boarding house with his elder brother, who also wrote fiction, and he began turning out mysteries in the classic mold by the late 1920s, primarily under the pen name Vernon Loder, whose work recently has been highly praised by vintage mystery authorities Nigel Moss and John Norris. (Moss calls Vernon Loder "a paradigm of the English Golden Age mystery writer.") Jack Vahey's other known pen names—those besides his two most notable ones, Vernon Loder and Henrietta Clandon--are John Haslette, Anthony Lang, John Mowbray and the hobbit-ish Walter Proudfoot; under the entire tribe, whose output included mysteries, mainstream, adventure and espionage novels, and school tales, he ultimately produced sixty-five books, making him a prolific author indeed. Vahey boasted that he once composed a novel over a span of twenty days at a table at the boarding house, afterward serializing it in both the United Kingdom and the United States under different pseudonyms.

By 1933, when Jack Vahey at the age of fifty-two created Henrietta Clandon, he had as Vernon Loder already published eight detective novels in five years, and no fewer than three additional Loder novels would appear in print in 1933. Many of the Vernon Loder titles were published in both the UK (with the prestigious Collins Crime Club) and the US (with Morrow, publisher of Christopher Bush and, shortly in the future, Erle Stanley Gardner and Carter Dickson.) Why, then, one might ask, did Vahey start publishing under yet another pseudonym?

When one reads the Clandons, the "why" becomes readily apparent, for Vahey with this new line clearly was attempting to do something different, and more ambitious, with his crime fiction than he had with Vernon Loder, et al., as pleasing as some of the Loder novels are. The Henrietta Clandon novels are the most carefully crafted mysteries that Vahey ever wrote, models of manners mystery which present to the reader wittily epigrammatic and cuttingly sardonic murder in its most deceptively cozy British guises of country houses and villages—quintessential malice domestic, as it were. Critics responded favorably to the Clandons, sensing an enticing new spice of mystery in the air, one which seemed exquisitely feminine.

Dorothy L. Sayers herself welcomed Henrietta Clandon's *Inquest* in the pages of the *Sunday Times*, where Sayers was the crime fiction reviewer from 1933 to 1935, as "an attractive and promising piece of puzzle making." She added that the "book is very well written, the dialogue being quite exceptionally fresh and well-managed, and the characterization good," before adding encouragingly: "This appears to be Miss Henrietta Clandon's first detective story; I hope we shall hear more from her again." Score one for the ladies!

Of a later Clandon novel, *Rope by Arrangement*, Sayers keenly pronounced, employing a most apt image, that the novel's merit lay "in a kind of quiet tortuousness; to read it is rather like working out an intricate little string puzzle by the fireside. . . . the tale makes very agreeable reading." Nor was Sayers alone in her praise of Clandon. Concerning *This Delicate Murder*, Torquemada (noted crossword puzzle designer Edward Powys Mathers) in the *London Observer* praised its "wit" and the "nearly watertight impeccability" of its puzzle. For his part crime writer Milward Kennedy, Sayers' successor at the *Sunday Times*, in reviewing the superb inverted poison pen mystery *Good by Stealth*, which recalls not only works by Francis Iles but ones by Anthony Rolls and Richard Hull, lauded the author's "gift for irony in the depiction of the criminal's mind." An able literary limner like Henrietta Clandon, observed Kennedy admiringly, "can suit style to subject, and even enable us to see character in its true colour though revealed by colour-blind eyes." Perhaps Anthony Berkeley, reviewing crime fiction as Francis Iles, summed up best when he declared that "Henrietta Clandon's novels are always welcome. She has developed a style of her own in crime fiction."

Sadly, the steady series of Clandon mysteries was abruptly halted after the appearance of the seventh Clandon novel, *Fog off Weymouth* ("quite charming narration," pronounced Torquemada), which was published in March 1938, just three months before Jack Vahey's death at age fifty-seven on June 15. I do not know what killed the author, but only three years before his death he had flippantly boasted, in a letter to the *London Observer* signed "Vernon Loder," that "I have not spent a day in bed in thirty-two years," despite the fact that "I add great quantities of salt to my food, and vast quantities of sugar to tea, coffee and lemonade." As a remedy against the chronic throat inflammation he had suffered between the ages of fourteen and twenty-one, he had taken up smoking eucalyptus cigarettes (forerunners of menthols, recently banned in the state of Massachusetts). Salt, sugar and cigarettes—perhaps Jack's death should not have come as a surprise. It will be recalled that thriller writer Edgar Wallace, who died from a diabetic coma and double pneumonia in 1932, consumed copious amounts of sugary tea.

At the time of his untimely demise Vahey resided with his wife, Gertrude Crowe Barendt, formerly a music teacher from Liverpool, at a flat in affluent Branksome Park in Bournemouth (today Poole). A final Vernon Loder, *Kill in the Ring*, a boxing murder tale far removed from the milieu of Henrietta Clandon, was published in October and, after that, Vahey, who left no children, was largely forgotten. His elder brother, Herbert Lowry Vahey, a more peripatetic author than Jack, survived him by two decades, but though he wed as well, he left no children. Jack's younger brother, Samuel Lowry Vahey, an insurance executive who migrated to Canada and later Houston, Texas, predeceased Jack by a decade.

Where did Jack Vahey get his mind for "delicate murder," his ability to compose a quietly tortuous mystery resembling "an intricate little string puzzle"? He was educated at Foyle College, Londonderry, Northern Ireland and in the city of Hanover in the state of Saxony, Germany (which perhaps helps explain his later marriage to an Anglo-German wife), and his favored hobbies were shooting and fishing, but perhaps he carried within himself something of his canny Scots-Irish maternal grandfather, John Lowry, who died in Belfast in 1886, when Vahey was five years old. Old John Lowry was a highly respected maker and retailer of watches and chronometers (a time measuring instrument used in marine navigation to determine longitude), who owned a big shop in the High Street and did regular business as well in London. Pieces which Lowry designed are highly sought collector's items today. (For example, the website of David Penney's Antique Watch Store offers an exquisite "top quality" nineteenth-century chronometer by Lowry with gold hands and a "very rare sapphire roller.") At the old man's death, he left an estate that was valued at, in modern worth, some 470,000 pounds (over 600,000 dollars), indicating that he was a top person in his field.

A well-plotted Golden Age mystery, after all, resembles not only a string puzzle or Rubik's Cube, but a clock--whether or not unbreakable alibis and railway timetables are involved. Vahey's grandfather John Lowry possessed more than the consummate skill to construct intricate mechanical devices, however; he had, as well, personal experience with criminals. In 1867 Lowry, sounding like detective writer R. Austin's Freeman famed medical jurist sleuth Dr. John Thorndyke, testified at the criminal prosecution of one Bernard O'Kane for allegedly passing counterfeit coins around Belfast. At the trial, it was reported, Lowry established that the coins at issue were fake, being made of "base metal." Eleven years earlier, burglars had daringly invaded Lowry's shop at 66 High Street. The watchmaker had spent the evening and early morning hours on the roof of his house, where he had been engaged in "comparing his time by transit observations of the stars" until one o'clock in the morning. During this time he heard noises on the roof, but took this to be merely the nocturnal perambulations of a cat. Later that morning, when the entire household had gone to bed, a felonious party took a pane of glass out of a skylight and with a rope descended into the house. Fortunately, "the shop being well secured, the goods locked in a large safe, a party well-armed sleeping in a room connected with the shop, and doors properly barred inside, the robber or robbers could get no farther than the kitchen and back room, from which they took several articles of dress and even some eatables," departing without detection. It is the sort of setting that with embellishment might have inspired Edgar Wallace's famous mystery *The Clue of the New Pin* (1923), in which a shady businessman who keeps all his spoils hidden away at his home in a massive basement vault, securely locked up at night to make it impregnable, is found shot to death, inside his own locked vault. There is no gun anywhere to be found, merely a single pin. . . .

Great outré stuff for a classic Golden Age mystery (though in violation of the rules of Father Ronald Knox and the Detection Club, a mysterious "Chinaman" lurks), which might have been just the thing for that earnest fellow Vernon Loder. In Jack Vahey's more up-to-date and sophisticated Henrietta Clandon tales, however, finical readers should rest assured that murder is something altogether more refined, a delicacy which can be served to polite society in the drawing room, along with buttered scones and tea. Just keep an eye out for arsenic and acid bon mots.

Inquest and *Power on the Scent*

INQUEST, the debut Henrietta Clandon detective novel, has as its setting that most fabled of locales in Golden Age mystery fiction: a house party at an English country mansion. The mansion in question is Hebble Chace, Wiltshire residence of Anglo-French Marie Hoe-Luss, widow of recently deceased English businessman William Hoe-Luss. It is said that William Hoe-Luss expired during a house party at his French estate, Château de Luss, from the accidental consumption of deadly death cap mushrooms; and now his widow intriguingly has reassembled all of the original guests from the fatal French house party for a second time, this time at Hebble Chace, with the addition of Hoe-Luss' English physician, Dr. Eric Soame, the narrator of the tale. When one of the houseguests at Hebble Chace falls to his death from an upper story window, after announcing his belief that there were no death cap mushrooms on the grounds of Château de Luss, the question arises: Did this person fall or was he pushed? Added to this question is another highly pertinent one: Was William Hoe-Luss actually murdered? Read on and find out in the novel which Dorothy L. Sayers hailed, when it was originally published in 1933, as "an attractive and promising piece of puzzle making."

Certain fictional Great Detectives, like Wilkie Collins' Sergeant Cuff and Rex Stout's Nero Wolfe, have famously had rather a nose for blooms, but in Henrietta Clandon's sixth novel, *Power on the Scent*, it is the murder victim—if victim of murder he is—who was a prizewinning grower of roses. When stockbroker Montague Morgan--renowned among flower fanciers as the originator of the "Rennavy Rose"--is found mysteriously dead in the garden at his rural residence in the English village of Malpertuis (pronounced Malpert), attorney William Power, familiar to Henrietta Clandon readers from three previous novels, is called into the case on behalf of his client, Morgan's dismal and disgruntled nephew Charles Sibbins, who would make an almost book perfect suspect in his uncle's death, if that death, as seems likely, indeed proves murder. For, Gertrude Stein notwithstanding, a rose is not always a rose—or, more exactly, a rose is sometimes something more than a rose, at least when that rose comes dusted with cocaine, like the prize specimen that was found in the dead man's lapel!

Power invites his good friends (and Clandon series characters) the Mercers, Penny and Vincy, insouciant husband-and-wife detective novelists who are ever eager for real life "copy," to Malpertuis to help him investigate the matter of Morgan's strange demise, which implicates as well beautiful widow Mrs. Davy-Renny and the several men who hovered around her, like bees to the most fragrant of flowers. Also on the scene are series professional sleuths Inspector Voce and Sergeant Bohm of Scotland Yard. With all this sleuthing power on the scent, murder surely will out!

Curtis Evans

Chapter I
SIX MONTHS AFTER

During the last ten years of his life, I was medical adviser to Mr Hoe-Luss.

He was simply William Luss at first. With an overflowing measure of prosperity, the Hoe was added unto him later. It was, like so many other things, optional for the first year or two. Then, substantiated by a hyphen, it was used, perhaps not compulsorily, shall we say, tactfully?

Willie Luss was not really a snob. But there is progress in a hyphen, while two names are demonstrably better than one.

When I first came in contact with him, he was already rich. When he died he left over a quarter of a million.

I had two good reasons for liking him. He was always pleasant to me; and could be relied on year after year to cover my income-tax and rent. He was never really ill, but often very nervous. Then he had a household of servants who, with considerable leisure at their disposal, could afford to be reasonably ill at various seasons of the year.

Hoe-Luss began as an iron-master and, later, formed some connection with a firm in Lorraine. He met and married Marie Hurst there (she was on a holiday with some relations at Metz), and this marriage was afterwards the source of considerable trouble.

He was fifty-three, and Marie thirty, at the date of their wedding. Her father—an Englishman of some note as a consulting engineer—died when she was twelve. He left his widow a quite respectable income, on condition that Marie was to be educated and brought up in England.

So Marie Hoe-Luss (née Hurst) became an Englishwoman. All that part of her, that is, which could be Anglicised. That which could not comprised: her dark, quick eyes, her (Norman) dislike of spending uselessly, her habit of gesticulation, and her physical charms, which were of a completely Gallic type.

It was perhaps natural that all Hoe-Luss's relations, with expectations equally natural, should refer to her as 'that designing Frenchwoman.'

I expect she did. She had a taste for intrigue of a petty type, and was a schemer by inclination. While her husband lived, she was kind to him—devoted, he said. I feel sure she had a strong sense of duty. He gave her a fortune; she did her best to repay him in the only way open to her.

I spent several holidays on his yacht. But, at her request, I believe, he put down the yacht, and in the last year of his life bought a large property on the Isère.

This was a rather fine property, including a large château, and a great many farms. These latter, I think, he leased out on some peculiar, but profitable, French system by which the farmer pays no rent, but divides his profits with the owner of the land.

It was at the Château de Luss (as he renamed it) that he died. I did not accompany him. He had a house-warming and a house-party, all (Marie legally) British.

I have heard so much about this sad event, from so many different sources, that I know very little definitely about it. It was hinted that Hoe-Luss died of eating fungi which he took to be mushrooms, or of fungi administered as mushrooms. It is obviously a matter of opinion. Marie of course would approve the fungi. The Gaul, the Norman especially, likes to use unconsidered trifles, which others disdain.

I believe there was some sort of fudged-up inquiry into the cause of death. But I am not familiar with the forensic medicine of our neighbours, and I am sure that the doctor called in did not send the unfortunate man's organs for the examination of a pathologist. He told the shocked house-party that the symptoms resembled those caused by eating fungi—*Amanita phalloidis*, perhaps. I am not sure of the exact species. And he was, to Marie's satisfaction, inclined to blame the fact on Hoe-Luss's English cook.

Marie knew that the English did not cook. This was not Chauvinism exactly, but an expression of her dislike for wilful waste and stringy vegetables. As she said, the English also did not know the difference between edible and poisonous fungi. They have only one sauce, and one mushroom.

One of his relatives, and the proverbial wild-horses could not drag the name from me, was ironically amused over the doctor's verdict. She said that the symptoms also resembled those caused by an irritant poison. But she knows very little of poisons, and I take that to be the result of unfulfilled hopes, and wrecked expectations.

Marie sold the château promptly. She grumbled at the probate's slow delays on this side. She had not realised that months must pass before an estate is settled, and a fortune handed over to the legatees.

She returned to Hoe-Luss's place in Wiltshire: Hebble Chace, Winstone. This was a fine house, of the Queen Anne period, standing high, and retaining most of its charming features, while perfectly and completely modernised as regards all those things that count.

I had a sort of expectation that she would ask me to come and see her when she returned from France. I was naturally interested in my former patient, who has left me the sum of five hundred pounds. But, although Hebble Chace is only four miles from my house, I was not asked to call. I wanted to call. There were still the expensive and leisured servants. But we doctors have a strict etiquette.

It was all the more surprising then, when, at the end of six months, I received a letter from Mrs Hoe-Luss asking me to stay a week. She was having a house-party. Some of the people I knew. And was this not the time when I usually took my holiday?

It fell in very well, for several reasons. I had arranged for a *locum tenens* that week. I had had a bad year, and would have to curtail my expenses for a while. I was anxious to know more about the English cook and the fungi; or, alternatively, the cause of death.

My own contribution to the debate, if any, was my knowledge that William Hoe-Luss had been passionately fond of mushrooms, and easily led by Marie. The data I had was very slender.

Had he eaten the dish of fungi *(Amanita phalloidis)* alone? And if so, why alone?

There are some people who cannot tolerate certain drugs, even foods, but I know of no one who can tolerate, in the medical sense, the poisonous varieties of fungi. There was no sickness, even temporary, among the members of the house-party at the château.

There was no proof that Hoe-Luss had eaten voraciously, or with a view to there being no waste. There was nothing left, however, of that fatal dish. The English cook, of course, threw the remains away. She gave evidence in a peculiarly British and aggressive spirit, saying that she never believed in eating weeds, and never would. She had thrown the 'muck' away.

It turned out that she had incinerated it. She agreed that she did so of her own volition. Even the female relation who made tendencious remarks to me admitted that Marie and the cook were at daggers drawn.

One of those men, so prevalent nowadays, who write detective stories, could have made a good thing of this. A cook with a grudge against her foreign-born mistress, with a fortune in prospect, might do something to throw suspicion on that mistress. Cook had done her duty under protest in this case. She said that Mr Hoe-Luss had gathered the 'weeds' in the park, and brought them to her to cook.

I don't think that he was seized with illness immediately after eating the fungi. I have been told that he went to his study, to work out some details of a business merger. He was found lying at the foot of the eight, narrow and crooked, stairs that led up to this chamber. He was quite dead then. Most of the guests had gone, it is said, to a picnic up the river. But there was some doubt about the times. And poisoning from these fungi is sometimes slow to develop.

I wondered about this new house-party. Since Marie had gone to live at Hebble Chace, she had cut down some of the staff, turned off one game-keeper, two gardeners, a groom, a chauffeur, and an able-bodied pensioner, who had lived on Hoe-Luss's bounty for many years. Also, she had begun to sell garden produce and flowers to a dealer. And now she was launching out in an entertainment to a number of people. Was this propitiatory, or premonitory? Every one of the relatives of her deceased husband had been passively unpleasant. Was she inviting them? And why, after ignoring me for six months, was she including me in the party?

I need hardly say that professional, not personal, interest led me to accept. A doctor does not like to see his patients die, but, if they must die, he is naturally anxious to know if any of his diagnoses were correct, and how far he had been able to distinguish between the fact and fiction of his patient's complaints. If you go so far as to suspect hob-nailed liver, for example, it is comforting and illuminating to hear that cirrhosis was the actual cause of death. It is crushing, but also valuable, to learn that the man you took to be a secret drinker is only, or was only, a martyr to indigestion.

Having been evaded by Marie for six months, it was strange that I met her out driving the day after I had accepted her invitation. She made her chauffeur draw up the car, asked me where I was going, and made me get up.

"I am glad you can come, doctor," she said, when I sat beside her. "You will be the eleventh. Yes, I am inviting all those who were with us at the château when poor William died."

"Have they all accepted?" I said lamely, for this seemed strange to me.

"Yes. Aunt Green and Sir Eugene Oliver are with me now. The rest come on Saturday," she said. "You have met them both?"

I assented. Aunt Green was really a cousin of Hoe-Luss. She was a sardonic old lady, and nobody's darling, I imagine. Eugene Oliver was a 'guinea-pig,' director of companies; flashy, sharp; a nominee of Caley Burton, the late Hoe-Luss's partner.

"I presume that probate is now a matter of the past?" I said. "It is always wearying."

She looked at me sharply. "You think so? Perhaps it is. Yes, your lawyers have made a bit out of it, and there have been duties and stamp fees to help out your Government."

"Everybody's doing it; has to," I murmured, as we drove into the village. "Well, I get off here, thank you."

"On Saturday, for lunch," said she.

"I hear you have a new cook," said I.

She smiled, but something in her eyes told me that this was where I definitely did 'get off.'

"I brought her from Paris, doctor."

"I hope she is a success," I said.

Chapter II
MISDEAL?

When I reached Hebble Chace on the Saturday, I found that only three more guests had turned up in time for lunch. One was Joe Hoe-Luss, the dead man's nephew, and his fiancée, Meriel Silger. And a Mrs Graves, who, I have been informed, had a good chance at one time of becoming Mrs William Hoe-Luss—a tiff, and the visit to Metz, alone intervening. I had not met her before, but she appeared to be a pleasant woman of forty or so, pretty for her age, very tolerant, very fond, one would imagine at first sight, of the woman who had supplanted her.

Joe Hoe-Luss was about thirty, and looked like a racing tout in good clothes. He was actually metallurgical expert to the iron firm, and superficially did not appear to be worried by the fact that his uncle had put him down for a hundred pounds, and a pair of London-made guns.

Meriel Silger had the air of a martyr to circumstances, and as this air had only been put on since Joe's uncle died, it had not yet settled properly on her face, which was pretty, if vacant of any noticeable intelligence.

"Joe was his nephew," she said to me once. "I do think—"

She dealt in these cut-off sentences, leaving you in no doubt as to their proper terminations. The fact is, according to Aunt Green, that Meriel became engaged to Joe when he was thought to be a holder of good cards. When all the honours went elsewhere, she felt aggrieved.

7 | INQUEST

I sat between Mrs Graves and 'Gene Oliver at lunch. Marie had Joe on her left and Meriel on her right, and talked very nicely to them about their marriage. She appeared to have forgotten that this was a sore subject. Or perhaps she hadn't.

Oliver looked at them, and then at me. "I suppose you heard all about it, Dr Soame? Rather odd, isn't it, that we should have the same crowd here that were over at the château when William conked out?"

He spoke quite softly, but Aunt Green heard it, and. cackled. "Hush, you young monster! Or at least abate your language."

"Oh, sorry," said 'Gene. "One gets into these slangy habits. But you did hear all about it?" he added to me.

Why did he want to know? I shook my head. "Something, of course. Certainly not all—unless that was all."

He nodded. "Reminds one of King John and the dish of lampreys—or was it John?"

I frowned at him significantly. "I am sure Mrs Hoe-Luss doesn't want the subject brought up again. She must be trying hard to forget it."

He giggled, and Aunt Green cackled again. "But how unkind!"

"Ask Meriel," said he. "Trying hard to forget it—that's decidedly good."

"And that is why we're here," said Aunt Green.

"Is there anything funny that I ought not to hear?" demanded our hostess suddenly.

"Certainly not," said 'Gene. "By the way, Joe, when is your fixture coming off? September, isn't it?"

"Ask Meriel," said Joe. "As I was saying, Marie, we have to cut out the idea of taking 'Hurdles.' The shooting is good, and I should have liked to try uncle's guns, but the rent's a bit above my figure."

"Well, everyone is hard up nowadays, or nearly—" said Meriel, and pouted.

Aunt Green whispered in my ear. "Dr Soame, you see our menagerie still growls over the bone! For a week too! A cheerful prospect."

You can see that I was in a fix. All these other people had got, or failed to get, what they wanted. They could afford to be unpleasant to Marie. But a country doctor when so many big places are empty is not in the happiest of positions. If I were to take sides, then I would have to grub a bit harder for my rent and income-tax.

"What about that merger that was in prospect at the time?" I asked Oliver hastily. "Gone west, I suppose."

He grinned. "Wait till Caley Burton comes. He'll tell you. You see, it was his proposition in the first place. He wanted William to join up with the 'Solidaris Tool Co.' Then our old friend discovered that Caley had batches of nominees who could have out-voted him, and there was the devil of a row."

He paused suddenly. Marie was looking at him. "I was just saying," he added, with his usual impudence, "that Burton was very keen on that merger with the 'Solidaris.'"

Joe flushed. "He wasn't the only one, young fellow!"

"I admit it freely," said 'Gene. "I was for it, all the time."

"Hammer-and-tongs, you see!" Aunt Green whispered to me. "How we love one another."

Meriel smiled most unpleasantly. "Sir Eugene is always frank. At least—"

Marie smiled at me. "You had better ask Mr Burton about it this afternoon, doctor."

I felt that this accusation of inquisitiveness was hard and undeserved. I had only mentioned the merger to get away from the acrid atmosphere of misdealt money.

"These big business affairs have an appeal to the layman," I pleaded. "How money is made, and so on."

"True," said Marie. "I am sure it interests you."

Joe cackled now, and Mrs Graves came to my aid. "I do think it is a quite fascinating subject," she murmured. "How some gain, and some lose."

"Who's being frank now?" asked Oliver.

"I have no idea what you mean," she replied timidly.

"All the better," said 'Gene. "But you wanted to know something more about the merger, Soame, didn't you?"

"Not at all," I assured him. "It was merely an idle question."

If this was an 'affair of vedettes' at lunch, I dreaded the idea of dinner; many dinners in fact. I had wondered why Marie invited this party to stay, I wondered still more when I realised that they had brought grudges for clubs, and hoped to lay them freely about her head, and each other's.

Oliver invited Joe and me to accompany him for a stroll in the park after lunch. But Joe said he was making up a four, and refused. Oliver took my arm, provided me with a cigar, and grinned at me affectionately.

"I suppose you know why we are all down here?" he asked me, as we walked across the springy grass a few minutes later.

I was not able to assure him that I knew nothing of the reason. I had begun to think that Marie, who was innately malicious, had asked them all down to upset each other. But it was difficult to put that into words.

"That business at the château," he told me, without waiting for an answer. "If you've ever played cards with Marie, you must know how keen she is on 'inquests.' This is an inquest."

"What?" I asked, in surprise.

"An inquest, my dear fellow. Who killed who, and so on."

"But surely that was decided, though there was no killing, strictly speaking."

"Everyone does not think so."

I looked horrified, and, better, I was horrified. "But there was no doubt about the plate of poisonous fungi?"

"None whatever. The cook cooked some. Wait a moment, though, there was a doubt if they were poisonous. The good woman threw the remains into a stove."

I smiled now. "Yes, I heard, or read, that. But since Hoe-Luss was poisoned after eating them, it is pretty evident that the fungi were not edible."

"Not so evident as it seems. There was the question of his neck."

"His neck? Whose neck?"

He stared. "Oh, I forgot. That didn't get into the papers. The French sawbones said it was irrelevant."

"My dear Oliver," I pleaded. "Do stick to the point. Are you suggesting that his throat was affected by the poison?"

He moved impatiently. "No, I was talking of his broken neck."

"His *broken* neck? Did he break his neck, and how?"

"That's the trouble," said Oliver sardonically. "I suppose bones can be broken after death?"

"Of course," I said. "But this is very surprising."

"That is what most of us said, until the doctor explained. He said William must have felt suddenly ill in his study, ran out for assistance, and tripped."

"And fell down the stairs?"

"Of which there were eight. The château is on so many levels."

"Then it may have been the fall that killed him, not the fungi? Is that it?"

"About fifty-fifty, Soame. Now you have an idea why dear Marie wants an inquest. I don't come into this. William never loved me enough to leave me anything, but some of the others imprudently remarked that William had no right to back Jenny Murphy in her theatrical venture, but, since he did, Marie might have scented trouble. My own opinion is that William was not a ready victim of Jean's, but simply out to help her."

"I wish you wouldn't start a fresh hare every minute," I said, rather helplessly. "I never heard of Miss Murphy, and I don't see what bearing this has on William Hoe-Luss's death either."

"I don't suppose it has," said 'Gene, drawing hard at his cigar. "I was just trying to make you see how dashed complicated the thing is. There are some people not homicidal in themselves, but provocative of homicide in others."

"But Hoe-Luss was a very amiable fellow."

"Amiable people are often most irritating," he said. "But I didn't mean that. There was this question of Jean Murphy and the dangerous age, you know."

"I don't know," I protested. "There's a lot of loose talk by laymen about things like that, but what does it mean?"

"The fact is," said 'Gene, "Marie has always been jealous of him. I don't think he gave her any grounds for it, but she once told old Madame Gavrault in my hearing that William was at a dangerous age."

"A silly remark," I said.

"I grant you, but silly remarks are responsible for many a spot of bother, aren't they? I'm not giving you my view, simply what I heard drifting about after William conk—died. He was fifty-five, wasn't it? and Jean is twenty-five, and pretty as a daisy."

"Are you exact in your simile?" I asked, seeing now what he was getting at. "Nothing orchidaceous about her?"

He laughed. "Nothing. A daisy just hits her off; fresh, simple, and pretty. Sound in wind and limb, and guaranteed free from vice, if you want another simile."

We had come to a great tree, felled, and lying on the grass. Oliver sat down, and smiled at me encouragingly.

"I see," I said. "In spite of these charming qualities, Marie persisted in thinking that the girl was making eyes at her husband."

"So they say. Personally, I never heard Marie link up Jean with her husband's supposedly dangerous age."

"And she based her suspicions—if 'they' are right—on Hoe-Luss's backing the actress in a venture?"

He nodded. "No one ever knew William to be interested in the stage. I don't think he went to the theatre three times a year. Then he lets it be known that he is putting up five thousand pounds, to give Jean Murphy a chance to play leading lady in a new play."

I sat down, and thought it over. I should never have suspected the man of being led astray by actresses, however pretty and simple. He was not that kind in my opinion. But we doctors more than other people are constantly being surprised by our patients branching out in new lines. As a man of the world, it seemed to me that these circumstances, unexplained, did give Marie some cause for worry.

"Did he pay over the money?" I asked.

"No. He was to pay it into the girl's bank two weeks after—well, he died before that, as you know."

"So he told Marie about it?"

"Absolutely. She invited Jean to the château. She had never seen her before. I admit that she treated her charmingly."

The gentle rain of Marie's charm was just as likely to fall on the unjust as the just, if it suited her book, so that meant nothing.

"So the play never came off?"

"No."

"What was it called?"

"*Springtide*, I believe. William had got the option of a—no, a short lease on the little 'Green Mantle' theatre. It was by a fellow called 'John Eisen,' she said. But she professed never to have seen the author, who was supposed to be a sort of natural hermit, living in the Highlands."

"And of course he might."

"Yes, it was that sort of play; pretty and ingenuous, full of the scent of heather, and that sort of tosh. It's my opinion," added the young cynic, "that the little devil wrote it herself."

"I suppose some of your charming party suspected that Marie had had a hand in her husband's death out of jealousy?" I suggested. "That isn't exactly a pretty thought, is it? Especially as there was so little evidence to back it."

"None at all," said he. "Of course, if it had taken place over here, there would have been a post-mortem, and an inquest, and things would have been buzzed off to that expert at the Home Office. As it was, I assume that all was right, but the medico being a pal of Marie's, so to speak, and functioning round the château and estate, if you know what I mean, did make people talk."

"The French doctor?"

"Yes. He lives in the little town on the edge of the property, and was called in to look at William, when they found the body."

He got off the tree-trunk, and strolled towards the winding drive. I followed him.

"The French professional man is at least as incorruptible as our own, I hope," said I.

"Very likely," said he, with a smile at me. "But they know which side their bread is buttered, too."

"What does Marie think?" I asked.

"She would like to think he broke his neck," said 'Gene, and turned, as we heard the sound of a car coming up the drive.

"Another crowd of jurors," he murmured. "Burton driving, and—yes—Jean at his side. Dr Geyle behind, I think."

"The French doctor?" I asked.

"No, D.Sc.," said he. "English, but attached to the Lorraine works."

Chapter III
A FRESH DEAL

THE world of business knew Caley Burton as one of the chief exponents of what they call 'big,' and socialists 'predatory,' business. But no man looked the part less. He was five feet six in height, wore pince-nez without rims, had sandy hair, weak eyes, an indeterminate chin, and a curious hesitating manner of speech.

He looked as if he ought not to be at the wheel of the big Rolls, but there was an expertness in his handling, as he slowed up beside us, that belied appearances.

I give 'Gene Oliver top marks for his description of Jean Murphy. If she was vicious, then vice was never more cunningly concealed. She had dark hair, the loveliest dark eyes, a perfect little mouth, a complexion which had not suffered from grease-paint or been stultified by cosmetics. There was something engagingly infantile about her smile and her gentle voice.

Anyone might have fallen in love with her, at any age, but I felt quite sure that Jean had not fallen in love with the middle-aged married man.

Geyle, on the other hand, looked a very *rusé* gentleman, very slick and spick-and-span, who had mastered his hair, and made it lie down, and had a complete command of his excellent features.

I knew Burton slightly, and he introduced me to Jean, and then to Geyle. She smiled, Geyle nodded, and showed his excellent teeth a little.

"We couldn't get over in time for lunch," said Burton.

"We mourned you," said Oliver, grinning at Jean, who smiled back unaffectedly, "Miss Green, and the doctor and I, not to speak of Mrs. Graves—No, we came out for a stroll, and we'll finish our martyrdom," he added, as Geyle tentatively opened a door. "Carry on!"

The Rolls resumed its majestic progress, and Oliver fell in at my side once more.

"In that loathly château," he said, "we had nothing to do but gossip. We met in study circles, my dear fellow."

"Studying what?"

"Man, and woman. The only absentee was Simcox. He spent his time in the park and country, gathering weeds, and labelling."

"Is that the fellow who wrote a book on the Field Orchis?" I asked.

"Perhaps he did—sort of thing he would do. But, as I was saying, we were dashed critical of each other, and Geyle came out about the worst. Aunt Green, of course, had something to say."

"What was it?"

"She told us that Geyle was, if not engaged to Marie, at least thinking of it, when William breezed in."

I don't know what Oliver wanted to prove to me, but he proved very convincingly the incompatibility of the party Marie had invited to the château, and the extraordinary fact that each had suspicions of the other, and was not behind-hand in mentioning them.

"But suppose it were so," I said. "Surely women have been in that position before without wishing to commit homicide?"

"Quite," said he. "But Miss Green has a down on Geyle."

"She's eccentric," I said.

"Eccentric people have often the sharpest eyes," he remarked. "Never do that which you ought not to do with an eccentric looking on."

"I suppose no one suspects you of having had a hand in the deed?" I asked, with mild irony.

'Gene threw his cigar stump into a bush. "Oh, I shouldn't say that. On the whole, no—not truthfully. Geyle doesn't like me. Hector Simcox is supposed to regard me as a parasite. That's the worst of this case, my dear fellow. Only our own motives seem pure."

"But that's very usual," I commented. "Now, I am ready to bet that no one dared to say Miss Murphy had anything to do with William's death?"

"You lose, doctor. The motive is obscure, but Joe has an idea that she is a dark horse. It was really most odd that William should back her. You get the truth about that, and Marie will love you for ever."

We had tea on the lawn, six or seven little tables being set out there, with coloured umbrellas over them, as if the place was an hotel. Marie had a little talk with me before tea, and pleasantly surprised me by asking if I would entertain Jean Murphy.

"A very charming girl, and a talented actress," she told me. "I do want to know more about the delightful play she was to have put on. It's fallen through now, of course, but I am so curious to know all about it. William, I think you know, was not at all devoted to the theatre."

The cloven hoof peeped out there a little, I thought. But, while the case of William Hoe-Luss intrigued me, and I was anxious to get to the bottom of it, I had no intention of acting as a spy for my hostess.

I think I wondered still more when I sat down at a little table under an umbrella with Jean Murphy, and did not observe any envy or jealousy on the faces of the other male members of the party.

Simcox, a pleasant, sandy-haired young man, with glasses, had turned up before tea, in the company of a dark young woman, with extraordinarily luminous eyes, called Fay Hobert. She was a designer of theatrical decors, and had formed a friendship with the botanist. The failure to put on *Springtide* had also meant a loss for her.

She and Simcox were at a table with Marie. Caley Burton and Mrs Graves were chatting to each other on our right. Meriel Silger was with Dr Geyle, 'Gene Oliver and Joe sat on the outskirts, smiling and chatting in a most friendly way, while Aunt Green sat by, and listened dourly.

"Isn't this place charming?" said Jean. "I love it. It's the first time I've been here."

"I know few more pleasant country houses," I said. "I expect you think it compares favourably with the château."

She shivered a little. "It was dreadful. I never liked it, and when poor Mr Hoe-Luss died, it was a terrible shock."

"Very," I agreed. "I have known him for years, and he was a very nice fellow. What a ghastly affair altogether. I don't wonder Mrs Hoe-Luss sold the place."

She looked about us, "Isn't it odd. Everyone is here now who was at the château then. I only noticed it a few minutes ago."

"Well, I suppose we are all her friends."

She nodded. "I suppose that is it. How charming she is, isn't she? I liked her from the first. And she was so devoted to her husband, poor thing."

"How unfortunate that your play was killed too," I remarked. "Any chance of getting it put on after all?"

She shook her head, "I am afraid not. I couldn't expect Mrs Hoe-Luss to finance me. There were the death duties, and so on. And it just happened that he had faith in me."

"I am sure lots of people must have faith in you," I said.

"Not the right kind of faith," she smiled. "It takes such a great deal of belief to make one spend money, doesn't it? I've never been a star, you know. I just had two small parts."

"But what a compliment then?" I suggested. "Anyone can hitch a wagon to a star, but to be picked out of a small part and put in the sky is something."

She laughed. "But it was strange, too. I never met the author of the play, and I never met Mr Hoe-Luss, before I heard of him through my agent. He simply asked if I would undertake the part of the heroine in a play, and when I said 'yes,' he wrote asking me to go to the château, to talk it over. William is not the first business-man who has wanted to sponsor a new play, without any knowledge of the theatrical business."

"How did he get hold of the play?"

"He told me he got it from a literary agent," she said. "He had the offer of a theatre—"

"I heard that you had the option."

"Oh, no. He had lent some money, it seems, and the short lease was part of the repayment."

"I am sorry. Do go on."

"Well, then he did not know what to do. He applied to an agent for a suitable play. *Springtide* was offered to him, and he liked it."

"And then he saw you?"

She dimpled. "I suppose he must have done. It was delightful, but he said sophisticated acting would have killed it."

"I never knew that he was a connoisseur of that sort of thing."

"He was repeating what the agent told him, I am sure. At any rate, he asked me to read the parts—Fay Hobert read some too. And then he said he was quite satisfied, and promised to finance it."

"And that is all?"

"Yes."

I wondered that she took it so cheerfully. "Where is the play now?"

"It went back to the agent," she said. "You see, the author was a funny sort of man, who lived in the wilds somewhere. He wanted it back. I'm 'resting' now. Mrs Hoe-Luss says she may get something for me, but I don't know what it is."

It was a plain enough tale, and I felt that I could repeat it to my hostess without a breach of confidence. Hoe-Luss had wanted to act as a patron to the drama, and had chosen this rather expensive way of setting about it. Malicious tittle-tattle about nothing seemed to be at the back of this ridiculous suggestion that Hoe-Luss's death was not accidental but contrived. It is amazing how suspicious people can become when their financial interests are threatened.

Geyle and the man they called Simcox drifted over to us presently, when we were smoking, and discussing the theatre, and Miss Murphy's chances of getting a new part. From Simcox's smile, it seemed to me that his former acquaintance with the girl had been a pleasant one. At any rate, he took her off to boat on the lake, and Geyle suggested that I should show him the park.

"I gather from Oliver that you live pretty near here," he said. "I often heard poor Hoe-Luss talk of you."

I knew the park very well, of course, and we strolled into it, while I wondered if Geyle, like some of the others, wanted me to watch him grind his little private axe, or disburthen his mind of suspicions.

"You met Oliver before, of course," he said, as we sauntered towards the path between shrubberies of rhododendron.

"I met him a good many times either here or at Hoe-Luss's house in town," I replied. "I think he is a clever fellow."

"Oh, clever—yes," he agreed. "He has a flair for following the right horse too. That was really at the back of the row at the château, you know."

It seemed to me that I was going to hear a great deal about this row at the château. It must have been an obsession with some of the guests, for there was no apparent purpose to be served by telling me of the affair.

"So there was a row?" I remarked, unwilling to say that Oliver had mentioned it, since I could detect a latent hostility to him in my companion.

Geyle smiled. "I'm a chemist myself; don't understand these business affairs, doctor. It interested the rest of us because Burton and Hoe-Luss had been partners for years. I don't understand the point at issue now, but Hoe-Luss was very angry with Oliver for taking Burton's view."

"I don't see in any case that a mere business quarrel is worth fighting over, now the man's dead," I said bluntly.

Geyle lit a fresh cigarette, and glanced at me. "Then you haven't heard? I quite agree, mind you, that the thing was best forgotten, but after the poor fellow was found dead, someone brought it up again. Aunt Green, probably."

"Very likely," I said. "She won't let the dead stay dead."

"And the atmosphere was damned uncomfortable for a while," he went on, as if I hadn't spoken. "Charges and counter-charges, you know."

It was evident that he believed Marie had told me something, and he was anxious to impose his own views.

"You were outside the whole affair in any case," I murmured. "Still, that sort of thing is uncomfortable even for the lookers on."

He nodded. "Yes. Still, I can hardly say that I was disinterested, altogether. The merger, if it had come off, would have resulted in a single head-office, don't you know—rationalisation. I've been with the French side for a good many years. And this is a rotten time to get a new post."

"But surely your experience—" I began.

"My dear fellow, money talks. A younger man could be had cheaper. You see, I am quite frank. The thing would have hit me, if it had come off. I said so at the time."

It began to appear that someone had suspected him too of a hand in what would have been an unholy affair. Oliver had suggested that he was a very old friend of Marie's. But if that had been the case, surely Marie, who had the greatest influence with Hoe-Luss, could have saved the job for him?

"I expect, Dr Geyle, that everyone's nerves were a little overstrained. A thing like that is apt to cause storms."

"What did Oliver think about it?" he asked.

"He said there was a good deal of gossip. He gave me the impression that it was a rather silly storm in a tea-cup."

"Silly! I should say it was," he remarked indignantly. "Some lunatic even suggested that that little Murphy girl was not all that she should be. Just because Hoe-Luss had promised to back her with a play."

"Which failed to materialise when Hoe-Luss died, of course," I reminded him. "It sounds like the echo of one of Aunt Green's spiteful remarks."

"Oh, there were others too," he mumbled. "That Silger woman, and Joe, of course. The moment they found out that there was nothing coming to them, they went up in the air."

I laughed. "The whole thing seems to have been filled with hot air," I told him. "Poor Hoe-Luss might have been buried quietly, and all this speculation with him."

"It ought to have been, doctor. I think it would have been, if the poor chap hadn't fallen down those stairs. But, as I said at the time, if a man has been sick, he is weak after, and a bit dizzy."

"Undoubtedly," I said. "Over here, I think, it would have been held that death was caused by that, and not by the mush—I mean fungi. It would be too pretty and delicate a problem to decide scientifically if he died of poisoning before he fell, or fell and broke his neck as the result of feeling sick."

"And the joke is," said Geyle, looking at me directly, "that that young ass Simcox tells me that there are no—*Amanita phalloidis*, wasn't it? in the park. I advised him to say nothing about it. I am quite sure he never searched the place, which is very extensive."

Chapter IV
INFORMATORY DOUBLE

Marie called to Geyle when we strolled up the park again, and he went over to see what she wanted. I continued towards the house, and met Caley Burton, carrying an armful of cushions, and Miss Hobert at his side. They were also going to boat on the lake to the east of the park, and Burton asked me if I would join them.

"We are really fleeing from Aunt Green," he added, with a smile. "Joe and his young woman managed to detach her, and she fastened on us, and resurrected William."

"Most horridly," agreed Miss Hobert. "Mr Burton and I are contemplating a flight to town on Monday. We both hate inquests."

I laughed. "It's not unusual. But is this an inquest?"

"It is," said Burton. "Six months too late."

"You might get Marie to speak to the old lady," I said. "I have known her to squash Auntie very effectively."

Miss Hobert grinned. "Then you don't know the real secrets of the prison-house, Doctor Soame? I thought everyone knew that Marie makes the balls, and Aunt Green throws them."

"Isn't it all rather ludicrous," I said. "Can anyone seriously tell me that people were actually accused of doing away with Hoe-Luss, simply because he fell downstairs after eating a dish of fungi?"

"Not because of that, and not to their faces," said Burton gravely. "But I dare say Marie told you that there was a rumpus, and all sorts of foolish accusations and rumours flying about."

"No, she did not tell me," I replied, realising that most of these people took me to be a confidant of Marie's, and were anxious that I should get my facts right.

Miss Hobert bit her lip. "Well that's how it was. Even poor Jean came in for some of the mud."

"There is one thing I should like to know," I said. "Who found Hoe-Luss at the foot of the stairs?"

"I did," said Miss Hobert, as we neared the thirty-acre lake. "I wanted to ask him about the decor, and no one told me he was busy on some business matter and didn't want to be disturbed."

"I see. You went to see him, and found him lying there. I suppose you noticed that his neck was broken?"

"Good heavens, no!" she replied, with a startled look. "I simply gave a yell, and bolted for help. I shouldn't know about his neck anyway."

Burton nodded. "I suppose a man may break his neck without looking as if he had?"

"Certainly," I said. "What next?"

"Well, I met Geyle in the hall at the foot of the staircase—the main one, and he dashed up, and saw to him. I know he isn't a real doctor, but he came down and directed affairs, sent for a real one, and so forth. Marie was in hysterics, you know."

"He was pretty useful certainly," added Burton, as we reached the boat-house. "A jolly good man in an emergency."

We rooted out a very nice punt, and presently embarked. Burton volunteered to paddle, and I sat with Fay Hobert in the stern.

"No one rang up the police, of course?" I asked, when we had started. "I forgot to ask that."

"Oh, yes, the doctor did," said Burton. "He said, as poor old William had died suddenly, the police must be informed. A chap came up, had a look at William, and then a long palaver with the doctor. It came out that William had been sick, and that was gone into, and the doctor and the police fellow saw the cook, and heard about the fungi."

I was interested now. The disjointed accounts I had had from Oliver and Geyle had left some important points obscure. "Then the doctor was able to decide that the fungi had caused death before Hoe-Luss fell?" Miss Hobert struck in. "Of course. He said the neck must have been broken after death, Dr Soame. He said Mr Hoe-Luss died, then fell forward down the stairs, and broke his neck."

"I understand now," I said. "I wondered how a doctor could ignore the broken neck without deciding exactly the sequence of events. If he had been unable to decide that, there would be grounds for resurrecting the matter, but with that verdict given, it ought to be allowed to rest. After all, there is no question of motive, if one excludes Mrs Hoe-Luss."

"She was the only one who scored," said Miss Hobert.

"Joe certainly expected to be helped on his way after his marriage," said Burton. "He was very nasty about it at the time. I don't say that he had the pluck to make any remarks to Marie, but I had to warn him that his insinuations were not only in bad taste, but dangerously libellous."

"He's indiscreet, to say the least," I admitted. "But surely he did not suggest that Marie provided the poisonous fungi?"

"He didn't say what she provided," remarked Fay Hobert. "He simply said that she scooped the pool. I am quoting his own phrase."

"I suppose the doctor said the death was caused by poisonous fungi?" I asked, "there are other poisons—drugs, which would produce somewhat similar symptoms."

Burton stopped paddling for a moment. "Yes, he did. He was positive about it. It would have been more satisfactory, I admit, if the cook had not thrown the stuff into the fire—"

"Wait a moment," I said. "How did she get the stuff without visiting—or without sending another servant to fetch it from the room?"

"She didn't," replied Miss Hobert. "Did she, Mr Burton? I heard that she cooked some, and there was some left over. He ate what was cooked, and she burned the rest."

"Did Marie dismiss her?" I asked.

This time Miss Hobert locked at me. "I don't know. Why?"

Burton paddled rapidly, and sheered the punt away from a little bay where Jean Murphy and Simcox sat in a skiff. "I know, of course. The cook was so indignant about being questioned that she gave notice. Marie brought a French cook back with her."

I agreed that I had heard that. "There you are," I said, "Marie did tell me so. It was a chance to get a cook who would fit in with her ideas of food."

"Naturally," said Caley Burton, "I never thought it was because there was any collus—I mean to say, nothing wrong."

"That is what I thought so annoying," Miss Hobert remarked. "It is bad enough to find people making mountains out of molehills at any time. In a case like this, it's dangerous."

I nodded. "It is rather dangerous referring to the affair as a 'case,' at all."

"You're quite right," murmured Burton. "Perhaps people will be tired of the gossip by to-morrow, and give it up. Otherwise, I do seriously think of finding an important engagement in town for Monday. I hate taking my pleasures so painfully."

Miss Hobert partially assented. "But I am still annoyed about Jean," she said. "The poor thing has had a nasty tumble. You can't get a chance of a star part in the West End, and lose it, and not feel rotten about it."

"You mean those insinuations?" said I.

"Absolutely. She's the only loser, too. And she was plucky. She said at once that the promise was washed out. She told Mrs Hoe-Luss that it was only verbal."

"By the way," I said. "It's rather thrashing dry thistles, now the thing is settled, but I hear your young botanist protests that those poisonous fungi do not grow in the park at the château."

Miss Hobert stared. "Then why didn't he say so at the time?"

"I have no idea. But he said so to Geyle."

Caley Burton looked puzzled. "How does he know?"

"Did he look?" asked Miss Hobert.

"I only heard what he said."

"I expect he is wrong," said Burton. "The French doctor mentioned the particular fungi, and he should know if it grows down there. But he is rather an important young ass, and proud of his knowledge."

"Was he there when the French doctor mentioned it?" I asked.

Miss Hobert shook her head. "No. If he had been, no doubt he would have told him, and the point could have been settled."

"Rather an important point, too," said I. "It would have complicated things tremendously."

Burton smiled. "We're still worrying at this rather stale bone. And I see someone signalling to us from the bank?"

"Aunt Green," I said.

Miss Hobert gave a little jump. "I quite forgot. I had promised to play tennis before dinner with Mr Simcox—(We'd better hail him)—Dr Geyle and Mrs Graves."

"Does Mrs Graves play?" I asked.

"Quite a good game," said Burton. "She used win 'pots' in her youth."

We hailed Simcox, who was just putting out again from the little bay in his skiff, and then set out for shore. When we saw Aunt Green, she said that Meriel and Mrs Graves had been on the tennis-court for ten minutes, waiting."

"You people had better hurry," she added. "Dr Soame and I will follow you slowly. My legs are not what they were."

"Then I'll wait for the other two, send Simcox up, and come along with Miss Murphy," said Burton.

As a doctor they may have thought it fit and right that I should hold the baby. But I had heard nearly enough of the 'case,' and

Aunt Green handles the pepper-box too violently to amuse one. It should be done so that the onlooker does not sneeze, in addition to those at whom it is directed.

I fell in beside Aunt Green, wishing that her tongue suffered the same disability as her ageing legs.

Chapter V
TWO HEARTS

"I never saw such an extraordinary party," said Aunt Green, with her irritating cackle. "Never!"

"You have been lucky," I returned.

"I forgot that you weren't at the château," she replied. "I can't understand why Marie wanted the same lot again."

"They are all very charming people," I observed. "At least, I think so."

"We are all charming to someone," said Aunt Green, though I never met anyone who used the word when referring to her. "We have to be. I have to be, though I hate humbug."

I let it go at that. There are many people to whom good manners are humbug, and hurtful things candour. Invariably, they are keenly sensitive to slights.

"I always enjoy coming here," I said, after a pause. "The park, to my mind, is one of the most beautiful in England."

"Though there are serpents even in this Eden," she chuckled, with a wave of her thin, much-beringed hand at something in the grass. "But now that we have a French cook, we shall be spared any dangerous mistakes."

The woman was actually pointing at a group of red spotted fungi, near the root of a beech.

"You are not fond of the French?" I asked hastily.

"Oh, yes, I am—in reason, doctor. Don't you think Dr Geyle is rather French-looking?"

I admitted that there was something in what she said. "The name almost suggests foreign extraction," I added.

She smiled. "No, he is quite English. Only he has lived there so long that he has Gallic tastes. I don't know if I told you that Marie was once very fond of him."

"I heard it somewhere," I replied cautiously. "Well, I don't wonder. She is an attractive woman still, and was very good-looking in her youth, no doubt."

"And he is good-looking too," she murmured. "I am sure Marie made the best choice, of course. Fond as one is of her, one can't help seeing that she has the French liking for the eligible *parti*, in a financial sense. They have none of our English nonsense about love in their system, have they?"

"Things are changing even there," I said.

Aunt Green did not believe it. It was only the anglophile, or cosmopolitan crowd, which adopted the sentimental approach to matrimony.

"I can't help wondering," she added, "if Dr Geyle hopes to hang up his hat here."

"It's rather early to speculate," I suggested. "There is nothing to go on."

"I don't know how Marie feels, of course," she went on, taking me what I knew was a very roundabout way back to the house; "but, of course, it would be a very fine thing for him. His tenure of that post must be most precarious now."

"Really?"

"Of course. Mr Burton was not very fond of him. He said at the time that he wondered Marie had the man to stay. Poor William was a dear, but he knew that Dr Geyle and Marie had once been on the point of an engagement. A new wife may not be jealous of her predecessor's portrait, but she can't *really* like seeing it there."

"I think you make too much of it, Miss Green," I said.

"It was thrust on me, more or less," said Aunt Green. "Dr Leclerc, of course, knew of the former affair, and he told me it must be embarrassing for Geyle too."

She was evidently anxious to impress on me the idea that these two hearts still beat as nearly one as was convenable in the circumstances. I did my best to get away from that ugly path.

"What happened to the English cook?" I asked.

"She gave notice," said Aunt Green. "At least, so Marie said. I believe she retired from cooking altogether, to a little cottage in Kent."

"She was not a bad judge," said I, using the term in its colloquial sense.

She grinned horridly. "That's what I say! So unusual, too, for an Englishwoman of that class to be saving. And only fifty."

"She was paid good wages, no doubt," I said.

"Must have been very good!" said Aunt Green.

"And Hoe-Luss probably left her something."

"Not a penny," said she. "Only servants with two years' service and over received legacies."

"And Marie, who disliked her, would hardly contribute," I said.

Aunt Green said nothing. She has the most hateful silences, when she is silent, of anyone I know. Her dumbness in certain crises condemns more savagely than anyone else's most decided speech.

"Where is Joe?" I asked at length. "Meriel, you said, was going to play tennis."

"He went off with Sir Eugene," said she. "Now that is a nasty, interfering fellow!"

"Joe, or Eugene?" I asked.

"Sir Eugene," she replied bitterly. "No manners, no respect for people older than himself. You know how he backed Mr Burton against poor William, don't you?"

"I heard of it from him," I replied. "By the way, the merger did not come off, did it?"

"I am not so sure. Mr Burton had set his heart on it, and he looks as pleased as a dog with two tails."

"Did the question of it only come up when you were all at the château?" I asked, before she could get under way with a fresh slander on someone.

"I don't know. I don't understand business. There was very little talk of it at the time. We heard more about it afterwards."

We were at last nearing the house, and to my relief I saw Marie Hoe-Luss waving to us from the porch.

"Do go in, and try over some of those new gramophone records for us," she told Aunt Green. "We want to dance to-night."

The old lady went away grumbling. Marie asked me to come and see a new bed her gardener was planning, and ignored the poor man's work the moment we reached it.

"Did you hear any more about that play, Dr Soame?" she asked me, rather eagerly I thought.

I hesitated. To tell the truth, I had been impressed by the general atmosphere of alarm, nervousness, and suspicion reigning among the guests. Some people tell you that they are not influenced by the atmosphere around them. They are quite mistaken. We are all more or less affected by the spoken or unspoken thoughts of others.

My head told me that all this scandal was probably baseless. William Hoe-Luss had died a natural death, in the strictest sense. But I began to let my intuitions get the better of me. And why was Marie so anxious to know about the play her late husband had promised to back?

"I am sure you know as much as I do," I ventured. "Miss Murphy apparently got an offer to play the part through her agent. Another agent—a literary one—found a play for your husband, and he decided to get Miss Murphy to play the principal part."

"Oh, quite," said Marie, rather impatiently. "But doesn't she know who wrote it?"

"No," I said. "She doesn't. It went back to the agent, I think. Someone suggested that she wrote it herself."

"Nonsense! The girl couldn't write a play to save her life, doctor. She acts charmingly, but that's another pair of sleeves."

I felt that that was probably true. Jean was not, I imagined, brainy.

"How did it come about that she was offered the part?" I asked. "I know some punters pick the names of horses out with their eyes shut, but it hardly works with actresses."

"And that's a pity," said Marie. "It's got so many pretty façades on the stage, with unlet rooms behind. Let me see—Yes, I took William to see *Verities*. Jenny was playing a very small part."

"But made it apparent to him that she had the real stuff in her?"

She shook her head. "William was no judge. I said the moment I saw her that she could act the star off the stage. William read the notices next day, and one critic he had great faith in said the same."

"So you were really at the bottom of it?" I said, and then I wondered.

If she had such a high opinion of Miss Murphy's talent, why had she so willingly accepted the girl's suggestion that William's death had terminated what was purely a verbal contract? On the other hand, there was Marie's saving disposition. A Frenchwoman likes her facts cut and dried. She must have known what a gamble a stage production was.

"She went to the lake with young Simcox, didn't she?" she added, as I made no comment. "Boating?"

"They went out in a skiff," I told her. "Simcox is a lucky fellow, if he has made an impression there."

She started. "Has he? I thought Arthur Geyle was her favourite."

It was my turn to be surprised. "Dr Geyle? Really?"

"They were tremendously friendly at the château," said she. "Mr Simcox was absorbed by his hobby—if you can call it a hobby."

There again the nasty atmosphere I had encountered had affected my judgment. Aunt Green had linked Marie's name with Geyle. Now here was Geyle (Marie's second string, according to that old gossip) presumed to be pursuing Jenny Murphy. Was Marie jealous again, or were the jealousies, first and second, phantasies of Aunt Green's meddling brain?

"I can find excuses for both of them," I murmured. "She isn't exactly what you would call a sparkling conversationalist, but she gives a delicious impression."

"I hate sparkling conversationalists," said Marie. "They're all fizz and sting. Not one in a thousand can sparkle without being unkind."

"At any rate," I said, "I've fallen in love with the girl myself. And I shall hate the successful suitor."

"I would sooner it was Arthur," she remarked. "He is a very old friend of mine, and I should like to see him happy."

She looked at me rather defiantly as she said that, and I understood that she was challenging me to believe a word of Aunt Green's insinuations. Everyone seemed to be on the defensive at Hebble Chace. If William had really died by accident, his guests at the château were still wonderfully worked up about it.

"Ah, you knew him in France?" I said.

"We were engaged once," she said calmly. "He broke it off. He was quite right, of course. I have very definite ideas about marriage."

"So wise," I murmured. "I dislike people who undertake to play games without mastering the rules."

She smiled faintly. "It was really quite simple. Arthur hates music. He doesn't dislike it. It is a torture to him. Now I have always loved it. I am still keeping on my box at the opera—though you know how much I have had to retrench, owing to these loathly death duties."

"You couldn't have compromised?" I asked.

"You may spoil the Philistines, but not compromise with them," said Marie. "Arthur is a Philistine about music; delightful, kind and generous, but what would you? I am sure now that I was right."

I nodded. "What is he going to do to-night when you dance? Surely the modern dance music will be a double pain?"

"Not a bit of it. It's music he dislikes, not noise. Still, he is sure to stay away."

"Not even the chance of dancing with Miss Murphy would attract him?"

"He doesn't dance. How can a man without an ear, and no idea of rhythm, dance, doctor?"

"Didn't Shakespeare say something about a man like that being fit for treasons, stratagems and spoils?"

"I have never read Shakespeare. He is too formless," she replied. "How is it that even poets make the mistake of thinking ill of people who haven't the same tastes as themselves? Arthur is charming. Now run and see the tennis."

I went to see the tennis. I have always wondered if the manner in which one plays games gives any indication to one's character. As I subsided into a deck chair at the side of the court, I looked at the four players, and idly tried to place them by their game.

Mrs Graves was all for position; but that might be because she was no longer so nimble. Simcox played a light and airy game; fast but inaccurate. Geyle was neat, quick, very steady, and rather cunning. Meriel's game was like her sentences, unfinished. She would make a tremendous dart to retrieve a ball, and give it up before she got to it.

I studied their faces. Mrs Graves preserved a sporting calm, and neither frowned at a mis-hit, nor smiled at a winner. Simcox was inclined to bubble over when he scored an ace. Geyle remained master of himself, as of his hair. He was polite, and mildly cheerful in fortune and misfortune alike. Meriel, as I should have guessed, claimed balls that had gone over the line, condoned her own faults, and quarrelled with decisions.

"You know that ball—" she would begin, then break off, and wrinkle her brows. She and Hector Simcox were, of course, getting the worst of it.

Jean Murphy had left Mr Burton, and came to sit by me. "I love to watch Dr Geyle," she said, rather naïvely. "He never seems to get out of breath, or out of temper."

"Except in places where they play. Mrs Hoe-Luss tells me that he can't bear music," I told her. "What is he going to do when you all dance to-night?"

She laughed. "I'm not going to. Mr Simcox hit my ankle with the butt of an oar getting out of the skiff. He is rather clumsy. It isn't really hurt, but I don't think I could dance to-night."

"If you'll allow me—" I began.

She shook her head, and laughed again. "Dr Geyle is taking me over for a drive to Hebble Abbey ruins—by moonlight."

"But how romantic!"

"You should have read that play," said she. "Now that was romantic. I loved every word of it. I am old-fashioned, you know. It does seem so silly to laugh at sentiment."

"It's just as prevalent as ever," I assured her. "Now that longer skirts have come in, it will begin to come out. But what will Mr Simcox say to this moonlight jaunt?"

She dimpled. "Mr Simcox is young."

"And you're not exactly an ancient," I suggested. "He could give you quite two years."

"He's very old about plants and flowers," she agreed, "but too silly about everything else."

"Has he proposed to you yet?" I asked.

"I mustn't tell you."

"You have. And it proves he isn't at all silly."

Jean pursed up her pretty lips. "Just an over-grown schoolboy, Dr Soame; nice and decent—and silly!"

"Is Geyle going in one of the house cars?" I asked.

"In Mr Burton's," she said. "He told me we could have it."

"I suppose you have told our hostess?" I asked.

"Oh, yes, she is sending supper with us. Isn't it kind of her. But don't tell a soul. Dr Geyle wants to talk over the play. He may find someone to do it, he says. Only, of course, I haven't got it."

Could this be some obscure ruse of Marie's, to get more information about that harmless, harmful play? I pulled myself up. In another day or two I should be watching faces, listening to chance words, playing the apparently popular game (with that particular party) of 'I spy.' I have often wondered do solicitors and barristers suspect everyone they meet? They hear so much. I do myself. But perhaps, like me, they regard it with detachment, as all part of the job, and do not let it colour their thoughts or lives.

"It was kind of Mr Burton," said I, after a pause, while I watched Meriel botch a poaching expedition, and blame her partner.

"He's very nice," said Jean. "I am sure he only made a fortune by chance, aren't you? He doesn't look as if he could push and shove, I'm sure."

"No; in that line, Oliver is the man for my money," I agreed. "He is just what we should take a successful man to be."

At that moment the tennis came to an end, and Jean looked at her wrist-watch, and said she must go up to dress.

But I noticed that she spoke to Hector Simcox before she went, and that Geyle watched her. She only waved a hand to him before she turned away.

CHAPTER VI
CLUBS ARE TRUMPS

I WAS relieved to find that at dinner the unpleasant topics which seemed to have devoured my afternoon were temporarily laid to rest. Mr Burton proved a valuable aid to brightness, and, with Jean Murphy unexpectedly witty, 'Gene Oliver a determined farceur, Mrs Graves developing an infectious laugh, and Aunt Green given subjects for humorous acidity, which were yet far removed from necrophilism, I was able to enjoy my food.

I thought it likely that the patients, having got rid of the accumulated bile in their systems (if you will allow me a medical simile), we might now settle down to a week of gentle amusement, without being haunted by William's restless ghost.

After dinner we danced, even Marie. Geyle and Jean had gone off in the Rolls, for a run before they settled to enjoy the moonlight at the Abbey ruins. I thought Hector Simcox looked rather glum about that, but it may have been something else. He danced at any rate, and recovered his spirits later on.

On Sunday morning, I went to church with Jean Murphy and Hector. The others breakfasted in bed. On our way to the little village, we met Mr Anderson, the squire, and he detached me, and began a long description of some cure he had heard of for his gout.

We doctors have to bear with people who, without realising it, are trying to teach us our own business, or at least that side branch of it which is based on profits and advertisements. Personally, I always advise them to buy what they want. It saves argument, and gives an impression of broad-mindedness, while, temporarily, curing the patient of his ignorant optimism.

The point here however is that I walked with the squire, and Hector Simcox proposed to Jean for the second time. She told me so afterwards, though not willingly. I know he complained afterwards of the sermon, and had a blighted look, which sat ill on his ingenuous face. This time, that is on the road home, he looked for rare weeds ahead of us, and Jean told me what a delightful time she had had on her moonlight picnic.

"You blasted young Simcox's evening though," I rallied her. "I don't think he considers moonlight picnics quite nice."

She looked at me anxiously. "You know, Dr Soame, I would not have gone, only Dr Geyle was very pressing. Marie didn't see any harm in it."

"Bless you, I was only joking!" I returned, more sure than ever that the supreme naïveté of Jean proved her to have been quite incapable of encouraging William Hoe-Luss, granting his susceptibility, which I also doubted. People often imagine that actresses are born vamps. They confuse the parts with the whole. Jean couldn't have vamped a ploughboy. "I think Mrs Hoe-Luss is a bit of a matchmaker," I added.

She coloured charmingly.

"He just told me the romantic story of the ruins," she said, "It was awfully interesting. And it was somewhat like the plot of the play I was to have done. I said so, and he made me tell him all about it. I do hope he may be able to do something for me."

"Did he say who his friend was, in the theatrical world?" I asked, "I mean a possible fresh backer?"

She shook her head, "No, he didn't. But he promised to do his best."

"It would be difficult to get a theatre perhaps," I said. "By the way, what about the one Hoe-Luss had the lease of?"

"Didn't you know? It was taken by Mr Vallam for a costume play, and that was taken off, and then someone else did a musical comedy, and now that's a frost. It ends next week."

"Pity Marie Hoe-Luss wouldn't put your play on," I said. "But when she is cutting down expenses, she is not likely to finance a speculative proposition. You don't mind me saying that, do you?"

She smiled, "Oh no. It's quite true. I'm not really conceited, and in any case, no one knows nowadays what will take."

Geyle came to meet us, and I joined Hector Simcox, while he walked behind us with Jean.

Hector made no mention of her as we strolled on together, but he did speak rather spitefully of Dr Geyle.

"I wonder what that fellow would think if I tried to teach him something about chemistry?" he asked.

"He would probably consider you ambitious," I replied.

"You bet he would!" said Hector. "It's his job. Mine is botany."

"My dear boy," I assured him, "you ought to be glad you never joined my profession, if that is a worry to you. There are two things in this world that the layman is cheerfully ready to undertake, without study or practice, writing and doctoring."

"I know," he said. "But when Geyle tells me that there are some of those fungi that killed Mr Hoe-Luss in the park at the château, I ask you!"

"Don't they grow in France at all?" I asked.

"They do," said Hector; "but what's that? They grow strawberries in Scotland, but not on top of Ben Nevis."

"Don't think I am doubting your knowledge," I replied. "But let us get this right. Is the soil in that park not suitable for this amanita thing?"

He bent down, and picked up a flower so small that I could hardly see it. "Quite all right—only the damned thing doesn't grow there."

"And you have been all over the park? I hear it is very extensive?"

"Huge," said he, throwing the flower away again, as if he had only picked it up absently. "Pretty well all over. The only bit I did not look over was the wood at the east corner bounded by the road to Varelles."

"But, look here, Simcox," I said. "Hoe-Luss said he had picked the stuff in the park, when he gave it to the cook. And if he didn't die of that poisoning, what did he die of?"

"Search me!" said he, inelegantly. "Hang it all, he may have eaten some fungi that were not deadly, and felt funny after. All I say is—and I say it again whatever that ass Geyle says—is that *Amanita phalloidis* does not grow in that park. I'll rag the blighter about chemistry to-night, you see!"

I smiled. "I suppose you are always on the look-out for rare flora?" I asked, to change the subject. "But I expect there are none to interest you down here?"

"Oh yes, there are," he said enthusiastically. "And I brought some stuff down with me—I had been collecting in Jura before I got Mrs Hoe-Luss's invitation. Like to see them before lunch?"

"Very much," I replied, for the young man was as ingenuous in his way as Jean was in hers, and you could not help liking him. "I've never been to Jura. Rather fine, isn't it?"

"I suppose so," he said, and I suspected that scenery as scenery was of no interest to him. He viewed the land merely as a habitat for rare flowers, or weeds, and interesting vegetation.

"By the way," I added, as we neared the house, "how did you fall in with Mr Hoe-Luss?"

Hector laughed. "It was rather funny, that. I was over in that part on a hunt, and he caught me trespassing; at least, one of his foresters did. He asked me quite politely to go up to the château, and who did I see there but Jean."

"Jean Murphy. You knew her before?"

He nodded. "When I was a kid, her people lived in the same village. Colonel Murphy was a great old sport, and a pal of my dad's. They went to London when I was bunged off to school. Anyway, as I was saying, Jean was at the château, and she made it all right with Hoe-Luss. He asked me to stay."

There was no one about the house when we went in, and upstairs to Hector's room. Hebble Chace is built in the form of a double-ended L, and his room (his bedroom, that is) is entered by a door in the centre of the corridor running parallel to the front facade. A dressing-room communicates with it, and has also a door opening on a passage. But this passage is the one that runs backward down the western wing of the double L.

We turned the corner into this passage, and Hector opened the door of the dressing-room.

"I don't dress here," he grinned, as he shut the door behind us. "The other room is big enough for a whole theatrical company to dress in. I'm using this to work in."

It was a pleasant room, with a two-mullioned window. Collecting cases stood in a corner, a table had been cleared, and on it were his microscope, a small box of dried-looking vegetation, and a sheet of strong, white drawing-paper, together with a tiny bottle of mucus.

"What's that—seaweed?" I asked as we approached the table. "I suppose I ought to call it *algae*."

"Call it Ferdinand if you like, doctor!" he chuckled. "It certainly isn't seaweed."

I am no judge of these things, but I bent over, and looked more closely at his specimens. "Looks like lichen rather."

He nodded. "It should, you know, for that is what it is; or they are, Dr Soame. I am on a little investigation at present. The lichen is not a popular plant, even more unfashionable than the aspidistra now. Naturally I am not trying to discover a new species. I am comparing variants at the moment."

"For a book?" I asked.

"Yes. I have a little theory, which I propose to develop. But that is a secret. If you care to buy my book you'll hear about it."

"If I'm not mistaken, there is lichen on the stones of this house, Simcox," I said. "But some dull kind, I am sure."

He smiled the superior smile of the young and informative, and took my sleeve.

"Walk this way, doctor."

He took me to the open window, and asked me to lean out. Twenty feet or so below us was the flagged path that ran round the side of the house. Moss and tiny rock-plants grew in the crevices, and it always seemed to me one of the most charming minor features of the garden.

"On the flags?" I asked.

"Nearer than that," said Hector, and indicated some patches on the wall, about four feet below the sill of the window.

"Now, isn't that luck?" said Hector, with enthusiasm. "I go to the château by chance, meet Mr Hoe-Luss, and get invited here, later, by his widow. She puts me here, just within reach of that!"

I felt as a layman does when a biologist invites him to look at some tiny ticks on a slide, and expects him to rave over their significance. The lichen to which he invited my attention was about as neutral and uninviting a growth as he could well have picked.

"I won't be hypocritical enough to enthuse over it," I said, with a laugh.

"You would if you knew," said Hector. "But that must wait. I want you to see my stuff from Jura. I made one or two finds, and I'm keeping them dark."

Of course I did my best to show an intelligent interest. My own experience has told me how trying it is to be worked up about something, to endeavour to share my pleasure with someone else, and then to be drowned in a butt of cold water.

My studies, while qualifying, to a certain degree helped me to appreciate his remarks. You learn a great deal more than the art of dissection when you are trying for your Conjoint. I admit that, while I am styled Dr Eric Soame, as a matter of courtesy (remember William's hyphen) I have the simple letters, M.R.C.S., L.R.C.P. after my name. In the country it is not worth while to go out for any more. You are Doctor anyway, even if you are a Fellow. And the fees are the same in any case.

I hope I pleased Simcox. I think I did. So little helps people to enjoy their lives, and it costs so little to make the effort. The boor who is only interested in his own tastes should be drowned.

"You must show me some more another time, Simcox," I told him, when a glance at my watch showed me that it was nearly lunch time. "And if you let me know about your book later, I will mention it to a friend of mine who is an assistant curator at Kew."

Hector beamed. "Righto! Well, now for a spot of water. See you at lunch."

My visit to his room had convinced me that he knew his job much better than I had imagined. This made me wonder anew if he could be so wrong about the fungi at Château de Luss.

There were other things that puzzled me, outside that. Joe was the metallurgist to the company in England, and in spite of his raffish tout-like appearance, I knew that he was qualified as a chemist. Naturally I do not mean a dispenser of medicines, nor do I suggest that Joe took any interest in toxicology, or a lethal pleasure in poisonous fungi.

But I began to wonder, since he was a metallurgist, if that was also the duty performed by Dr Geyle in Lorraine. A doctor of science could do that job very well, if he tried. That led me, of course, to ask if Joe would have had a bigger position, and greater emoluments, if Dr Geyle went, or if Geyle suspected it. The talked-of merger seemed to interest them more than such things do interest mere specialists.

But here I was worrying again at that old affair. I washed my hands of it in my basin, and went down to lunch, determined to be no party to any further futile speculation.

Chapter VII
SPADES!

Lunch was mercifully taken up with a general discussion of an article which had appeared in one of the Sunday papers. Some bright person had asked and answered the question: "Are Women Generous?" It was about as silly a question as "Do Men Swim?" but that is not the point. Each Sabbath scribe knows his public, and presently we were at it hammer and tongs.

Curiously enough, most of the women said "No," and at least half the men said "Yes." Marie said they never could afford to be; Jean, unwontedly cynical, but perhaps sincere, said that if the virtue was more appreciated they probably would be. Eugene Oliver was, strangely enough, on the side of the angels.

"They are the only really generous people," he observed. "They are always ready to give what they haven't got."

"Especially if it's ours," grunted Joe.

"How can they give it—" began Meriel, then subsided and went on with her fish.

"Scientifically, I suppose we ought to define first," said Hector.

You can judge from that, the sort of nonsense we talked. It is always easy to be epigrammatic if you don t care a rap for common-sense, and only listen to the other fellow without understanding, while you get your own contribution ready.

Still, it gave us a respite from that other oppressing topic, and that was something.

Marie had something up her sleeve for after lunch, and drew the women away with her, leaving the men to do what they wished. Hector Simcox yawned, lit a cigarette, and went up to his lichens. Mr Burton led the way to the great hall, and we settled to talk, sip coffee, and smoke.

It was a blazing hot day outside and the cool of the fine timbered hall was very refreshing, especially when we could look out through the door, and see the crisped grass, and the heat mirages dancing lazily over the lawns.

Joe broke the silence first. "What a bore Simcox is with his damned weeds," he grumbled. "Wish they'd choke him!"

Caley Burton laughed. "He certainly impresses himself, that young man. But I suppose he does know his job?"

Geyle smiled. "Omniscient young blighter!"

Eugene Oliver stuck his legs straight out before him. "Here, here!" he protested. "The young feller has gifts, and he wants to show them when people begin to doubt."

"Who doubts?" said Burton, "and what?"

Oliver puffed at his cigar, shifted it to the corner of his mouth, and replied, "T'other side of the water."

"At the château, d'ye mean?" said Joe.

"Well, what he said you couldn't find there," replied Oliver, lazily. "Those amondillas, or whatever you call 'em."

Soon, I should never have the pluck to look a fungus in the face again.

"Of fungus hot, and fungus cold,

"Fungus new, and fungus old—" I misquoted.

"But seriously," said Joe, while Geyle watched him with quiet eyes, "he would know, wouldn't he?"

I answered for Oliver. "Simcox could certainly tell one variety from another."

"Then what?" began Joe.

"It seems to me a question of locale," put in Geyle. "I for one am not fool enough to say the fellow doesn't know what they are. The point he made was that they didn't grow in the park."

"Well then," said Joe, "if he looked all over the park, and you say he knows his job, then they didn't grow there. Q.E.D."

"Absolutely," said I. "I put that question to him myself this morning. I asked him if he had been all over it. As you people know, I wasn't at the château. I never have been."

"What did he say?" asked Geyle.

I told him, and added that it was a wood, near some village called Varelles, that Simcox had not explored.

"I know the place," said Joe. "It's about fifteen acres and a sort of irregular triangle—good pheasant covert."

"But some distance away from the château," said Burton.

"At any rate," said I, "Hoe-Luss probably strolled there, and found the stuff. Simcox left that spot alone."

"I noticed that he roped you in before lunch to see some of his specimens," remarked Geyle, putting down his coffee cup. "What was it—flowers or veg.?"

"Lichens," I told him.

"Stuff what grows on walls," said Joe.

Burton laughed. "I thought it was something to do with gates to a churchyard," he observed.

"You mean lych-gates. Natural too," said Geyle. "Only Soame here has the pronunciation wrong, or you have. Let's switch on the B.B.C."

"I'll get a dictionary," said Joe.

"Don't!" said Geyle. "All the dictionaries are like the croquet mallets in *Alice*. I find 'humur' for humour now. It used to be 'umur' or 'yumur,' the Y version a bad second."

"Anyway, we have the stuff here," said Joe. "Or is it stone-crop?"

"I haven't seen any stone-crop on the walls," said Geyle. "There is some on the roof of the old stable."

"It is lichen," I informed them. "There is a patch below Simcox's window, a special kind of variety, or hybrid, or something."

"Did he scrape some off for you?" asked Joe.

"No. It is about four feet below the sill. But he means to have a go at it later," I said. "You see, he is comparing specimens for variations. It may have something to do with Mendelism. I am not sure."

Burton yawned, appearing to have had enough of the fungi from France. He wanted to know what Mendelism was, but I turned him over to Geyle, who was much better up in the subject, and asked Joe what were his views on the steel tariffs.

But Joe was brief in his remarks on that topic. It was clear that he was as anxious to get back to the fungi as I to get away from them. Meriel, it appeared, did not like Simcox, nor was Joe himself very sweet on him. He thought the youngster would have been better advised to keep his mouth shut about the stuff William died of.

"It keeps focusing people's minds on Marie," he complained, in a low voice. "As you must know by now, she came best out of it by a good many lengths. And then our friend G. here. We all know he and she were sweethearts years ago."

"You might as well suspect Mrs Graves, who was a sweetheart of Hoe-Luss's," I said scornfully. "She was there too."

"Oh, leave me out," cried Joe, rather vexedly. "I don't suspect anyone. I merely say other people talk, and the sleeping dog advice is right for here. The young pup!"

I saw that Geyle was not listening, but lecturing to Burton, who looked intelligent, and nodded from time to time.

"If it meant anything, it would clear Marie of all suspicions," I said softly. "No one would suggest that she broke his neck."

Galey Burton was at last convinced that he knew enough about Mendelism to satisfy him. He turned to me.

"What are the others doing? Hadn't we better join them?"

I got up. Marie had not made any plans for us, but I did not relish the idea of sitting out the afternoon with Joe, and listening to his perpetual grousing. As I rose, Jean Murphy passed the front door, carrying a book, and wearing a wide, shady hat.

Geyle was off like a shot. Joe grinned at me, and made a gesture. Burton said he would have a walk round outside the house, would I join him? I did not suppose he was going to canvass a new angle of the affair of the fungi, but I was taking no risks.

I excused myself, and went off. In the drawing-room I came on Mrs Graves. She, I felt sure, would not be reminiscent. I asked her would she like to see the view from the hill behind the house, which was a magnificent one, looking over the valley of the Orwen. She got up at once, and agreed. It appeared that she loved scenery. How long would it take?

On a hot day, of course, it took longer, but I was sure we could be back for tea. Marie had taken Fay Hobert, and Aunt Green, in the car to a farm where they bred greyhounds. Miss Hobert thought of buying a couple to enter for races. Mrs Graves and Jean Murphy had cried off.

"I am very fond of Jean," said my companion, as we took the shady path that led upwards through the hanging-wood behind the Chace. "So is Marie."

"And so," I said, smiling, "are others. But perhaps men's affection is not such a compliment."

"It's different in kind, anyway," said Mrs Graves. "Who are your choices?" she added.

"Geyle seems to be the only man really in the running," I told her. "The rest nowhere."

"Not even that boy Simcox?"

I shook my head. "They were children together. That is always a handicap, isn't it?"

She smiled a little wryly. "Did you know that William and I were neighbours at about the same age, Dr Soame?"

I wiped my brow furtively. Curse those fungi! Were they on the conversational menu again?

"I did not know that."

She smiled. "With doctors I am always frank. I feel that they can detect the complexion beneath the cosmetic. I wear well, you think?"

I had to laugh. "You show no signs of it, which is another matter. What is the secret?"

"Don't worry!" said she. "I never do. But this is a digression, isn't it. We were talking about these young people. That boy is very much in earnest about Jean, you know. Only, being young, he is in deadly fear of showing it. He's frightfully hipped."

"How can you know, if he is shy of showing it?"

"Well, you see, I am old to him," she replied amusedly. "I may appear to you a well-preserved forty-five, but Hector naturally places me among they aged. He talked to me a bit about Jean, and I am sure he is dreadfully cut up at the prospect of losing her."

"He never had her," I said. "I gathered as much from her—a tribute to my age too, I suppose. But I shouldn't worry, if I were you. He is young enough to get over it."

"That isn't always true," she commented. "Age gives a sense of proportion and perspective. At the moment our young friend thinks the world at an end."

I felt annoyed. All this modern talk of the disillusionment of youth seems to me as exaggerated as the fuss about bandits, just because there have been a few hold-ups on the road.

"What has the present generation to be disillusioned about?" I asked. "There were wars before 1914, and soldiers had to undergo amputation without anaesthetics, and live afterwards without pensions. And young people never had half as good a time as now. Of course, I don't believe that the majority of young people are disillusioned—only the novelists who write about 'em."

"You find Hector trying?" she asked.

"No, I rather like him," I said. "There's more in him than I thought. Only it seems silly, his crying for the moon when he knows someone else has the long ladder. But I expect you are mistaken. Things always sound worse than they are."

"Oh, I didn't say he was suicidal about it," she laughed; "but he is upset, I am sure of that."

She duly admired the view, and smoked a cigarette with me on the apex of the hill. Then we went down again, to find that Caley Burton had stumped down to the village to post a letter, Joe and Meriel were drowsing in chairs under a lawn cedar, and Geyle and Jean were not visible. I heard afterwards from her that they took out a punt on the lake. Hector Simcox came down for his tea, just as the car returned with Marie, Aunt Green, and Fay Hobert.

The latter had chosen two young greyhounds, which were to remain at the farm for another fortnight. She had got them cheap, and the cynical Aunt Green prophesied that they would turn out as rubbishy as most bargains. All the others turned up then, and the argument became general. Were the good things of life ever cheap?

We sat on the lawn for an hour after tea, and then the disintegration began again, and everyone drifted away to his own chosen haunt, singly, or in couples. Hector Simcox went off solitarily, to find in the park some variety of the wild orchis.

I was very hot after my walk, and sitting out had not cooled me. So I had a bath, and then went to my room in the right wing to write letters. There were at least ten notes I should never have penned if it had not been for my growing boredom. I had expected great things from my visit to Hebble Chace. None of them had come true. The inquest, if it were one, was proving as dull as a funeral.

When we assembled for dinner at eight, Simcox's place was vacant.

"Where has that boy got to?" asked Marie, glancing at his empty chair. "Has anyone seen him?"

Geyle nodded. "Well, about an hour back. I looked in to see his collection of lichens. Rather interesting."

"We shan't wait," said Marie. "I expect he will turn up in a minute or two."

But he did not turn up again at that table. It was agreed that he must have taken some mad whim to try the park, or the woods, for something in the botanical line. A footman sent up to his room said that it was empty.

Chapter VIII
MY PSYCHIC BID

Collectors of all kinds are apt to get so enthusiastic in their quests that one never looks for them in the appointed time at the appointed place, or worries if they do not turn up.

We fully expected to see Hector Simcox, since it was a fine summer evening, turn up late, with a box full of botanical odds and ends, and shouting loudly for supper.

But at half-past nine, the tender-hearted Mrs Graves spoke to Marie about his absence, and Marie glanced over at me.

"I wonder would you run up to his room, Dr Soame, and see if he dressed for dinner? I can't think that he did, if he was going collecting."

Of course I volunteered, remarking that I wondered if the footman had only tried the dressing-room. "Which is now only a workroom," I added.

I left them, and went upstairs. His large bedroom disclosed no signs of his dress clothes! How like the boy, to get into a boiled shirt, and start out on a hunt for his beloved specimens.

But, to be sure that he was not absorbed in some botanical dissection, I opened the communicating door and stepped into the dressing-room.

As I had expected, it was empty. There were the same things on the table as were there when I visited the room with him that morning. In addition, there were a few small flowers in a flat tin box. I was sorry I had not remarked the number of his collecting-cases, to tell if one were missing. But it hardly mattered, I thought. He must have gone out.

I went back, and told them, and they settled down to their games again.

Jean and Geyle sat together, and seemed much interested in each other. I felt sure that they would make a match of it, and I hoped that she had chosen well. I do not like that smooth type of man myself, but that was a personal prejudice, and may have meant nothing.

I read a novel that interested me a great deal, and it was half-past ten when I shut it, and thought once more of Hector. It was quite dark outside now, and I wondered where the dickens the young fellow had got to.

Joe appeared to have the same thought simultaneously.

"Where is our wandering boy to-night?" he asked suddenly.

They all looked at each other. He had been forgotten, and Marie frowned.

"I think he is a very silly young man," she announced. "He must know that we weren't warned he was going out."

I volunteered again to see if he was in his room. Perhaps he was hipped about Jean and Geyle. Sulky, perhaps, and simply slid off to bed without coming down. But I did not find him upstairs.

"But surely that's absurd?" said Burton, "and unmannerly!"

Oliver laughed. "Oh, come, Burton! That's a bit too much."

Jean looked across. "Hector was like that as a boy," she said. "He would dart off without notice, and give his people something to wonder about."

We settled down again for a little. It was Burton who, in spite of his last remark, said that we ought to see what had come to Simcox. Geyle backed him up, and finally, having once more determined the fact that he was not in his room, we did get up a search-party, sallied out—the men only of course—with electric torches, inquired at the two lodges, and returned without having seen or heard anything of Hector.

Marie was still up when we got back. The others had gone to bed.

I don't know why I slipped out again. I had nothing to go on but a feeling that Hector had not gone into the park. I left Marie talking to the others, and went round to the flagged path beneath the young man's window.

I found him there dead. A glance at the injuries to his head assured me that he had not survived the fall a moment. It was quite dark then, of course, but in spite of my professional familiarity with death, this sight gave me a dreadful shock. I had begun to like him. And he was young, and this was such a terrible end to what might have been a prosperous and happy career.

I ran back to the house. Mercifully, I found that Marie had gone upstairs, also Caley Burton, and Joe. Dr. Geyle was fiddling with his electric torch, and talking to 'Gene Oliver.

"Where the dickens did you get to?" he asked me.

I told them what I had found. Oliver swore, and his face turned pale.

Geyle was more composed. He muttered something about it being a dreadful thing, and volunteered to come out with me. Oliver baulked. He said it was damned funny, but he could never look at blood without being sick. Was there anything he could do, short of that.

"Yes," I told him. "Ring up the police station, and ask the constable to come up. Luckily I am police surgeon. But we had better get a footman to help carry him in. Not a word to anyone else yet."

We got a footman with strong nerves, and went out. Geyle was the kind of man I wanted in this emergency. He wasted no words, and had had the foresight to cut into the billiard-room, and bring a piece of chalk with him.

He said he thought, for the purposes of the inquest, it might be useful to mark where the body had fallen. I agreed. I did not think it was suicide. Probably Hector had had a cut at getting those lichens, and overbalanced. But an inquest would certainly be necessary, and I intended to ring up the coroner early next day.

Having marked the spot, we got the poor fellow into the house, and decided to put the body on the billiards-table. I asked Geyle if he would scout about outside, to see if there was anything to indicate that Simcox had been hanging out of his window when the accident happened. Then I dismissed the footman, with strict instructions to say nothing to anybody about the affair, and set to work to make my examination.

The body was completely clothed; evening-clothes, and white shirt, the black tie very neatly tied, and a cigarette case and matches in the pockets. I thought that might have a bearing on the evidence I should be required to give at the inquest. People who are mentally afflicted are incalculable, but the normal man who, for some passing reason, or on impulse, thinks of suicide, is unlikely to take pains to dress himself correctly before taking his life. The very neat bow also suggested that Hector was not emotionally disturbed at the moment when he tied it. Then, though the cigarette case and matches might have been put mechanically into the pockets when he dressed, their presence there made me believe that he had fully intended to go down to dinner.

In any case, the question of suicide would involve Jean Murphy. I did not want to have her dragged into the inquest. The idea that he was jealous beyond reason only rested on a remark of Mrs Graves, and you must be very unreasonably jealous to fling yourself on to a flagged path beneath your window.

Gene Oliver, a complete ass for once, had telephoned the police, and then informed Marie of the occurrence. I had forgotten to warn him sufficiently sternly, or rather, counted on his common sense. Marie had fainted, and Jean Murphy, who occupied the bedroom, had come in a hurry to see what was wrong.

Luckily, Mrs Graves arrived on the scene, and Caley Burton. They revived the swooning woman, and got the sobbing girl back to her bedroom, where Fay Hobert volunteered to sleep with her for that night.

I heard some disturbing sounds, but did not go up. Geyle came in, said that ass Oliver had told Marie, and there was trouble upstairs, and then sat down on the 'bank' to watch me.

The chief injury was a fractured skull. There were other fractures, of course, but the fall on his head had killed Simcox instantly. I said so to Geyle, and then noticed that he had some small object in his hand. "Incidentally, he broke his neck," I told Geyle.

He started. "Good heavens!" His tone was so queer that I thought he was recollecting another acquaintance who had also broken his neck. "By the way, Dr Soame, I picked this up on the soil just beyond the flags."

We had procured a sheet when we went in, and I now drew it over the body, and sat down by Geyle to look at the thing he offered me. It was a medium-sized pen-knife, the bigger blade opened, the handle one of smooth ivory.

"It's clean," he said, "so it wasn't out long. The dew these nights would soon rust it."

I agreed. "Do you recognize it?"

He shook his head. "No, I don't."

"It may be his," I suggested. "I had better put it away, and not handle it."

He seemed surprised. "Why not?"

I had an idea, of course, and told him. "It just strikes me that, if this belonged to him, no one in the house may be able to identify it. I certainly never saw it, and you didn't. But we can easily trace it by his finger-prints."

Geyle nodded. "Good. I can manage that, if you like. I have seen it done by old Foodheimer, who used to teach us physiology. He was called in by the Metz police now and again."

"I think we'll leave it for the present," I said, and rolled it up in my handkerchief, till I could get upstairs. "We'll ask first."

Geyle assented. "What do you think happened?"

I explained my theory. "That knife seems to complete it," I said; "there are two alternatives, suicide or accident."

He looked surprised at that. "My dear fellow! Suicide?"

"Mrs Graves has an idea he was deeply in love with Jean Murphy," I told him.

He bit his lip at that, but shook his head vigorously. "You don't mind if I say that's rot! I know he was fond of her; very fond of her, you may say. But you don't tell me that an educated man like that commits suicide because he—No, I told you I was with him about seven. He was quite cheery then, and on Mrs Graves' theory, I must have seemed to him the villain of the piece."

"Very well. I only gave it as one of two alternatives," I told him. "The other is accident. He showed me that lichen under the window, and I gathered that he was going to get some of it later on."

Geyle slapped his knee. "That's it!"

I was glad that he saw my point. "This knife, you see. If he had it in one hand, ready to scrape off a bit of the lichen, and suddenly slipped, it would be jerked out of his hand."

Geyle nodded. "That's it. Poor young devil. Think of losing your life for a bit of fungi."

I don't quite know why the word startled me, but it did. Lichens are parasitic fungi (sometimes parasitic on each other), but I had never thought of them as that.

"An ill-omened word," I murmured.

"So it is," said Geyle, "so it is!" He changed the subject very quickly. "Why isn't that copper here yet?"

The 'copper,' P.C. Harris, turned up a minute later, and was shown in by the footman. He was a man of forty, tall, not unintelligent, and, if excited by the unusual nature of the occurrence, not inclined to be swept off his official feet by it.

I explained what had happened, while he took notes. Then I drew back the sheet, and roughly explained the nature of the injuries. Harris took that down too, and the body was covered up once more.

"Now you had better see the place where I found him, and then you can go back, and ring up the superintendent, and report," I said. "I am afraid an inquest will be necessary. I shall communicate myself with Mr Lay, the coroner."

"That would be best, sir," said Harris, and turned to Geyle. "Who is this gentleman, sir?"

"Dr Geyle, a guest here, who has helped me," I said.

Geyle nodded. "I suppose it was all right moving the body, officer? We marked the spot where it fell."

Harris agreed. "'Tisn't like a murder, sir, and Dr Soame here being our surgeon," he put it that way apologetically, "it's all right. But I think the dead gentleman's room ought to be locked up, sir."

I rang for the footman, but Geyle volunteered to go up, lock the doors of the bed- and dressing-rooms, and bring the keys down to us.

We borrowed his torch, and with it and mine we went out, and examined the flagged path. "We'd better get it cleaned up before the ladies come out to-morrow," I said.

Harris had a better idea. We should get some sacking, or a tarpaulin, and cover it over till the superintendent saw it.

"You and Dr Geyle were the only gentlemen to come out here?" he added. "Except the footman?"

"Yes. I don't suppose any of the other guests will be required to give evidence at the inquest?"

"No, sir. I think not. Your idea is he fell when trying to get some of—of that stuff that grows on walls?"

"Yes," I said, and then we went to a tool-shed in the back garden, covered the spot where Simcox had fallen, and went back to the billiards-room. Geyle was there with two keys.

Chapter IX
THE WRONG SUIT

"This is the thing that makes me believe Mr Simcox was trying to remove some lichen," I said, showing Harris the pen-knife. "It was found by Doctor Geyle here, just off the flagged path. I assume that the young fellow had it in his hand when he fell."

Harris looked at it. "It does look like it, sir. Shall I take that?"

53 | INQUEST

"I shall give it to the superintendent to-morrow," I said. "I want to make sure it is—or was—the property of the dead man."

Harris made a note, shut his book, and put it away, and said he would go back to report. I did not see that there was anything else he could do, so I saw him out.

"I'll lock this room, then we had both better get to bed, Geyle," I told my companion. "I may get Dr Marsond up later, but there is no hurry now. Go up as quietly as you can. We don't want an excited crowd worrying us for details."

I slept further down the passage where poor Simcox had his bedroom. Geyle was in the other wing of the L. I was held up for a moment or two by Burton and Joe, who opened their doors, as I made some slight noise in passing, and had to be told what I thought had occurred. But I refused to go into details, and went on to my room. I heard someone whimpering as I passed Jean Murphy's door, but no sound from Marie s room.

By the time I got to my room, I felt I needed a smoke. I put on a dressing-gown, and sat down in an easy chair to have a cigarette.

Someone had jested about this being an inquest got up by Marie. By Jove! we were now to have an inquest in earnest. There was a horrid coincidence about that that worried me. And I was dreadfully sorry for the young fellow, and for Marie too, who had only got over one tragedy to run into another, in this ill-omened conjunction of guests.

There they were; with the exception of myself, the same crowd who had stayed at the château when William Hoe-Luss died. No wonder Geyle had started when I remarked: "Incidentally, he broke his neck." Fortunately, no one would comment on that at the inquest. When it was decided that Hoe-Luss died primarily of poisoning by fungi, the irrelevant detail was not mentioned publicly.

Fortunately again, I said to myself, this was a clean-cut issue, a simple accident, with no money motives involved; just a young, eager botanist, who tried to get a specimen, and lost his life in the attempt. The edelweiss of the Alps has been responsible for a score of somewhat similar tragedies. It would be unpleasant for our hostess, but it would soon blow over.

I suppose I should have gone to bed then, and tried to get a sleep, to clear my mind. If you keep on thinking round a problem, you are apt to lose your sense of proportion, and get lost in a maze of wild theories and silly speculations.

I don't know why it was that Hector Simcox's white shirt came into my mind. It wasn't white or smooth when I found the poor devil. But it did come into my mind, white and smooth and clean, as he had dressed for dinner—dressed so carefully too; with that black bow-tie such a marvel of neat handling.

I repeat that you must judge a man's state of mind when you consider evidence like that. Hector was not mad, and in any case we had decided that his death was an accident. Very well then. I had to take him as a normal, sane young man; rather dandified and particular about how he looked when he was about to dine.

It was true he was impulsive in some ways. But he was scientifically-minded; a trained man. A wild lover may be a meticulously accurate draughtsman. Hector may have been emotional with regard to Jean, and yet calm and careful when at work at his job.

But why did I think only of the white shirt? I don't quite know. I have met keen shots, who hated seeing birds that were shot through the eye. Human nature is funny. A man takes more care to keep his broad white front unspotted than his evening-clothes. And the white shirt is easier cleaned, or washed. But that is not the point. Watch any man dressed for dinner, and see.

As I lit a second cigarette, I saw the whole scene in my mind's eye. Hector decided to get some of that lichen. He took the pen-knife, and leaned down out of the window, slipped, and fell headlong.

But that white shirt! Hang it, he would be crushing it, either against the sash at the bottom or the dirty sill beyond. He had had all the afternoon to get the specimen.

Well, I went to bed at last, and when I woke, though I remembered the affair with horror, I had a clearer head, and began to wonder if my late night speculations were not rather imaginative. I looked at my watch. It was just seven. I got up, had a bath, shaved, and thought I would have another look at the body before the others got up. Then I remembered that the policeman had taken the keys.

I looked out of my window, and saw that an under-gardener was at work not fifteen yards from the path.

I went out of the house, and told him on no account to remove the sacking we had put over a section of the flags, but to warn anyone else on the staff that it was to be avoided.

I knew Lay, the coroner, was an early bird. I rang him up next, and informed him of the accident. He was very sorry, but both country coroners and country policemen nowadays are not greatly excited by accidental deaths. There is always some venturesome motorist, or cyclist, or unfortunate pedestrian, to be dealt with.

You must remember that the superintendent of police there knew nothing of the extraordinary atmosphere into which I had been brought, nothing of the rumours and counter-rumours regarding Hoe-Luss's death. No doubt he took Simcox's mishap to be a mere question of a fall from a window.

So he did not turn up until ten. By that time, I had asked everyone in the party if they recognized the pen-knife as having belonged to Hector. No one did. No one had seen him use a pen-knife for any purpose. And no one claimed the pen-knife as his own.

That latter fact rather worried me.

That is not quite correct. I remember I did not see Aunt Green. She was driven to the station at a quarter to ten, after what was described to me by Oliver as a most unholy row with Marie. I did not hear it, but when I asked Marie about the knife, she said something about Aunt Green being intolerable. "That woman shall not enter my house again!" she said.

I expect Aunt Green could not keep her tongue from speaking evil. I was not ill-pleased that she had gone.

Poor Jean did not look like an actress when I saw her. Her eyes were red and swollen with crying. She was certainly much upset by Hector's death, and it was with the greatest difficulty that I managed to extract from her the fact that he was an orphan. Mr Simcox had been killed in a motor accident on the Stelvio ten years ago, and his wife, Hector's mother, had not recovered from the shock. There were, as far as Jean knew, no living relatives.

Only five came down to breakfast: Caley Burton; Oliver, who looked as if he had not slept a wink all night, and was trembling with nervousness; Joe, sulky and pale; myself, and Dr Geyle. Geyle was composed as ever, his hair lay as smoothly on his head as if he had devoted an hour to its subjugation.

When Superintendent Dale turned up with his sergeant, and Dr Marsond, whom he had decided to bring, I took them all into the billiards-room. Dale had a look at the body, and then suggested that Marsond should undertake the post-mortem. I agreed. Some preparations were made, Marsond had brought his instruments with him, and we left him to it.

Dale and the sergeant and I went into the little library. They had heard the constable's report, and consequently brought with them the apparatus for bringing out finger-prints.

Dale smiled as he told me that. "I don't think it will be necessary, doctor, for I expect you were able to trace the ownership of that pen-knife."

I shook my head, and handed the thing over, still wrapped in my handkerchief. "No. But that does not prove it was not his. How many times does one produce a pen-knife in company?"

He laughed. "Not often. You explain its finding, I suppose, on the ground that the dead man had it in his hand when he fell."

"To remove some lichen for a specimen, Dale. He was a keen botanist."

"I see," he murmured. "Well, get to work on this handle, sergeant, and let us know what you find."

"There will be at least two prints on it," I told the sergeant. "Dr Geyle found it and brought it in, and I took it from him."

Dale wanted to see the bedroom, and I took him up the backstairs, which were at the end of the western L of the house, near the three bath-rooms in that wing, to avoid meeting any of the house-party. I showed him the room and dressing-room, and then the patches of lichen on which poor Simcox had set his heart.

"Doesn't look as if he had even started to work," said Dale, leaning far down, while I hung on to the tail of his jacket. "We'll assume that he overbalanced almost immediately. I don't wonder."

"I took that to be so from the state of the knife blade," I told him. "It was dirty where it struck the soil beyond the flags, but the blade did not show any signs of having been scraped against stone."

He nodded perfunctorily. "I suppose so. Well, we have all the evidence we want for the inquest, I imagine. I am a pretty tall man and, as you saw, I had to do some wangling to get a proper look at that stuff on the wall."

We were going down the passage again when Burton came after us. He had just come upstairs from the hall, and had a telegram in his hand. He had been called to Lorraine on business, but was anxious to know when the inquest would take place. He thought he ought to be present, and would put off his departure for a short time if necessary.

Dale smiled, and said it would not be necessary. The inquest would be purely formal. But Burton did not agree. His was the bedroom next to Simcox's, and he had heard nothing of the fall.

"My evidence may help to fix the time of death," he said. "In any case, I think I shall stop, to support poor Mrs Hoe-Luss."

"That is a matter for yourself, sir," replied Dale. "There is nothing in the affair to worry about. In a case of accidental death, the exact time is not important."

Burton said he would stop anyway. I hoped inwardly that he was not going to make trouble, and had not been, like myself, speculating incautiously on fantastic possibilities. He left us, and we went back to the library.

The sergeant had done his job, and did not seem very satisfied about it.

"I can only bring out four prints, sir," he said to Dale. "That will be Dr Soame's finger and thumb, and Dr Geyle's."

Dale smiled. "Now we have begun the job, we may as well finish it. Go to Dr Marsond with my compliments, and ask him to let you take prints from the fingers of the body. It must have been Mr Simcox's knife, for the doctor says no one claims it."

The sergeant went off, and we left the house so that Dale could examine the spot where Simcox had fallen.

I noticed that two servants had thrust their heads out of a window on the top floor, where they slept, but no one else appeared interested in our proceedings.

Dale inspected the spot carefully, then said that he thought no purpose could be served by further delay in washing the path. "I'll get that gardener on to it," he said, as a man came near us. "It will only give one of the ladies a nasty shock later."

"You see, the affair is obvious at a glance," he added, when he had given the reluctant gardener that job. "Of course the poor fellow might have got off with a broken limb. He was unlucky!"

Marsond's post-mortem was naturally limited to the injured regions. And it did not take long. He came to see me, and told me that he agreed with my views as to the cause of death. I could sign the death certificate with an easy conscience.

"Poor devil!" he added. "A fine healthy fellow, but he must have been crazy to do what he did. I say, Dale, what day is the inquest?"

"We can make it Wednesday, I think," said the superintendent. "It is a straightforward affair, and we needn't keep Mrs Hoe-Luss harried any longer than is necessary. I'll send men up for the body when I get back."

Marsond drove off, and we went in search of the sergeant. He was still puzzled. It seemed that Simcox's finger-prints did not coincide with those on the handle of the pen-knife, or I suppose it is more correct to say that they did not appear on it at all.

"Never mind," said Dale, looking at his watch. "It can't have much bearing on the accident after all. Mr Simcox leaned out, overbalanced, and that's all there is to it."

He was a busy man, and had important matters to attend to. He saw Marie, explained things, notified her about the inquest, and promised to clear the business up as soon as possible.

I was to go to Winstone, the town where the county business was transacted, to speak to the coroner, and sign the death certificate.

I felt relieved. It was another bright, sunny day. The mists that had fogged my brain had cleared. The thing presented itself to me now more sharply and simply defined.

I lit a cigarette, and determined to go for a sharp walk. But Joe had seen me, and as I started across the park, he came after me, and took my arm.

Chapter X
DID SIMCOX WANT TO CUT?

I expect you have gathered from my observations that Joe Hoe-Luss was not a favourite of mine. His constant grousing, his appearance of raffishness, and his temperament were repellent to me. I determined to stop any futile discussion of the matter by telling him at once that there was no doubt about the accident.

I told him what Dale had said, and added, "I am going for a five-mile sprint, just to work it out of my system."

I hoped that would send him back to the house, but he declared that he wanted exercise badly, and lengthened his step to suit mine.

"Old Aunt Green didn't think it so simple," he urged, as we walked. "Gosh! you should have heard her. Marie turned at last, and told her to put a sock in it."

I was annoyed. "There has been far too much gossip and backbiting ever since I came here," I said sharply. "If there is so faint excuse for her, on the ground that she has nothing else in life to do, there is none for other people."

He grinned. "That's what I say. By the way, it was a rum go about that knife. It doesn't seem to have any home to go to. Or did you find it was Simcox's?"

"No," I said shortly, "I didn't. But it is of no importance, and does not affect the issue."

"Fellows in my job are trained to observation, and Simcox, though he was always grubbing in the ground for roots, kept his hands nice, and his nails well manicured," he murmured.

I looked at Joe. What was he hinting now?

"My dear fellow," I said, "what has manicure got to do with it?"

"It disproves the vulgar possibility that the poor fellow was cutting his nails with the knife, standing at the window."

This was too silly and, I thought, flippant. "Don't be stupid! The knife was to remove the lichen from the wall."

Joe's look at me contained so much genuine surprise that it made me momentarily uneasy, and it became slightly contemptuous.

"Good heavens, man! And you saw Simcox's specimens, and talk tripe like that. Damn it! where are your eyes?"

Joe is not tactful, but this time I forgave him, since I saw that he had observed something which had escaped me.

"Pretty good as a rule," I said, "and in the usual position. Why?"

He shrugged his shoulders. "Strange! Why, Simcox was a scientific worker, a delicate worker, as he had to be. And the specimens were set up remarkably well; a work of art, even to a fellow like myself, who has a different field."

"I did notice that," I replied stiffly. "My eyes were equal to that observation."

"Then your brain wasn't," he said, rather rudely. "I suppose you wouldn't perform operations with a sickle, would you?"

"A glimpse of the obvious," I said.

"Quite. I meant it to be. Here is Simcox, a trained botanist. He wants to secure a specimen of a delicate growth, adhering to a wall, for scientific purposes. He wasn't a blue-bell raider, grabbing up plants by the roots," he added, rubbing it in.

I started, and stopped. "You mean that knife?"

"Of course I do. A rotten half-crown pen-knife, not even sharp, the blade flat, and you took it to be the tool with which he proposed to shave specimens off irregular stones."

I admitted my mistake at once. I have read novels, written by clever men in their own line, about tiger-hunting in Africa. I had made the same kind of mistake. "That's clever of you," I said, "very clever."

He grunted. "Extremely simple, if you ask me. It simply yelled to be seen."

"No one else noticed it," I said feebly.

"There may be reasons for that," said Joe, grimly.

I headed him off from that line. "Then it simply means that someone unknown happened to drop a pen-knife in the garden near where the poor chap fell."

"Yesterday," said Joe; "dropped it yesterday, and forgot this morning that he ever owned it."

"Perhaps you know to whom it belongs," I said.

"I don't," said Joe. "But it wasn't manna from the sky."

I nodded. "No. But after all, the fall is explained more clearly that way. As you say, the knife is not suited to delicate botanical work, and I don't suppose Hector had it in his hand at all. When you come to think of it, he wouldn't try to get the stuff after dressing."

"I should say not," said Joe.

"But he might say to himself that he would have a go at it first thing this morning, and just look out to see it before he went down."

Joe seemed more satisfied now. "Yes, that would cover it. What worried me was that tripe about the knife being used for the lichen. Anyway, this is a nasty jar for Marie."

"In what way?"

He raised his eyebrows. "Of course, coming so near on top of the other rotten affair, Soame. First her husband breaks his neck; and then young Simcox. That was what made old Auntie talk, you bet. She has her knife in her and Geyle."

"Wait a moment," I said. "Why drag in Geyle?"

"I didn't," he protested. "And I only heard the tail-end of the row. Of course Geyle was in with Hector about an hour before—he says it was an hour anyway, and she is always hinting that Geyle and Marie are still hoping to make it up."

"Now that is nonsense," I told him. "She is most anxious that Geyle should marry Jean Murphy. I think the girl's too good for him, but that is how it stands. She told me so herself."

He grinned in his sceptical way. "I suppose you always take your patients' word for it? By the way, are you going to sign the death certificate, or does that other johnnie do it—the fellow who made the post-mortem?"

I considered that point. After all, Marsond had done that, and he was the right man to sign. But now I wanted to get away from Joe and his innuendoes, so I remembered that I had to see Lay, the coroner. I hurried back, with Joe at my heels, and drove off to Winstone.

Lay heard what I had to say, and agreed that Simcox had most likely leaned out to take a peep at his beloved lichen, and gone overboard.

"It won't take long to get that settled," he said. "Sorry poor Mrs Hoe-Luss has this other bother on top of the recent tragedy, but you can tell her in confidence that a couple of hours ought to wind up proceedings. Marsond will sign the cause of death, you say? Good! See you on Wednesday then."

When I drove off, I ran into Major Tobey, the Chief Constable. He was coming out of a shop where they sold fishing-tackle, and hailed me.

"I say, Soame, what is this about an accident up at the Chace?" he asked, when I drew up.

"If you are going home, let me drop you," I said, admiring, as I had always admired, Tobey's six feet of athletic frame, that of a man of forty (not the sixty of actuality), and his handsome sun-burned face, with its neatly cut grey moustache, and the bright eyes that helped to make his smile so attractive. "I'll tell you as we go along."

We had been great friends ever since he came to Winstone ten years before, and I often turned in at his place on winter evenings for a chat and a smoke.

He was well fitted for his job, intelligent, quick, but sound; and had become a member of the Bar since his retirement from the Army. I felt that here, if anywhere, was a fitting recipient of any confidences I might wish to make. I didn't trust anyone very much up at the Chace, except perhaps Jean Murphy, and I had done some rapid and troubled thinking since I talked with Joe in the park.

Whatever I said to him, that knife was significant. Who owned it, dropped it so recently, and forgot to mention it? It was a cheap thing, and I would make inquiries among the household and garden staff when I got back. Meanwhile, why was it just beside the spot where Hector had been killed?

Then my mind had gone back to his evening-clothes and that white shirt. I had stalled off Joe, who might be fishing indirectly for information by talking of Simcox leaning out to look at the lichen before he went down. But I felt that my explanation did not explain. He knew the lichen hadn't flown away, and if he wanted a really close glance at it, he would have had to do the kind of gymnastics Dale had indulged in. Actually I had no proof that Hector had meant to get it from the window. If removing the stuff was such a delicate job, he would have got a ladder, and gone up.

I did not intend to explain these doubts to any of the mob up at the Chace. They seemed to have enough subjects for suspicion and innuendo as it was. But I began to be glad that I had not to sign the death certificate. Of course I should be merely registering the cause, which was obvious; fractured skull and broken neck. But I did not care to give evidence about the fall.

And yet, why not? Nobody profited by the fellow's death, not even Geyle, who would have no motive for trying to remove an unsuccessful rival.

I told Tobey the details roughly as I drove him to his house, a detached one with a nice garden, near the borders of the Cathedral Close. But when I mentioned the pen-knife, he pursed his lips, and irrelevantly asked would I come in to lunch.

I wanted a chat with him, so drove in, and left the car on the drive. He took me into his study, gave me a cigar, and said we had a clear forty minutes.

"That knife, you know," he murmured, sitting down opposite me. "Did you or Geyle own it?"

I laughed. "You haven't been listening," I said. "Our finger-prints were on it, but only because we handled it when found."

"I know. Yes. But the blade was open, according to your friend. And there were no other finger-prints on the handle, according to the sergeant. Didn't that strike you as odd?"

"It didn't," I replied, staring. "But it is. What do you think it means?"

"In an ordinary case," said Tobey, "I should say that the owner was wearing gloves, or cleaned the handle."

"But this hot weather—and in the garden. Who would wear gloves?"

"A woman might—getting roses," said Tobey.

I went on to tell him my doubts about a man—especially a fellow like Simcox, who was a dandy at night—irretrievably creasing and soiling his white shirt after dressing, and he agreed that that was a more valid objection.

"But, I say, Soame," he remarked, "what's biting you? What put you up to this worrying?"

"You mean why do I not accept it as a perfectly straightforward case of accident?" I asked.

"Yes. You are not one of those fools always wanting to play the detective. But here you are trying to show me that this orphan botanist might have been done in. Reason and motive most obscure!"

That is how it must have looked to him. It was difficult to explain what I meant, unless I showed him how the atmosphere at the Chace had disagreeably affected me since I went there three days ago. I knew he would judge better than I was able to do, if my feats were real, or imaginary ones generated by contact with that lot at the house.

I did my best to tell him, starting with my talk with 'Gene Oliver, and finishing with Joe's hints that morning, and the echo of the row between Marie and Aunt Green.

"Evil communications affect more than good manners," I added. "I wouldn't have believed that about two days' gossip could make me begin to wonder how many hopeful homicides go to a house-party."

Tobey had listened attentively, puffing at his cigar. He nodded now, and appeared to find my new distrustfulness not unwarranted.

"The talk you heard does make it seem that many of the guests regarded Hoe-Luss's death as suspicious," he said. "Interested parties are often devilishly apt to libel people, when they are disappointed in their expectations. But granting, for the sake of a hypothesis, that Hoe-Luss was murdered (arrant nonsense, of course!), the one person in the whole house who seems to stand clear of it is this young fellow Simcox."

"That is what worries me."

"It should be the other way. There was no motive to get rid of him, so it was probably an accident."

"You think so?"

"Until I have evidence of motive I am bound to. We must take it that, for once, he forgot that he was all dressed up, and in his enthusiasm had a last peep at the lichen."

"Lay thinks so, from what I told him."

He assented. "You must have a nice party up there at the Chace," he went on, throwing his cigar-butt away into the fireplace. "Full of malice and all uncharitableness, by Jove! They seem to sit round and talk of poisonous fungi, and its uses and abuses."

"Something like that, with intervals," I said, smiling. There was a sudden spark in his bright eyes. "Wonder over at that French place they didn't call this chap in to vet. the fungi, if you know what I mean."

"There wasn't any left," I said. "So he couldn't see the stuff, and wasn't asked for an opinion."

"Naturally not."

"Though he had a very decided one," I went on, "but did not mention it till lately. I suppose he thought it was irrelevant what particular fungus killed Hoe-Luss."

Tobey sat up. "I don't think you said anything about that."

"No. It was only that Simcox swore there were none of that particular species in the park at Château de Luss."

"Did he tell you so?"

"Yes, but Geyle hinted at it first. Simcox told me afterwards that he was quite sure."

"Then how did he explain the death?"

I told him, and he appeared much interested. "It wasn't in the papers. So Hoe-Luss had a broken neck, and now this young chap has a broken neck. Coincidence, I suppose."

"At any rate," I informed him, "that made another fuss yesterday—or, rather, more gossip. Joe Hoe-Luss worked round to the subject in the afternoon, and I told them what Simcox had said."

"Told whom?" he asked.

"Well, all the men. Geyle knew already, of course. He was there, and—"

"Wait a moment. Dr Geyle is the doctor of science who is supposed to have been a suitor of Mrs Hoe-Luss before her marriage?"

"Yes. He was there; Caley Burton, Hoe-Luss's business associate; Joe, Sir Eugene Oliver, and, of course, myself."

"Did they believe it?"

"I am sure they did not."

Tobey looked at me thoughtfully. "I presume that, but for the meal of fungi, *amanita* or something else, they would have had to fall back on the broken neck as the cause of death?"

"I suppose so. That too, apart from the food taken, might have been an accident."

"Quite. But this old Miss Green, who appears to be a bit of a pest, wanted to work it out that it might be no accident."

I agreed. "I wouldn't listen to her."

"Perhaps not. But, Soame, taking it as another hypothesis, if there was no accident, someone in that house was most anxious that the broken neck should appear secondary, the fungi the primary cause?"

"You don't think—" I began.

"I am only speculating. Following that tentative line of argument, Simcox was a real danger."

"In what way?"

"Barging round telling people that the stuff that was supposed to have killed Hoe-Luss was not to be found in the park at the château."

I could not deny that. It rather frightened me. "You mean that gives a motive?"

Tobey looked at his watch. "Granting this, that, and the other thing—none of which may have any relation to fact. Let's have a spot of lunch and forget it."

Chapter XI
WHY DID HE PLAY THE KNAVE?

But there was that in this case, as in the case of William Hoe-Luss's death, that made it peculiarly hard to forget. Halfway through luncheon, Tobey apologised for opening the subject again, and asked me if Caley Burton was the financier. "For he has a reputation for being pretty ruthless," he added.

"As mild a man as ever cut a throat," I agreed. "I know he had a row with Hoe-Luss, over some merger that fizzled out, but I cannot say that he quarrelled with Simcox. Mind you, I don't say that Burton wouldn't be capable of homicide. I don't know enough about him. But naturally I am aware that many business-men, who would sacrifice a rival without mercy, would not hurt a fly, if it came to physical action."

Tobey smiled. "Elementary. When you told me that yarn about the château, I wondered about that theatrical episode, and the part the girl played in it. You mean to say that Hoe-Luss, with no judgment of affairs of that kind, proposed to launch out not only with an unknown play, but an unknown star?"

"That explains itself, Tobey. A man experienced in theatrical business wouldn't do either."

"I see. No. What sort of young woman is she?"

I began to tell him, and he interrupted me with a laugh. "My dear Soame. We'll never condemn her out of your mouth. I want to know really what motive, other than affection and admiration, could make the man back this compound of Venus and Priscilla."

"I am sure she never tried to vamp him," I replied. "But what about him? How did his wife take it?"

"She has been very kind to Jean, and appeared to like her. I don't believe the poisonous gossip about her being jealous of the girl."

Tobey pondered. "Hoe-Luss's death severed the connection, at any rate, and not only saved five thousand pounds (which would have undoubtedly gone west), but left Mrs Hoe-Luss a fortune," said he. "That is nothing more than what I take to have been the gossip at the château."

"Quite," I agreed. "The venomous gist of it was a hint that Mrs Hoe-Luss might have removed her husband out of jealousy, knowing at the same time that she would inherit his fortune. The absurd point about that, of course, was the fact that he died of eating fungi he had gathered himself. The only thing to bolster it up was that she dismissed the cook afterwards, who has now retired."

"Just a moment," said he. "I know the ordinary G.P. isn't a toxicological expert, but would you say that the symptoms of poisoning by fungi in that case might resemble symptoms produced by a drug?"

"I was not there, but from what I heard, I should say yes."

"Whereas, if it had been decided that Hoe-Luss died of a broken neck, that verdict would exonerate his widow?"

"Yes, I should say so."

Tobey was an intelligent man. "That in itself seems to put paid to part of this Aunt Green's gossip, Soame. The verdict was given by this French doctor. It was hinted to you that Mrs Hoe-Luss had him in her pocket. Had that been so, the verdict would have cleared *her*."

I said that that was so. I added that the only motive Geyle could have to assist Marie in such a fiendish thing would be a desire to marry her and the fortune.

"What I mean is this," said Tobey, ignoring my remark. "If Hoe-Luss died of a broken neck, it would not suit someone's book to have it known that he hadn't eaten *amanita*. You mentioned Simcox's statement about that to four men, Geyle, Burton, Joe Hoe-Luss, and Sir Oliver—Sir Eugene Oliver. If Simcox met with foul play, then anyone of the four might be at the back of it."

"Or any woman, who knew, and I must say most of the gossip got round," I remarked. "But surely you said just now that it was an accident."

He frowned. "I did. But I keep on wondering what made the fellow lean over far enough to fall out. What you told me of Dale's contortions came back to me. When Simcox showed you the lichen, did you lean out?"

"Not like that," I said quickly. "We put our heads out of the window, and he just indicated the patches."

"You could see them without being anywhere near the over-balancing point."

"Of course."

"And before he fell, we take it that he was not proposing to get a specimen. He would not inspect them either, for he knew what they were. And that knife, Soame! If it doesn't belong to any of the servants, or any of the staff outside or the guests, how did it come there?"

That, of course, had stuck in my own gullet, and prevented me from readily swallowing the simplest explanation of the accident.

"You remember the 'Brides in the Bath' case," he went on conversationally. "The brute simply put a hand under their knees, and hoisted them up, so that their heads went under. Now Simcox, if he leaned out of the window, could have been tipped over by a quick movement of the same kind. I am rather inclined to have experiments made."

I started. "But won't that muck up the inquest?"

"I don't think so. Lay could direct the jury to a verdict of broken neck, with no direct evidence to show how it was—or rather the preceding fall, was caused. We can work on it independently."

"You and I?" I asked.

"No," he astonished me by saying. "After all, I am here to see justice done. What you have told me about preceding circumstances has made me change my mind. If there is a case here too, it is a big case, and involves large interests, not bounded by the county."

"What do you mean by that?" I asked bluntly.

He looked grave. "This man Burton for example, with his companies, and the finance that hangs on them; the widow, who certainly profited; this Sir Eugene fellow, who apparently looked more sick next day than any of the others—a nominee of Burton's, you said?"

"Yes. Well?"

"Well, if I have it investigated, I haven't got the material here, or the men. Dale is a good fellow, but he would not pose as a detective of parts, though there is no better administrator of police routine than he. And my small detective staff is not trained for this kind of job. If you will make inquiries about that knife, and let me know, I will think matters over. If I decide to proceed, I shall consult Scotland Yard."

"Good heavens!" I cried. "Bring them in?"

He nodded. "Yes. Think of that knife again, with no prints on it but yours and Geyle's. Of course, Geyle might have brought it to you, so that his prints would be explained. But take any knife, new or old; people do handle it, prints do get on to it, from the shopman's fingers, as he shows it, and so on. But this was clean, except for the ones I mentioned. I think we might have an experiment first though. Mrs Hoe-Luss would allow us to try that, if you told her that it was necessary for the purpose of the inquest to know exactly how Simcox fell out."

I nodded. "Yes, but what would you do?"

"Our people have the dead man's clothes, Soame, and we know his height and build. We can get a man to wear a white shirt, identical in size, and make him lean out, to see where the mark of the sash, or stone sill, would come. I know Simcox's shirt was in a mess, but not all of it, and an expert would find part of the soiled line, however invisible to the naked eye."

"And the line of pressure would be at least microscopically apparent?" I agreed.

"Yes. The second experiment could be made by one of our fellows, who is about the dead man's height. We could have a sheet held below by men on the path, and our fellow would lean over till he over-balanced, with someone above, and another outside, to mark his exact position when he went over."

I was rather worried. What would Marie think if all this fuss was started again. But, naturally, I knew that Tobey had his job to do, and if Hector Simcox had really been killed, I was as anxious as anyone to have the guilty punished. The idea of someone butchering that harmless boy, just to shut his mouth, filled me with rage.

"I'll do my best to get her permission," I said.

We had come to the end of luncheon, and he rose, and offered me a cigarette. "Look here, Soame, it's too bad to put it on you. If you'll drive me over, I'll talk to the good lady myself. Incidentally, I would like a look at that dressing-room."

"I wish you would," I said.

"I will. If you meet any of these gossipers, make it very clear to them that I'm an old Army man, rather stuffy, and a stickler for accuracy and routine, who won't abate a jot of the rites and ceremonies. I want them to feel that whatever is done is only part of the official machinery to arrive at a proper verdict on an accident. Got that?"

I had. "Must all the guests stay until it is all cleared up?" I asked.

"No, we have their names and addresses."

"Because Burton was called to Lorraine, but elected to stay till after the inquest," I said.

"Shows a public spirit, but is quite unnecessary," he told me. "They can leave when they like, except Geyle, who found the knife, and saw the body after you—and the footman, of course, but he will be here."

I suppose most of the people at the Chace wanted some fresh air, and were not anxious to stay in the house. When we arrived, we found that Marie had sent them out in two cars, to see the castle at Howith, and have tea in the village.

She was rather surprised, when I introduced Major Tobey, and listened to his nicely put expression of sympathy. But she did not seem worried at all when he asked if he might have some experiments carried out to discover the cause of Hector's fall.

"You see it is rather difficult to determine," he remarked, "and the Home Office is apt to get sniffy if we are lax in these matters."

"It does seem extraordinary," she replied, evidently taken with him, "that Hector leaned out like that. Must I be here while you make the experiments, Major Tobey? I was rather anxious to go to Winstone to do some shopping, while my guests were out."

He assured her that it was not necessary, asked if he might use the telephone, and bowed himself out.

"What a handsome man!" she remarked to me, as I was about to follow him. "England certainly does score in its police."

"A delightful fellow, but a trifle fussy about details," I said. "I think the spit-and-polish school in the Army, to which he belonged, is given that way."

When I joined him, he had finished telephoning to Dale for some men to be rushed over with the necessary apparatus for the experiments.

"We'll have the place to ourselves," he said, rather joyfully. "I think I shall glance into that dressing-room now."

"Caley Burton had the room next to it," I told him, as we went up, "or rather next to the bedroom, only facing front."

"Ah, the wicked financier!" he smiled. "Did he hear nothing?"

"He says not. But he was having a bath, part of the time, and the bathrooms are at the very end of this wing," I explained, as we went down the main passage. "Three at this end of the double L."

He followed me into the dressing-room.

"Where is the lichen he showed you?"

I took him to the window, and pointed down.

He just gave it a glance, and pursed his lips.

"He'd have had a ladder for that."

I was fully aware now, of course, that no man could work at that sort of job head down.

But Tobey took a great deal more interest in the room than Dale had done. He examined it every inch, and then stepped back to the door to glance at the window. "What now?" I asked, as he lingered.

"We must give the accident theory the benefit of the doubt," he murmured. "Soame, suppose you were the weed-gatherer, and in a silly moment decided to shave off a patch. How would you go about it?"

"If I were so silly, Tobey, I would, of course, lean over as far as I could, midriff on sill, and—"

"And what would you do with your toes, fair experimenter?" he asked.

"Hang on with them."

"I thought you would."

"I'd have to."

He nodded, and looked serious again.

"Have a look at the paper?"

I took that to mean the wall-paper beneath the inner sill. I had a look at it, and noticed two dents, caused, I had no doubt, by the toes of Superintendent Dale when he leaned out. He was a taller man than Hector Simcox, and Tobey agreed with me that he was responsible for those marks.

"There aren't any others," he added. "What did the youth do? And if he felt himself going he would be bound to give an extra kick, or attempt to hang on."

"That's true," I replied soberly. "This is a rotten business!"

Chapter XII
MAJOR TOBEY CALLS

I LEFT Tobey a few minutes later, and started on my progress in quest of the owner of the pen-knife. I did the indoor servants first, then went the round of the gardeners, the odd-job man, and the three game-keepers. Some of these people had no business to perambulate on the flagged path, but I had to be thorough, and even ended up at the two lodges, where there were children, to make sure.

But no one owned the knife, or owned up to it. I began to get worried. If the knife had not been accidentally dropped where it was found, the assumption was that it had been thrown after Hector, to provide a hint of accident.

I felt very angry. The crime, if it were a crime, had no extenuating circumstances, no personal grudge, or anger, or vengeance behind it, as far as I could see. Simcox had made an innocent discovery, and proclaimed it as legitimately and innocently. On that account, some callous brute had summarily and cruelly closed his mouth for ever.

I saw now the real point of Tobey's remark that this case extended beyond the bounds of the county, out of his jurisdiction altogether. There was nothing whatever in Simcox's discovery to disturb or alarm anyone, save the person or persons who had conspired against William Hoe-Luss's life.

But that conclusion pulled me up with a round turn. It involved so much. Hector's murder was senseless unless Hoe-Luss had been murdered too. If I accepted the theory of murder here, I must accept it at the Château de Luss.

It seemed to me that Marie had a motive in the former case, and Geyle, too, if he was really only flirting with Jean Murphy as a blind. I determined to find out from him if the merger had really fallen flat. If so, Caley Burton seemed more or less clear. He and Oliver had been pushing hard for it. There was no doubt of that. Was there some other person, working in the dark, who was determined to prevent the merger of the two companies, an end secured by the murder of Hoe-Luss? If so, then I had to assume that Hoe-Luss, even after the quarrel with Burton, had come round to his view. Joe? Well, Joe did not like Geyle. Two of a trade never agree, says the proverb.

I gave it up. I went back to the house in time for the end of the second experiment. It had taken me more than an hour and a half to hunt up those who might have owned the pen-knife.

To my surprise I found Joe watching. He said he had got fed up with the castle, had a bickering with Geyle, and given them the slip.

"I hate castles anyway," he added. "I caught a country 'bus and got put down at the north lodge."

I don't think I believed him, but Tobey did not appear annoyed at his presence, so I laughed and agreed that we did not all admire antiques.

"So I was just in time for the end of this show," he said. "Dashed if I didn't think they were practising fire-drill at first."

He glanced over at a policeman in plain clothes, who was just gathering himself up after falling into the sheet held beneath the window.

"Major Tobey must have been a Sapper," I remarked. "He has the careful mathematical mind, Joe. One of those fellows who lives on the Euclidean Q.E.D."

"Looks like it," said Joe, "and there's a copper making a rough plan. A fellow can't fall nowadays without provoking a demonstration."

I thought it better to remove any suspicion of my collusion with Tobey, so I said I wanted my tea, and went in to have it, leaving him to watch as long as he liked. Had he come back to have a search on his own, or had he suspected that something was up? I could not say.

Tobey must have understood. He gathered his men at the end of the job, and took them back to Winstone. Before he left, he appeared to have convinced Joe that this was all routine.

When the rest of the party came back in good time for dinner, Marie had returned from her shopping, and Joe was not referred to, except by Mrs Graves, who told me that he had been most disagreeable, till at last even Meriel had told him to shut up.

We couldn't sit mum all the evening, so fours were formed for bridge, mostly Contract, and Geyle took a hand at Marie's table, as her partner. I believe he was a brilliant player, and he was well fitted to stand an 'Inquest' if Marie started one at the end of a rubber.

But that night, though they both held bad cards, and were down considerably, she did not seem anxious to inquire, or have an autopsy over the play.

I was happy in sitting with Jean. She had once learned bridge, to the extent of making her partners wonder if any homicide was justifiable when the victim was so pretty and so charming. Auction had frightened her away from the idea of playing Contract. I was the gainer, or would have been in other circumstances.

She still looked unhappy and troubled, though of course she had partially recovered from the shock of hearing about Hector.

"I am so happy to know that Miss Green has gone," she said to me, in a low voice. "Hateful, lying, venomous old woman!"

These were strong words from her, and I took it that Aunt Green's latest innuendoes against Geyle had been somewhat worse than usual.

"Look here," I said, "I won't play the doctor, Miss Murphy, but just give you the advice any man of common sense would give you. Give the whole lot here, as a matter of fact. Harping on this, or the other bad business, doesn't do a bit of good. Drop it! Aunt Green is the sort of person any sensible person discounts at once. She has got into the habit of libel. Let me hear what you did at the Castle. I have never been there, though I am sure I ought to have gone."

She wasn't one of the deep, brooding kind. In fact, if she had not been so lovely, I imagine that she would have been dubbed shallow. She seemed glad that I had given her a lead out of the morass of suspicion, smiled a little, and talked about their afternoon. It had evidently been a happy one for her. She and Geyle had got detached from the party, and explored on their own.

Unless Geyle was a perfect monster of cunning and dissimulation, he was her destined husband. She coloured prettily every time she spoke of him.

Burton cut out presently, and came to talk to me, while Jean went to sit beside Marie.

"Joe tells me there was a kind of experiment this afternoon," he remarked. "He scoffs at it, but I was wondering why it wasn't done when the superintendent came here."

I nodded. "Yes, it should have been. But common or garden accidents don't wring the withers of matter-of-fact country policemen. Someone, as you know, was silly enough to hint at suicide, and Tobey heard of it, and pricked up his ears. I told him how silly it was, and it was agreed that, to save everyone pain, this should be tried out. By the way, Tobey said you needn't stay for the inquest."

"But I shall. You see I was in the next room part of the time between seven and eight. I saw Geyle go into the dressing-room about seven."

"As he said, yes. But you forget that the window of your bedroom faces front. The wall to the side of your room had no window."

"Well?"

"If there was any sound made by Hector, that would dull it."

"Yes. But what I mean is this. I went to have a bath about twenty-past seven. I heard Geyle and Simcox murmuring as I passed the door."

"Are you sure of the time," I asked.

"It's the only time I am sure of, except that I got down to dinner at eight. I did not look at the clock again, but a bath as a rule takes me fifteen minutes—if no one is hammering on the door," he added, with a smile, "so we may take it that Simcox must have fallen between eight and half-past eight."

"He was always punctual at meals," I said.

"Yes, someone used to chip him about it."

"Hoe was next door," I said, "on the other side. Did he hear nothing?"

Burton shook his head. "He says not. I know he went up early, and he says he dressed before half-past, and went into the library to write a letter or two."

I managed to change the subject at last, and turned the talk on business, gradually edging from rationalisation to the American law against certain types of mergers, and asking him to explain its incidence. He was well up in the subject, and explained at some length.

"Uncle Sam is rather grandmotherly in those matters," he ended. "I think the law does no good to business."

"I expect you had to get up the subject when there was the question of the merger between your company and the other," I said.

He shook his head. "I have lived in America, and knew the ropes long ago."

"Did that business fall through after all?" I asked.

He nodded. "Yes, unfortunately. Hoe-Luss was a bit conservative. He was quite shirty when I mooted it first. In fact, we had a row over it. But I was able to prove the advantages to him, and he was working on the papers when he died, poor chap."

This was new to me. "Is that why he wanted to be alone?"

"Yes. He said I was too good at special pleading, you know. He would go into the thing by himself, where I couldn't get at him, to sway his judgment. But I didn't mind, I felt sure he would come round. Then, of course, he died, and the thing went west."

"Who could revive it—Joe or Marie?"

"Neither of them want to," he said. "The idea would have been to make one head office, and technical staff. Geyle is the better man, from that point of view, though Joe is quite a clever fellow at his job."

This interested me. It seemed, as I had suspected, that there was more than personal dislike between Geyle and Joe. A completed merger would have meant a choice, and I could see which way Burton would have voted.

But in some way I suspected Burton. Why did he insist on staying for the inquest when there was no need for him to do so? Fellows like that have so many secret interests, and do so much wire-pulling, that you find it hard to decide exactly what is their motivation. I mean that, to take a case, the uninitiated may think a man selling shares suggests that he has no faith in the company. But men like Caley sell sometimes because they have great faith in a company themselves, but want to undermine the faith of others, so that they can buy in cheap.

"I suppose it was a blow to you?" I asked.

"At the time, yes; now, no," he replied. "The 'Solidaris' has now branched out on its own, and has a new process that is going to be very profitable," he twinkled, and added, "Now we're the shy party. We don't want a merger."

The card parties broke up suddenly, Jean Murphy went to bed, as did Mrs Graves. Oliver came over, and sat down by my companion, Joe joined us too, and I got up and went over to Meriel, who was looking discontentedly at the little group, and shutting some money into her bag, with a vicious snap.

"Bad cards?" I asked her.

"Rotten partner," she said. "I wish all the men—"

She stopped short, and tossed her head. Then she nodded to me casually, and left the room. Marie smiled after her significantly. She said good night to Fay Hobart, and came over to me.

"I am afraid you have not had a very pleasant visit," she said. "Isn't this whole business hateful? It's poisoned everything." She paused, and added, "I've told the others there is a fine of ten shillings if it is mentioned again. Was I right?"

"Absolutely," I said. "It's been a blight."

"Mr Burton goes on Wednesday, after the inquest," she said. "Miss Hobart and Jean are staying on for the present. Joe has volunteered to stay his week, to support me. Meriel goes on Wednesday."

I was going to say colloquially that it was a regular jail-delivery, but checked myself.

"The house will be pretty empty."

"I should like you to stay your week, if you will be so kind," she remarked. "Your friend, Major Tobey, is *so* thorough. Perhaps you will act as interpreter."

"Of what?" I said, laughing.

She lowered her voice. "My maid, Annette, happened to look out of a window this afternoon, Dr. Soame. What was one gentleman doing in a white shirt—penance?"

"A mere test," I said. "Part of the routine."

She did not appear convinced. "Oh, come! The ordinary fatal accident even in England is not made the occasion for a police reconstruction."

"You had better ask Tobey, then," I said lightly. "What else could it portend?"

"I wish I knew what suit Major Tobey was calling," she said. "Oh, I fine myself ten shillings! I led you into it, so there is no forfeit for you.—What I really wanted to say is that while you are here, if you don't mind, will you have a look at the under-housemaid? She isn't strong, and her family has a history of phthisis."

"Certainly," I said, "if you wish it."

She beamed. "Poor William had so much faith in you, Dr Soame. It is a great thing for us that you live so near. I said so to Lady Bensham when I met her in Winstone to-day. She has just come to live at Holly Abbey, and wanted to know the name of someone dependable. She is a martyr to rheumatism, and of course intends to keep up a large establishment."

"Very good of you," I murmured. But I felt uncomfortable. It did look so perilously like bribery and corruption. I had been ignored for months, now I was to be taken up again.

Geyle had sat down by himself in a corner, and was smoking a cigar. Looking that way, I saw he was watching us, and smiling gently.

Chapter XIII
UNDERBIDDING

During the next day nothing happened. The self-denying ordinance worked very fairly, though there were three ten-shilling fines put into the hospital-box before the guests realised that one question was taboo. On the Wednesday, there came the inquest.

Mr Lay, the coroner, was brisk and brief. He listened to the two or three witnesses, heard what I had to say, and the technical details of Marsond's autopsy. You could see that the jury was impatient. A murder might have held their interest, but why this fuss about a young fellow who fell out of a window when governed by a fantastic impulse to look at some 'moss stuff'?

Having no idea what had happened, and no anxiety to know exactly, they remained vacant and half-deaf until Lay began to sum up. They brightened when he said that the cause of death was clear, some of them nodded when he added that, in the absence of direct evidence, no one could say how Simcox fell. They might take it that he bent to look at the lichen and overbalanced. But it would be wiser to record the cause of death, and add that there was no evidence to prove why he fell. The jury officially said Amen to that, and the business was over.

Mr Burton went off to Lorraine. Meriel and Miss Hobert were driven with him to the station to catch the London train. Miss Hobert had decided after all to go home. There was some question of seeing an actor manager who was going to stage a new play.

I examined the under-housemaid, told Marie that I could not find anything wrong with her, except a slight debility, which was due to other causes, then drove over to see Tobey.

He had made no overt move yet, as far as I knew, and I was anxious to know if he had communicated with Scotland Yard. That question answered itself when I reached his house, was shown into his study, and found him in the company of a well-dressed man, whom he introduced to me as Chief Inspector Mattock.

Mattock, apart from his height, and his military build, looked like an elderly actor. He was rather handsome, with a good mouth, a bold nose, large, grey eyes, with a contemplative look in them, and very large white hands, particularly apt in gesture. His voice was quiet and free from roughness, and his smile, which was not rare, was very attractive. We shook hands, I was given a seat, and Tobey asked me if I would mind just running over the tale I had told him once more.

I did, of course, and Mattock sat still, and made no notes, but kept his mouth shut, and his large hands lightly clasped together until I had come to an end.

"Well, Mattock," said Tobey, "do you agree with me?"

"I do, sir," said the other. "I had a talk with my superintendent over your report and request yesterday evening. We both agreed that the matter called for investigation. Now, Dr Soame, I must ask you a few questions."

I answered his questions as best I could, and he looked at Tobey, and fell again into silence. Tobey drew a sheet of typed paper towards him, and spoke to me.

"Now, Soame, I am sure you will be interested to hear the result of our experiments the other afternoon. I'll mention the result of one, the fall from the window staged by one of my men. He didn't fall in the exact position in which we, or you, found Mr Simcox."

"He didn't?" I cried.

"No, but that is inconclusive. It was near enough, and I presume that Simcox, though killed immediately by the fall, might, or his muscles might, have made some convulsive movement, shifting his position slightly after he struck the ground."

"It's possible."

He went on. "The second experiment, carried out by a man wearing a white shirt, similar in size to that worn by the dead man, was more helpful."

I shivered a little. That meant murder; the poor fellow's sacrifice to an innocent discovery! I looked at Mattock, who was watching my face steadily.

"How exactly?"

"The expert who examined Simcox's shirt was able to point out a faintly soiled crease, more or less horizontal on the shirt, which showed where the garment had met the sill of the window, the lower sash, rather. Its position did not correspond to the crease, also soiled by dust, on the shirt worn by our man. That was higher up on the breast."

"What do you deduce from that?" I asked.

"Our man bent down as far as he could, as if inspecting the lichen. His shirt met not only the sill, but the—"

"You mean the outer edge of the sill, as well as the window sash," put in Mattock.

"I did mean that. In other words, Soame, the marks suggest that, while our man was bending well over, more or less in the position you saw achieved by Dale, Mr Simcox was leaning out at a much more upright angle. We took the most careful measurements, knowing his height."

"So he was not looking at the lichen?"

"No, I am sure he was not."

"And yet he was facing the window," I said. "Surely, if someone else was in the room he would not have his back to them?"

Mattock made a suggestion. "He may have been talking of something in the garden beyond, and leaned forward to show it to the other person—"

I noticed that he did not name the sex. "The other person would come behind him, and have the opportunity."

"At all events," said Tobey, "that experiment, and the knife, make me pretty sure that Simcox was not the victim of an accident."

Mattock nodded. "There was talk of poison in the other case?"

I agreed. "But a peculiar and not very reliable source, Chief Inspector. Miss Green would slander the Archangel Gabriel on very little provocation."

He smiled. "I understand. But the truth sometimes proceeds from the mouth of slanderers, as well as babes and sucklings, doctor! We know something of that at the Yard."

I am the police surgeon, of course, and it seemed likely that I should see a great deal more of the case than I had expected to; from the inside that is. It was obvious that the earlier tragedy should be cleared up if we were to get at the truth in the present case, so I gave Mattock what information I could, and then waited for him to speak.

"The hint then was that Mrs Hoe-Luss, apart from being the chief beneficiary under her husband's will, had another motive for killing him, this prior attachment to Dr Geyle. Dr Geyle's training would enable him to understand the dosage and value of certain poisons. I don't see that this covers the poisoning by fungi, which were picked by Mr Hoe-Luss himself," he remarked.

"Yes, poisonous or innocuous, no one had denied that he picked them."

"Someone, however, who knew he was going to take a meal of that kind, might give him, in some other form, a poison which would produce symptoms closely resembling those he exhibited, sir?"

"Of course, if he, or she, knew. Dr Geyle was near at hand when Miss Hobert found the body."

"Apparently he was not far away," said Tobey.

"And this cook, who retired from her job. Where is she now?"

"She retired to a little cottage in Kent. Miss Green told me that. I heard from one of the others since that it was a mile or so from Edenbridge."

"My sergeant, who is with Superintendent Dale now, had better go there, and see what he can pick up," remarked Mattock to Tobey, and turned again to me. "Dr Geyle is now apparently turning his attention to a Miss Jean Murphy, a young actress, doctor. I can't quite understand that play that was to be put on. Where is it now?"

"I understand it went back to the literary agent who supplied Hoe-Luss with it. I don't know his name."

"But surely there must have been a contract between Hoe-Luss and the author, if the play was accepted? Death would break the contract of course, but the agreement would give the name of the principals, surely?"

I said I did not know, but would ask Jean Murphy. Mattock then wanted to know in what order the bedrooms at the Chace were occupied, relative to that in which Simcox had done his work. I borrowed a piece of paper from Tobey, and put it down.

MAIN FRONT, from West to East.
    Sir Eugene Oliver—Mrs Graves—Meriel Silger—Joe Hoe-Luss—Mrs Hoe-Luss—Jean Murphy—Aunt Green—Caley Burton.

EAST WING, running north and south.
    Dr Geyle—Miss Fay Hobert.

West Wing, north and south.

Mr Simcox (bedroom, and dressing-room)—Myself.

I passed it to Mattock, and he looked at it carefully. "So Mr Burton's room had a party wall with the dead man's bedroom, sir? The dressing-room adjoined that, and was next to your room?"

"That's right."

"I presume that you would have heard a fall or a cry if you had been there when Simcox overbalanced?"

I agreed. "Yes, my windows were wide-open. Let me see. I sat out for an hour or so after tea. Tea was late, for Mrs Hoe-Luss had taken some of the party on a drive to a farm. Roughly, I think I went indoors about six and had a bath. That would bring it to about six-twenty. I dressed again—no, wait a moment! I felt hot, and did not care to change twice. I remember I put on my dress-trousers, and a dressing-gown, and sat down to write a lot of letters. They were not very long ones, but I finished I think by seven, and then dressed."

"So you heard Dr Geyle come into the room next door?"

"I heard voices," I replied, "but I think Geyle must have entered by the bedroom door, and then walked through the communicating door to the other room. At any rate, I only noticed the voices."

"They did not sound loud, or angry?"

"Certainly not. It was a sort of buzz I heard. They must have spoken softly. In fact, I was not aware who were the speakers."

"And then you dressed?"

"Yes, I finished dressing, and finding it early, went to the library, where I sat alone, reading. The voices were still buzzing when I left. Mr Burton informed me a short time ago that he went for a bath about twenty-past seven, heard voices in Simcox's room as he passed, and usually takes about fifteen minutes in the bathroom. That would bring the time he went back to his bedroom to about twenty-five to eight. He says he heard nothing, but then there is no window to his room on the side, and Simcox's bedroom is between his room and the bathroom."

Mattock could have found this out for himself, but I knew that his was at present only a fishing inquiry, and he was not anxious to let it be known that murder was suspected.

"Is there anything against him, doctor?"

"Only the row with Hoe-Luss over the merger, which he explained to me quite simply," I said. "All the same, I am not very clear about his financial motives, and he was in the room next to Simcox in this case. He could have slipped in and out of the rooms."

"Would there be no servants on that floor?"

I explained that all the rooms had hot and cold running water. I believed that one of the footmen did valet Burton and Joe, but he laid out their things earlier than twenty-past seven and would go below again. Mrs Hoe-Luss's maid might be upstairs, but I could not say at what time."

"And Sir Eugene Oliver?"

"I don't know if anyone valeted him, but he is in the other wing."

"Any line on him, sir, except that he did not go to look at Mr Simcox, when found, and was looking sick?"

"I don't know of any, except that he was on Burton's side in the business transaction in France," I replied. "Of course, like most of the others, he kept hinting at something being not quite square at the Château de Luss. But you couldn't tell if he was repeating gossip idly, or because he wanted some of the hints to stick."

"And this nephew of Hoe-Luss?"

"Well, I don't quite trust him, and don't like him, but I must say that it was he who told me the pen-knife would be no use to a botanist anxious to secure specimens. That is in his favour."

Tobey intervened quietly. "Or was meant to be? It cuts both ways. A man who commits a murder may be subtle enough to lay false clues for a purpose."

"You mean, sir," said Mattock interestedly, "that by throwing down the knife, he created the impression that it was not suicide, but murder; and by pointing that out, did two things: made you feel that he would not give himself away—and directed attention to a man who had visited Simcox some time before dinner?"

"Well, it's possible."

The detective took up the telephone, called the police station, and asked that his sergeant should be instructed to go at once to Edenbridge, Kent, look up a retired cook, formerly with Mrs Hoe-Luss, and get from her certain details. He was to ask if Hoe-Luss himself directed her to cook the fungi, and what they looked like. The sergeant was to procure on his way a cheap book illustrating the various poisonous species, and show it to the woman. He was also to give his impressions of her character, credibility, and bearing when interrogated. Then Mattock turned again to me.

"You must forgive me asking you so many questions, doctor. I am anxious to hear what you think of the other guests."

I said that Meriel was discontented and bitter, but I could not see any motive in her case. Mrs Graves had, I heard, been a sweetheart once of the late Mr Hoe-Luss, but what could she gain by his death, which left his fortune to the woman who had supplanted her?

"Especially as she never hinted at anything wrong at the Château de Luss," I added. "She certainly did not give me the impression that Mrs Hoe-Luss was a murderess."

"Only Miss Green seems to have been as daring as that," said Tobey. "And Miss Hobert?"

"Miss Hobert was a friend of Miss Murphy's, connected with designing for the play. She is an athletic young woman, but I see no motive there."

"Or, if there is one, it is connected with her friend, and this play which didn't come off," murmured the Chief Inspector. "I suppose we could not get an exhumation in France, if it came to the point?"

I shook my head. "Hoe-Luss was cremated."

They both stared at me. "Then it couldn't have been a mineral poison," said Mattock, "if there was any likelihood of the French doctor suspecting. Unless, indeed, he was in the game. What about the ashes?"

I shook my head again. "That was in his will at least. I do know that. It stipulated that he should be cremated, and his ashes scattered in the garden of sleep at Golder's Green. The will was drawn up before he bought the château."

"I suppose his wife knew of the contents?"

"Probably. I am not sure," I said, "the cremation would naturally destroy any vegetable poisons in the body."

"So that the question if *Amanita phalloidis* did or did not grow on the soil of the park was rather important."

"Yes, but that was a guess. There are other poisonous fungi as well as that species, Mr. Mattock," I told him. "I can assure you of that."

"Don't assure anyone else of it," he said, with a faint smile. "He may be unaware of it at the moment."

"Miss Murphy did not gain, but lost, by Hoe-Luss's death?" Tobey asked me, as the detective pondered.

"Both she and Miss Hobert, who was to design the decor."

"Where are the bathrooms in the wing you and Mr Simcox occupied?" Mattock asked.

"At the end of the wing," I said. "There were four empty bedrooms beyond mine, most of them small, then came two bathrooms in a line, then one across the end of the wing. A passage runs the full length, on the inner side, and gives access to the rooms, and bathrooms. No, I am not quite correct! There is a servant's stair to the upper storey, where the staff sleep, which has a landing near the bathrooms, the upper portion of that stair is panelled in."

"I'll show you the plan of the Chace, in *Tamrell's County Seats*," Tobey told him. "Well, Soame, we are much obliged to you. But we must not keep you all day."

I got up, and looked at my watch. "No trouble, Tobey," I said. "I am anxious to have the brute caught. I'll help all I can."

Chapter XIV
MARIE CUTS IN

It was quite true that Hector Simcox had no living relatives. But he had a solicitor, who came down, and informed us that he had drawn up a will for the deceased. There was almost fourteen thousand pounds to be devised, and that went for a Chair of Botany (or towards a Chair) in the legator's old college.

That certainly disposed of any motive in the matter of his death, as far as expectant legatees were concerned. He was to be buried on the Thursday, and when that ceremony was over, Meriel Silger was to join Joe at a house in Northumberland, where he was invited to fish the Coquet. 'Gene Oliver was due in London, where he played polo for the "Red Polls"; Mrs Graves was returning to her flat in Hertford Street. As far as I knew, only Jean Murphy, myself, and Dr Geyle, proposed to stay out our week.

When I left Tobey and the detective, I called to have a talk with my *locum*, and to get my morning-suit and topper, for the gloomy business of the next day. Then I went back to the Chace.

Oliver was quite himself again, and arguing with Joe over blood-sports, of which he claimed fishing to be one.

The trouble was that Oliver, as he said, might be suffering from a memory of something once seen in childhood, and was unmanned by the sight of blood. This, however he might fight against it, precluded him from joining in the shooting and hunting he might otherwise have enjoyed, for he appeared to be both fond of horses and natural history.

But, as Joe tried to explain, appealing to me for biological details, fish were cold-blooded, and not gifted with a nervous system of a highly-specialised kind.

"I've seen a polo-pony take a nice toss," he added. "I bet it suffered more than a trout, hooked in the grisly lip."

"Killing for the sake of killing," said Oliver. "No, you can't convince me, Joe."

Joe sneered. "Well, I am jolly glad I am going to have a spot of fishing after this racket," he remarked. "Do you fish, Geyle, or are you one of those who let your humanitarianism run riot?"

There was a palpable sneer, too, in this, and I saw Jean bite her lip, and Marie look hard at Joe, who grinned. But Geyle merely smiled, and smoothed down his hair with his fine hand.

"I? No, I don't think so. I am a bad shot, and a poor fisherman, but I've tried both, and may again."

Jean exclaimed that Joe expected everyone to like what he liked. He laughed, and looked straight at her, saying in a mocking way that he was sure everyone shared his admiration for her.

"Oh, don't be an ass!" she snapped. "You know what I mean."

Marie intervened. "What about this evening? I don't think I care to play cards. You had all better start a game of snooker. Dr Soame, you play, don't you?"

I don't, and she knew it. Billiards is one of the games that I cannot even begin to play now, and what billiards I formerly attempted was hopelessly spoiled by my inability to pot a ball, which is essential in snooker.

After dinner, Joe, Geyle, who was an expert, Oliver and Mrs Graves played snooker. Jean did not understand the game, and she and I and Marie went into the small drawing-room, and sat down with books and cigarettes.

Jean went up to her room for something, twenty minutes later, and I knew that Marie intended to cut into the game at which Tobey, Mattock, and I were taking a hand.

"Now, honestly, doctor," she began, in the most surprising way, "how many lies have you heard about me since you arrived on Saturday?"

What are you to reply to a question like that? I did my best.

"Lies, Mrs Hoe-Luss? I don't know. I have heard a great deal of unkind gossip."

"And you don't know how much of it to believe?" she asked mockingly. "Do you know why Miss Green had to leave so suddenly?"

If people ask for it, they ask for it! I nodded. "I imagine, because she was making the kind of accusations of which she seems to be a past mistress. Why, I don't know."

"Because she hates me; they all do," said Marie. "Don't trouble to deny it. Ever since I married, I have been the 'designing Frenchwoman.' A half-truth at best, since I am half-English. Joe thinks I ousted him from his uncle's affections. How funny that sounds if you know! Meriel wants to marry money, but was too previous. Now that Miss Green has gone, I may tell you that she practically charged me with poisoning William."

"In so many words?" I said.

"More, if possible," she replied grimly. "You know, of course, that the evidence of sickness in my husband before his death was put down to poisonous fungi."

"Yes."

"The symptoms somewhat resembled those of a man who has been poisoned with arsenic," said Marie, as quietly as if she were telling me that the evening promised to be fine. "And you know that William was cremated. Do you think I poisoned William?"

I jumped that time. She was a most amazing woman, but I did not know what she was getting at. "No," I replied, quite truthfully. "If you ask me, I think my French confrère was quite wrong. I believe that Mr Hoe-Luss broke his neck."

It was my turn to startle her. Two red spots came out on her cheeks, and her eyes glistened. "The cause of death, you mean?"

I nodded. I had refreshed my mind with regard to fungi, before dinner. In this country it is not a subject that the ordinary practitioner worries about.

"For this reason," I told her, "the symptoms of poisoning by fungi may appear within an hour, and death may take place within twenty-four hours. It was only a few hours at most from the time Mr Hoe-Luss took that meal until he died. At the worst, the verdict ought to have been broken neck following sickness caused by what he ate."

Her colour subsided and she looked disappointed. "Yes, on the toadstool theory, doctor. But he might die sooner *after arsenic*."

"Of course; of a large dose. I expect the doctor was misled by the *post hoc* fallacy. He knew that your husband had eaten poisonous fungi, he found him dead, and evidences of sickness. Naturally, he would not suspect, either that you had poisoned him, or that he had broken his neck and died of that."

"Why not?"

I smiled. "In the first place, that kind of case is not common enough for us doctors to suspect poisoning, whenever we see sickness; especially when the widow is eminently respectable, and normal. No one can go through life looking for murders, and fraud. Your devotion to your husband, and his to you, no doubt reached his ears. Then he was a country doctor, in a very provincial quarter of France. You corresponded to the wife of a squire here, if not more, and the ordinary squire's wife, even here, is Caesar's wife as well!"

She did not smile at that. "Be frank with me, Dr Soame. You were a long time at Major Tobey's, and I hear that he has a man down from London, who came from London in the company of an obvious plain-clothes policeman."

"How did you hear that?" I asked incautiously.

"The squire's wife in the country hears a good many things," she told me, and did smile this time. "Surely Miss Green's voice has not reached so far?"

Was she afraid that Mattock had come down to rake up the affair at the Château de Luss? It looked like it. She was aware that Aunt Green was quite capable of the atrocity of an anonymous letter, and the prompt appearance of Mattock on the scene must have seemed inspired. It would be cruel to let her think that, so I told her in confidence that I believed Tobey had some doubts as to the correctness of the verdict on Hector Simcox.

She was all eagerness again now. "But surely he was killed by that fall from the window?"

"Yes," I said. "He was, as far as we can judge."

I had let myself in for something unpleasant. Marie sat up. "Well, what was wrong with the verdict, wasn't it complete enough?"

I wriggled. "Something like that."

She made a gesture of impatience. "Why he fell, eh?"

"Yes, I suppose so."

She sat silent for a minute, then. "I see. Someone was behind it, is that the suggestion?"

I nodded. She asked hesitatingly if any one of the malignant gossipers had mentioned Dr Geyle. I hardly knew what to say. I believed that Dr Geyle was in love with Jean, and that Marie approved. But it was on the cards that Dr Geyle had set up this other business when the storm of gossip arose after William's death, and that, had nothing been said to make people suspicious, he would have continued to be Marie's suitor.

"No one knows anything about it," I said. "It will be inquired into."

She reflected gravely for a moment or two. "But it is too extraordinary, doctor. That venomous old woman could at least produce a motive for killing poor William, but what motive is there here?"

Never tell a woman half a secret! Tell it all, and she may forget it, or overlook its significance. Tell her half, and she will not only drag the rest from you, but find glosses in your silence, and quite unmeant clues, in your narrative gaps. I fell back on the Hibernian parry.

"What do you think could be the motive?"

"I said there was none. Major Tobey, of course, must have some method in his madness."

"It couldn't be jealousy?" I fenced.

"Whose?" she demanded indignantly. "You are not absurd enough to suggest that there was jealousy over Jean?"

"No," I said, and added hastily that I wondered what was keeping the girl.

But Marie was not going to let me off. "Now, Dr Soame, I can see you are hedging. If what you say is true, this will be a most unpleasant business for me, especially after the last trouble—I want your help. Ridiculous as they are, Miss Green's charges have done me a great deal of harm. There is no saying where it will end. I believe poor William broke his neck by a fall down those stairs. If that could be established, it would put an end to this dreadful talk."

I saw what she meant. I did not remind her that, if it were proved that Hector Simcox broke his neck as a result, say of a push, it might even be contended that Hoe-Luss's broken neck was not wholly due to giddiness, or any such impersonal cause.

"The cremation did a great deal to make any such reconstruction impossible," I remarked. "Unless you could find a motive there as well."

She turned rather white. "How do you mean?"

It had to come out. "If it was proved that your husband was pushed or thrown down those stairs, and that Simcox's fall was not accidental," I murmured, "the person who had a motive for removing both might be more easily identified."

"One man killing both?"

"Unless you like to assume that two of your guests, at successive house parties, have homicidal tendencies." She recovered a little. "I see. If we could find someone who wished both Simcox and my husband dead, is that it?"

"We could be pretty certain, yes."

"You are sure of that?"

"Fairly," I told her. "If you wish to fix your position in a fishing boat, you take marks—a line from the boat through objects on shore, and then another line from it to objects on another part of the shore. Where the two lines converge is your position."

Jean suddenly made her appearance, to my relief.

Marie as suddenly said she would go to watch the snooker. Jean, who had no intention to explain her long absence, sat down by me, and took a cigarette.

Now was my chance. "I have been thinking about that charming play," I observed. "It made an impression on you. I wonder who the agent was?"

She smiled. "I don't know. Mr Hoe-Luss said he had got it from an agent, but he did not tell me his name."

"You never saw the agreement?"

"Oh no, that wasn't my business. I suppose Mrs Hoe-Luss sent it back."

"Then she would know who the agent was? You see, I am foolish enough to have fallen in love with the play from your description of it."

I was quite sincere in saying that. There were so many plays on at the moment depending on legs and vulgarity for their success that I should have liked to see Jean in her innocent romance.

"I don't know," she said. "I suppose she must know, but she never told me. I gave her the script."

I talked to her until it was latish and she went upstairs, then I turned towards the billiards-room, and met Marie coming away from it.

"I was wondering," I said, since she was now more or less in the secret of the official investigations, "if Oliver was working in his hatred of blood-sports with a purpose, and his aversion from blood. He looked pretty sick when he heard of Simcox being found."

Marie was quick enough to understand, but she shook her head. "I don't think so. I heard that about him some years ago—about his being upset when he saw blood anyway."

"I see. It was just an idea of mine," I said. "By the way, I was talking to Jean about that play. I wonder if you could give me the name of the agent to whom you returned it?"

Marie did not ask me why I wanted to know. But she looked me straight in the eyes—no guarantee of sincerity that, of course—and said she had forgotten.

Chapter XV
ONE SPADE

The funeral was over. It was a most cheerful day, with the sun shining, and a blue sky, but I think I never felt so gloomy before. Hector was so young, and his taking-off so callous and casual.

As I called at my house to change into less dismal garments, I determined that I would not rest until I had helped to arrest the brute who was responsible.

Oliver did not go. It seemed that he had an aversion to funerals as well as blood-sports. I had a talk with Tobey and Mattock in the afternoon, and mentioned it to them.

"I don't know what you think of it, and I cannot supply a motive," I observed to the detective, "but I told you before how shaken Oliver was when the body was found, and to-day he did not go to the funeral."

Mattock folded his hands, and put his head on one side. "The murder, Dr Soame, was a particularly callous one. Then, if Sir Eugene Oliver was guilty, I should think he would have had more *nous* than he showed. For example, looking so distressed at the time, which gave him a guilty look; failing to attend a funeral, which would give people who were suspicious of him an idea that he might not wish to attend the last rites over a man he had killed. A murderer generally tries to cover up."

"Right enough," I conceded. "I merely wanted your views about him."

Mattock went on. "Another thing—he was apparently cheerful and normal until you came in to say that you had found the body?"

"Oh, quite."

"Good point," said Tobey.

"The murderer would of course know that the body would eventually be found," said Mattock, "he would surely be more apprehensive and nervous before it was found? He would hardly preserve his cheerfulness soon after the murder, and exhibit signs of guilt or emotion hours after?"

"In any case, we can get at him at any time," said Tobey, who knew that I was merely trying to place all the information I had at the man's disposal, not to play the omniscient detective. "Going to town, isn't he?"

"He is due to play in a polo match on Saturday," I said. "He is a member of the 'Redpolls,' and can be found at their ground most afternoons in the season, I have been told."

The detective nodded. "Right. At the moment I am more interested in Mr Burton. His story about the merger does not fit in very well with what Sir Eugene told you. He had a row with Mr Hoe-Luss. I wondered too why he left so hastily for Lorraine."

"I suppose that could be ascertained?" I remarked.

Mattock smiled faintly. "I had a cable sent to the chief of police at Metz, doctor, asking him to have secret inquiries made. We can't get away from the fact that of all the guests, next to you, he had the best chance to slip into and out of Simcox's room without being seen."

"When he had his bath?"

He shrugged his shoulders. "A bathroom is always a good site for an alibi. You go in, turn on the water, wet a towel, and the bathmat, do a little splashing, then attend to your business outside, and return to wait for a few minutes before going out."

"I suppose you haven't heard from Metz?" I said.

"Yes. We heard this morning. Mr Caley Burton has not turned up there yet. You are sure he was going to the city?"

"Quite," I said, "the offices of his company are there. He casually mentioned the fact that 'head office' had called him."

Tobey nodded. "Suspicious, though not damning, of course. I wonder if he went to the château?"

"Why?" I asked.

"He was one of the four men who heard what Simcox said with regard to the fungi," said Tobey. "We must inquire there too, and at once."

He and Mattock telephoned to Scotland Yard, and when they had spoken in turn, the sergeant who had been sent to interview the retired cook at Edenbridge made his appearance suddenly; a thickset man, with close-cropped hair, a pugnacious chin, and a paradoxically mild voice.

"Oh, here you are, Cromer," said Mattock. "Sit down, and let us hear what you've got."

Cromer began at once. "I saw the woman, sir," he said, "she has a nice little cottage, and nicely furnished too. But there is nothing in that to hint that she had retired with a large bribe. I made inquiries, and found that the cottage had belonged to a cousin, a local butcher who has come into a bit of money. He married his cousin—the cook's sister, and his wife prevailed on him to hand over the cottage and its contents."

"For nothing?"

"Well, not exactly, sir. There was a villa left by the same person to the two sisters. He persuaded the cook to take the cottage and furniture as her share of the villa."

"I see. Now how did she strike you?"

"Most respectable, sir, though a bit hot-tempered. I should say she was a trustworthy woman."

"Exhibited no feeling against Mrs Hoe-Luss?"

"No, sir. She said she thought Mrs Hoe-Luss intended to give up the English place and settle at the château. She didn't like foreigners, and she wasn't going to learn French cookery at her age."

"Natural enough," said Tobey. "Did you ask her about the fungi she cooked?"

"I did, sir, and she went off the deep-end rather, when I mentioned it. She said she was in her kitchen when the kitchen-maid came in with some toadstools—that was her word, of course. The girl said Mr Hoe-Luss had met her in the garden near the back, handed her the stuff, and said he wanted it cooked. She had cooked several 'messes of stuff' that 'nothing would have made her eat,' before that, and she duly cooked the fungi, and had it sent up to her master."

Mattock glanced at me. "Unfortunate for Hoe-Luss that the cook had been asked before to cook stuff of that type."

"In France," I said, "they eat a dozen species that are suspect over here, and rather laugh at our caution. I mean edible varieties that are not familiar in England."

Cromer went on. "I had bought a cheap book on mushrooms and toadstools, sir, with coloured illustrations."

He took a little book from his pocket, and passed it to Mattock, who handed it on to Major Tobey. "You showed it to her?"

"When she had calmed down, and I had explained that no one was quarrelling with her cooking, or expected her to know the difference between the poisonous and non-poisonous varieties."

"I suppose you will tell us that she was unable to remember which was which?"

"No, sir. Naturally enough she didn't pick the right picture at once. But the colour did it. As I gathered from your instructions, sir, that *Amanita phalloidis* was in question"—his pronunciation of this was dreadful—"I showed her that first. She was quite certain that there was no little ring round the stem, and she was also sure that the colour was not a yellow olive, but reddish."

I started. "Then why the dickens did the French doctor say that it was *amanita*?" I cried.

Tobey nodded, but Mattock did not agree to our objection.

"I expect these things when cooked are not of the original colour," he said.

"I thought of that, sir," remarked the sergeant, rather proudly. "She said she cooked them well—burned them, I expect she meant, for you could see she hated the idea of even doing them."

"And then the French doctor would have no experience of cooked *amanita*," I said. "Apart from the effects of partial digestion. The French cook much that we leave, but they don't poison themselves for frugality's sake."

"I expect not," said Mattock. "Carry on, Cromer."

Cromer asked to have the book back. "Now this was what she thought it was, sir," he observed, indicating a highly-coloured illustration on one plate, "Emetic russels."

I suppressed a smile. "*Russula emetica*," I said. "Poisonous, but not virulently so. If he ate this, the effects would not be so serious, and might take even longer to develop."

"*Emetica* suggests sickness?" said Mattock.

"It would undoubtedly cause sickness," I told him. "The doctor, seeing that he had died in a comparatively few hours, and suspecting fungi, would take it that the species was the more deadly one."

"Must have been a bit of a fool all the same," said Tobey.

I agreed. "The country parts of France have a number of doctors who are about as inefficient as they can be, for qualified men. In the big towns, you get competence, but as I know from my experience in the war, some of the country practitioners were a scandal. At one hospital, where I helped, the surgeon was quite surprised to see a Paris surgeon put on overalls, mask, and gloves."

"May I take it, sir, that Mr Hoe-Luss did not die of eating this particular species?" Mattock asked.

"If he was in his normal health, as I knew it, no," I said. "Certainly not that alone, and not in such double-quick time."

He nodded, and turned to Cromer. "You see from what the doctor says that the death was either due to Mr Hoe-Luss breaking his neck, either accidentally or otherwise, or was caused by some poison introduced into the dish of *russula*. You appreciate the fact that a man might put poison in a dish of fungi, thinking that it would be blamed for the result?"

"Yes, sir," replied Cromer, who was as intelligent as most men of his rank in the C.I.D. "I questioned her to see if there was any point at which any foreign substance could have been introduced into the stuff. She said that no one but the kitchen-maid came into the kitchen, from the time she brought in the stuff until the time it was cooked."

"And after that?"

"It was taken direct to Mr Hoe-Luss by a footman, one who is at the Chace now, sir. Unless he or the kitchen-maid can be suspected of tampering, I don't see when the poison was put in."

"No chance of Hoe-Luss committing suicide, and for his—I mean for the sake of the insurances on his life, wishing it to be thought an accidental death?" Tobey asked.

"I can't say, sir."

"We know there was some talk of this Dr Geyle," remarked Mattock, "and Mrs Hoe-Luss. He may have discovered something. He was devoted to his wife?"

"Very devoted," I replied. "But that does not explain Simcox being killed, does it?"

Chapter XVI
DID SIMCOX CALL?

"Were you seeing that policeman again?" Marie asked me, when I returned. "Why don't you ask him to come here to see the place?"

"Perhaps he doesn't want it known that he is investigating," I said.

"What, here? Everyone knows it; the inn-keeper, where he is putting up at Winstone, knew who he was at once. Chief Inspector Mattock is apparently well known to the readers of certain Sunday journals," she added, with a sniff, "even the maids are gossiping about it, I believe."

"Personally, I was not sure if you would welcome him," I said rather clumsily.

She stared. "Why not?"

"I mean to say the worry—the publicity."

"Preferably, I should say, to people in the country asking why he doesn't come out into the open, and who is paying him to keep it dark."

"Absurd, of course, but I'll tell him," I returned. "To-morrow."

"I shall write him a note, and have it posted this evening," she said.

Even doctors know the value of bluff nowadays, or some of their hypochondriacal patients would be worse than they are. Marie's willingness to let Mattock investigate meant nothing.

Oliver button-holed me before dinner, and remarked that he had heard me christened Watson. "Not that I think you such an egregious ass as the great man of that ilk, Soame," he added handsomely. "But we hear you are now acting as Mentor or bear-leader to the great Mattock. I wish I knew what it was all about. Couldn't you give a friend a tip?"

"There is no secret about it," I replied. "It seems possible that Hector Simcox was pushed out of the window."

He laughed, then dug me in the ribs. "I said you were not like your great predecessor, Soame—he hadn't a grain of humour in his composition."

"Mine isn't functioning at present, Oliver," I informed him. "You asked for the facts, and you've got 'em now."

His face fell. "Honest? But damn it! how do you work that out?"

"I don't, Mattock has gone into the matter, and he is sure that Simcox did not fall accidentally."

I was wondering if he would tell me that Geyle had been the last man to see Simcox, or would have to give an account of himself. He didn't. He frowned, and asked what was the motive.

"The law doesn't need to prove motive," I said.

"Legally no, but between you and me, what evidence is there?"

I was not going to drag up the affair at the château, but left that to Mattock's discretion.

"Did it ever occur to you that no one heard Simcox call out?" I demanded.

"Are you sure?"

"Quite. Now stoicism is all right in its way, but I doubt if any man would find himself falling out of a window without crying out, screaming, or something. It would be forced from him."

Oliver rubbed his chin. "Yes, that's true. But I suppose it would be true too if he was thrown out, as you suggested. And would he be thrown out without a struggle?"

I told him the theory about the brides, and the adaptation of the method to young Simcox. He lighted up then, and nodded vigorously.

"I see; yes, of course. He was bending out to show something to his visitor, and the visitor hooked a hand suddenly under his knees and sent him over. By Jove! that's logical enough."

"And that visitor must have been in his room within a very limited period," I said. "Where were you? I mean between half-past seven and eight?"

He smiled. "My dear Watson, I must protest. I was in my room. It is in the other wing, as you know. But don't let your humble servant allow his remarks to hinder you. He could, for example, have got into the west wing by the back door, having left by the servant's door in the east wing—"

"Up one back stairs, down another, in fact," I said. "But that would mean a long journey and a trip across the passage on the top floor between the two wings."

"It would," said Oliver. "But I wouldn't be such an ass as to go along the main passage on our floor, where anyone might pop out and perhaps see me stealing along."

"We'll investigate that," I assured him, smiling. "Mattock is coming up to-morrow I believe."

"Geyle was the last man to see Simcox alive," I added, since he made no comment.

"Don't worry about that," he returned. "Geyle would hardly do that if he proposed to hoof young Simcox over. And Geyle is the lucky man with Jean, don't forget. He wasn't jealous of Simcox, though it may have been the other way about."

We were naturally a small party at dinner though Mrs Graves, Joe, and Oliver had postponed departure. Marie was unnaturally cheerful, I thought, and Geyle kept glancing at her with a slightly puzzled air. Jean and Oliver began chipping each other, as if their hostess's relief had been communicated to them.

Marie suggested cards afterwards, and she and Joe played against Mrs Graves and Oliver. Marie only smiled when Dr Geyle and Jean said that they would like an evening stroll in the park, and asked me if I would join them. Naturally I didn't. I began to wonder if Geyle was our mystery man after all. What better bluff than to visit openly the room of the man you mean to kill less than an hour before his death? And what guarantee had I that Simcox's death was premeditated? Shoving a man out of the window (for you cannot say that a man who falls twenty feet is certain to be killed) is more like the result of a hasty impulse in anger. It was true, however, that Geyle did not look a hasty man, and had never showed himself one in my experience.

There were French windows to the room where we sat, opening on a tesselated pavement which, with a sort of glass awning over, had been some vandal owner's addition to the fine old house. I took a chair out there, and enjoyed the golden view across the park, and, what I never see without a sentimental lightening of the heart, the rooks coming in from their wanderings, circling and cawing, against the evening sky.

I had a book on my lap, but did not read it, just smoked and watched and listened. A fret of gnats danced just in front of me. They too were part of the summer, doubly cursed when they bite, but part of the lovely panorama of the season to my mind.

Mrs Graves came out to sit by me for a few minutes, Oliver playing dummy. She asked me rather nervously if it was true that a detective was coming to the house.

I said in a low voice that I believed so. "Look here, Mrs Graves," I added. "We shall all be roped in to help. There is one thing that puzzles me. You see, I was not at the château, and I have no idea of the cross-currents there. Was Mrs Hoe-Luss jealous of—of anyone?"

She seemed rather surprised at my question, but she nodded. "Yes, I think she was. She is temperamentally a jealous woman."

"You mean that really?"

"Yes," she smiled faintly, "my connection with William is an old story, doctor. I was very fond of him once. I thought I could marry him, I was just nineteen, and he was the first man who proposed to me."

"He did?"

"Yes, and I asked time to think it over. He had to go away. His father sent him to their New York branch for six months, so I had plenty of time. Then," her voice softened, "I met George Graves, and knew that I had never been in love with William. You don't make any mistake, you know."

I nodded. "I must take your word for it."

"But I am afraid Marie was jealous even of me at the château," she murmured. "And of Jean, and Miss Hobert. Funny, isn't it?"

"Not unnatural," I said.

"But with William, who never thought of women!" she said. "I don't think she was in love with him, but she is jealous of all she possesses. Some people are like that."

"I thought she admired Jean, Mrs Graves?"

"When you are jealous of a man you don't so much mind it being seen," she suggested, "but people do not care to let you see that they are jealous of what they merely own."

Marie suddenly called to her, somewhat impatiently, and I was left to consider this new facet of Marie's character.

I believed Mrs Graves. She spoke as if she knew, and I believe she did. So Marie had been jealous of Jean too; jealous perhaps of those hours the girl spent with William talking over the play. It was strange how that play had disappeared, how Marie had forgotten even the name of the agent who supplied it to William; how the hermit author had not demanded the carrying out of his contract. Did William's death really end that, and did the author know it. I have met some authors. They are often intractable people, and grossly ignorant of law.

Joe came out to me next. He is a curious fellow, and seemed to be worked up about something. I was soon aware that he had, like most of Mr Galsworthy's characters, a curious dislike for the police. He talked of them, not as our natural protectors and allies, but as if they belonged to a privileged corporation of bullies and evidence-twisters. I don't like people who have that obsession, any more than those who are obsessed by what they call 'nosey-parkers.' It is my own private opinion that these individuals are what the vulgar call 'dirty dogs.' No prying person, or policeman, can catch you out if you run straight. If you don't, well, be damned to you! is my feeling.

"What's he want down here," Joe asked grumpily.

"Probably to congratulate you on your insight, Joe," I said. "You gave me the tip about the pocket-knife being the wrong sort of tool, and I passed it on."

He grunted. "H'm, yes, I thought it very pretty at the time, but what would a fellow do. He might know that Simcox kept the real article locked up in a little instrument-case."

"I didn't know it, Joe," I remarked.

He gave a queer glance at me, then turned, and went in before the dummy hand had even been played out.

Chapter XVII
BURTON'S DEAL

Tobey brought Chief Inspector Mattock to the house next day at half-past nine. Marie was having breakfast in bed, so was Joe. Geyle and Jean had got up unbelievably early, for a morning stroll. They had developed an understandable love for nature and solitude. I hoped it would all come right, though the man was a great many years older than Jean.

If Oliver was about, he did not show himself then.

I had a talk with Mattock and Tobey, sitting outside the French windows where I had sat the previous evening. And I heard some news which surprised me.

It was evident that Mattock took the Burton side seriously. Scotland Yard has, of course, a great fund of information at its disposal, some of it with regard to people in high places, who have not yet come into contact with the law. In any case, Mattock had telegraphed in different directions, and netted at least one fact.

Caley Burton had not gone direct to Metz. He had gone to Lyons, and taken train to the little place near the Château de Luss. He had stayed a night at the 'Boule d'Or,' and been out for some hours in the middle of the day.

"Since Mrs Hoe-Luss wrote to me, and welcomed the investigation," said Tobey, "Mattock intends to ask her to wire to the people at the château, asking if Burton was seen there."

"Why?" I demanded.

Mattock looked at me. "Do you know anything about the propagation of—well, fungi, doctor?"

"They seem to have no difficulty about propagating themselves," I said. "That isn't a very learned or informative remark, I am afraid, but it is all I know."

"The fact is, that Mattock and I have been trying to account for the digression and its purpose," said Tobey. "Any of the men who heard you repeat Simcox's denial that certain fungi grew in the grounds of the château, must have heard you say that Simcox had not explored one small wood, near Forelles, I think you said? Burton, as one of them, would not know that the cook down in Edenbridge had identified the stuff as *Russula emetica*."

"I am still in the dark," I remarked.

Mattock took up the word. "I have a good many experts I can consult in London, doctor, but, pending their opinion, Major Tobey and I were wondering if fungi could be collected in one place, transferred to and planted in another."

"Good heavens!" I cried, the light breaking in upon me.

"For, if Burton could do that, and get us to look in that little wood, he might take it that he had proved to us the existence of *Amanita phalloidis* in a part of the park," said Tobey.

I certainly did not understand why Burton had gone to the château, when he had proclaimed the fact that he was called to Metz on business. Then Oliver had not told me that Hoe-Luss had eventually come round to Burton's views about the merger. Tobey's theory was horrible, but not out of the question.

"As these things spring up everywhere, and seem very tenacious of life," I agreed, "it may be possible to transplant or propagate them. I don't know. But I suggest that, if Burton makes any communication on the subject, the investigation over there should be placed in the hands of a trained botanist."

"It will be," said Mattock grimly. "Now, before we start to work, sir, may I ask if you heard any more about that play from the young lady? I had a questionnaire sent round the literary and dramatic agents already, and not one has any knowledge of placing a play with Mr Hoe-Luss, or any play called *Springtide*."

I felt rather worried by the attention he was giving to Jean. "I asked her and Mrs Hoe-Luss about it. Mrs Hoe-Luss says she forgets the name of the agent, and Miss Murphy says she was never told it."

Tobey looked at Mattock, who raised his eyebrows. "That's odd."

"When you see her you will believe her," I said.

The detective permitted himself a faint grin. "We'll hope so, sir. Now I had better see the two rooms, and I think we should have a long ladder to put up the wall outside, for no one can examine it properly head downwards."

I arranged that the gardeners should get a ladder and place it in position, and we went upstairs and into the dressing-room once occupied by poor Simcox.

Pending instructions from the lawyer, nothing had been touched, and the Chief Inspector examined the specimens of lichen most carefully—rather to my surprise—before going to the window.

"Beautiful bits of work," he remarked, as if he was a connoisseur in lichens. "I do a bit of model-making myself, and though it's a clumsier job than setting up delicate specimens, it makes me appreciate the skill shown. You can take it that he never scraped off this stuff with a pen-knife."

He went to the window, opened it, and leaned out to look at the lichen patches, drew in again, for the ladder was not yet in position, and began systematically to examine all the objects in the room. When he came to a little, locked, leather-case, I suggested that it contained, as Joe hinted, certain tools for detaching and perhaps dissecting botanical specimens.

"Mr Joseph Hoe-Luss told you that?" he asked, "I see. Well, this is a simple lock, and I had better have a look."

He had no difficulty in opening the case with an instrument from his pocket, and admired the instruments inside for a minute or two. "Neat as ninepence," he murmured. "He had the right stuff for the job here."

By this time the ladder was adjusted, and we all went down to the garden, and to the flagged path.

We met Marie on the way, and I introduced her to the detective, who was very polite, and asked her very courteously if she would spare him a few minutes when he had finished the job outside.

She was very calm and almost amiable, hoped that he would find out who had perpetrated the crime, if crime it was, and added that she would be glad to answer any questions he cared to ask.

"Handsome woman, of a type," said Mattock, as we left the house. "I can see she has a will of her own."

A constable had turned up. He was the man who had done the stunt fall from the window, as being the nearest to Simcox in height and build. He was now sent up to the room above, and asked to stand leaning out of the window at a certain angle.

Mattock took a steel tape measurer from his pocket, and mounted the ladder. He measured the distance from the crown of the constable's head to the ground, first at the most upright angle, and then several times at lower angles, the constable bending outwards, and downwards, as directed. He did not ask for a repetition of the experiments carried out by Tobey, since he had a typed report on them.

I confess that I did not see what bearing this had on the case, but Mattock went on to measure the distance of the nearest patch of lichen from the window sill, and also examined the fungi closely, remarking afterwards that none of the growth had been in any way disturbed.

The ladder was taken away, and the party returned to the house. As we reached the front door, Jean Murphy and Geyle came up from their walk and I introduced Mattock, who smiled amiably, and hoped he would have the opportunity of a little chat with both of them, later on.

"I have to see Mrs Hoe-Luss now," he added. "Perhaps in a quarter of an hour's time, eh?"

Geyle smiled, and said that would do for him admirably. Detectives he appeared to take in his stride. Of course I had now got to the point when I no longer accepted sang-froid as proof of innocence. Apart from Oliver, all the guests had failed to show the embarrassment which is supposed to be a proof of a guilty conscience.

Jean said nothing, but nodded acquiescence. She did not appear to be afraid, but was naturally unused to being confronted by detectives. I think she was reassured after the first minute. Mattock had such a normal, civilian air. Saying that her shoes were wet with dew, and she must go and change them, she left us together, and I led them into the billiards-room, and got a box of cigarettes. That is to say, Geyle and Tobey, for the Chief Inspector went off to interrogate Marie.

I noticed Tobey having a good look at Geyle, who was lighting a cigarette, his hand steady, and his face calm.

"Rotten job this, Major," he remarked, seating himself on the bank. "Something fishy about young Simcox?"

"About his death," said Tobey gravely. "Yes. I am afraid there is. But we're gravelled for a motive. Have you any idea? No one else seems to have."

Geyle did not shake his head. He puffed for a few moments, and reflected. "I never thought of it. Can't say that I do. He was an outsider, in a way; I mean he got to the château by accident, and seems to have been asked here by Mrs Hoe-Luss because he was a guest at the other show."

"Which you would think she would want to forget, not to revive, Dr Geyle."

Geyle smiled, "Bless your heart! she's not like that. I'm an old friend. I know."

"Then what was her motive for asking this young man again?"

Geyle made a gesture. "Didn't Soame tell you?"

"I gathered that there was some spiteful gossip, and it was hinted that Mrs. Hoe-Luss brought her former guests here to analyse—no, clear it up."

"An 'inquest.' Pretty near it," said Geyle coolly. "She never said so explicitly to me, but I took it to be that."

."And where did Simcox come in?" Tobey asked carelessly.

Geyle replied slowly. "He was sure the French doctor was wrong in his verdict about Hoe-Luss's death."

"But not at the time."

"No. He seems to have made the remark since."

"Quite. He made the remark, and Dr Soame communicated it to some of you here, Mr Burton, Mr Hoe-Luss, Sir Eugene Oliver, and you?"

"Did it occur to you that Simcox's death might be connected with that remark he made?"

"How could it, my dear fellow. Like the rest of us, I took it to be an accident. The last day or two I have heard talk of detectives and so on, and naturally concluded that there was something wrong."

"You can't envisage any motive for killing Simcox connected with his refusal to believe that Mr Hoe-Luss died of poisoning by fungi?"

Geyle looked alert. "Oh, I shouldn't say that, Major. That pestilent old woman, Aunt Green, made the most abominable suggestions, which it would be very hard to disprove now scientifically."

"Since Mr Hoe-Luss was cremated?" said Tobey. "Quite so. I feel now that I should have pressed for a thorough autopsy. It could have been done in Metz quite well. But as things stand, the old woman's charges cannot be disproved. Simcox's dogmatic statement would of course help. I do see that, in face of it, some interested party might hope to benefit by removing him."

Tobey thanked him. "Dr Geyle, you are a great friend of Mrs Hoe-Luss?"

"Yes. I was something more once, but she broke it off," said Geyle frankly. "I am engaged to be married—to Miss Jean Murphy."

I stared at him. Evidently he had proposed that morning on their walk, for I had not heard this before. Tobey congratulated him, and so did I. He thanked us, and smiled.

Tobey tried a new angle. "We don't know very much about the details of some business that led to friction between Mr Burton and the late Mr Hoe-Luss," he said. "Can you give us any help?"

"Not much," replied Geyle, "Burton and Oliver wanted a merger between companies. Hoe-Luss didn't. I didn't, for smaller, but sufficient, reasons. I am only a servant of one company, and I knew I might lose my job."

Tobey nodded. "I see. You are quite frank. That rather exculpates Mr Burton from a possible suspicion that he profited by Hoe-Luss's death. It was the other way about, wasn't it?"

Geyle smiled again. "My dear fellow, I am not a financial expert. All I can say is that the merger did not go through. I can add that, mere scientist as I am, I never take financiers' avowed aims as gospel. There are the tricks of the trade, and that projected merger got a great deal of publicity; more so from the fact that it was admitted the two associates did not see eye to eye."

"So that you cannot say if Hoe-Luss's death was or was not unwelcome?"

"Ultimately I cannot. I can analyse the constituents of any metal, and give you a true and correct list of them, but I cannot do more than speculate on what is in a man's mind."

"Thank you," said Tobey. "Now, Sir Eugene Oliver. He was on Burton's side in this business matter. He is also a younger man than either of the others."

"Not so young as he looks, but certainly younger. Yes. He was a friend of Hoe-Luss. He met him hunting first, and they used to play polo together at Sir Ernest Grain's ground near Rugby. Hunting was a passion with Hoe-Luss, and—"

"Wait a moment," said Tobey. "I understand Oliver had an aversion from blood-sports."

"Yes," said Geyle. "It was Oliver's first hunt, and his last. He is a fine horseman, and was invited to a meet. He met Hoe-Luss at the covert-side, and they were both in at the death. Oliver fell off."

"What?"

Geyle nodded. "Fell off. Sick, you know, and fainted. Hoe-Luss got him away, and made some excuse for him. It's a physiological fact that such things happen; even with juvenile medicos in the dissecting-room," he added, with a glance at me.

"I know," said Tobey. "Well, he was a friend of Hoe-Luss, but a business associate of Burton's, and backing Burton in this matter?"

"So they say. He has a good head for business, and good judgment. He was sure the merger would profit both companies."

Mattock came back, and said he would like a word with Geyle. He asked me to tell Miss Murphy that he would be ready for her in ten minutes.

At the end of both these interviews, he and Tobey left. Geyle was unruffled, and said he quite liked the policeman. Jean was certainly puzzled rather than alarmed. I took the opportunity to congratulate her on her engagement, and feel sure that she was very happy in it.

Oliver and Mrs. Graves had definitely settled on leaving next day. I suddenly decided that I had business in town too. Jean was happy. I had taken a great fancy to her, and was most anxious to do what I could to clear up what I was sure was only a mistake.

Chapter XVIII
WHAT MR BUSBY DECLARED

I HAVE said that my acquaintance has included a few authors. One of them, a very prosperous man, once gave me lunch in town, and introduced me to his agent.

Mr Busby was small and stout and rubicund. Every feature, except his eyes, declared him to be an innocent at home and abroad. But when you met his quiet and calculating stare, you realised what part of his face had helped to launch a thousand books.

Head of a large agency, he had a department devoted to the drama. I never met the head of this department, but my friend knew him (all novelists want to be lazy, and write plays), and Busby himself was no mean judge of the drama, or, what is more important, the commercial gentlemen who run it.

I determined to run up to town for the day and see Busby. My friend contributes a few hundreds a year to his support, and Mr Busby himself is an accessible little man—on occasion.

I told Marie of my trip, though not its reason, and she promised to have me sent to the station with Mrs Graves and Oliver.

Curiously enough, for the rest of that day, no one seemed anxious to discuss the case of young Simcox, not even Joe. Mattock and Tobey did not come up again, and sleeping dogs were undisturbed for once.

I went to town next day with Oliver and Mrs Graves. Dead silence about the case. We talked of Jean and Geyle, and Mrs Graves wondered if that would mean her leaving the stage.

"She has never been really of it," said Oliver. "She can only play one part—herself."

"I think that is true," said Mrs Graves. "I saw her twice. She is a perfect darling, but twenty or thirty years ago no one would have engaged her. They wanted actors then, not people who murmur in drawing-rooms, however lovely and ingenuous."

"There was the *ingénue*, of course," said Oliver, "but she was the result of artifice, not realism. She had to act the innocent, not to be it."

I had never seen Jean act, and this was a line I wanted to hear more about.

"But she made an impression on William Hoe-Luss," I said. "A five thousand pound impression!"

"She would on anyone who was not utterly heartless," Mrs Graves observed. "Granted the right play, the part she takes outside the theatre, she is most moving. But where is she going to find plays to suit her, now that the dirty little Freudians abound?"

"Of course sentiment is out of date," said Oliver. "We're too sophisticated for that nowadays."

"We listen to crooning tenors ululating to jazz bands," said she. "But I agree that isn't sentiment; it's slushy, sloppy sentimentalism, whined through the nose. Still, it ought to remind us that we are not very sophisticated yet."

"I am sure she will retire," said Oliver.

Mrs Graves looked at me. "I was with William and Marie when he saw her act, Dr Soame. He looked quite absorbed, and Marie did not like it."

"I begin to understand now," I told her. "Jean had a part that suited her, and William, no judge of acting or the drama, was so struck that he determined to back her in a play."

"While Marie, knowing there was a theatre lease to be used up, half consented," said Oliver, smiling. "Though that's not what Aunt Green says!"

Mrs Graves' car was waiting for her at the terminus, and she volunteered to give me a lift. I was set down at Bloomsbury, after she had reached home, and went at once to the offices of Mr Busby.

Naturally I had taken care to pencil the name of my friend on my card, and, after ten minutes, an author with a discontented face came out of the private office, and I was shown in.

Mr Busby received me with a smile, gave me a cigar, and asked if I had taken to authorship.

"Perhaps some little brochure on the functions of the kidneys?" he permitted himself a grin. "Novelists are so damned fond nowadays of describing their characters' innards, and there is a future for a medical novel which people can read, without having to hide it on occasion. A doctor's name on the back makes all the difference!"

"I came to talk to you about a play," I said.

"Horrors!" he exclaimed. "I am stacked with plays."

"Not mine," I said.

"You relieve my mind," remarked Busby. "Whose is it?"

"I don't know," I told him. "It was called *Springtide* and was written by a sort of amateur hermit."

"It would be," said Busby. "Only a hermit has time to notice when spring comes in nowadays, or the compiler of a bulb catalogue. But wait a moment—*Springtime—Springtide*? Hang it all, is that the crime play the police are on the track of?"

I had forgotten Mattock's questionnaire. "I suppose it is the same. But I gathered that it was about dew and roses, and the bloom on the rye, and that sort of thing."

"Evidently written by *two* hermits, male and female," said Busby. "Is there a regulation now against the propagation of roses and dew?"

"I had better explain," I said. "I want to discover who wrote the thing, for there is a kind of mystery about it."

"A complete mystery to me, Dr Soame. I never heard of it, and I told the police so."

I said that the star was to have been a young actress named Jean Murphy, and he looked intelligent.

"Oh, I did hear something about that proposition many months ago. Some hard-faced business-man, who had the fag-end of a lease, and proposed to scatter the largess on some fairy—"

"No," I said, "your facts are right to a point. But Mr Hoe-Luss, whom I knew well, was not a man to encourage fairies of the type you mean."

In confidence, I told him all I knew about the play and its vicissitudes and Hoe-Luss's death, with the subsequent falling in of the contract. He listened thoughtfully, and when I had come to an end, asked me a question.

"Let me get a glimpse of Mr Hoe-Luss. He was a clever, prosperous business-man, with no experience of the theatre. He was greatly struck by your young friend's acting, though his interest in her went no further than that?"

"Correct."

"Apart from his devotion to his wife, he was a tough nut in business; not very artistic or aesthetic. He procured a play from a hermit, whose name no one knows, sponsored by an agent, equally un-get-at-able, whose name his widow forgets, and the police are unable to trace."

"You sum up admirably," I said.

Mr Busby grinned. "What is the strong, silent man most famous for in real life?" he asked.

"A false profundity?" I guessed.

"Not on your life!" said Busby. "The strong, silent man is your hyper-sentimentalist, and is thoroughly ashamed of it. That is why he has to appear strong and silent."

"You may be right," I agreed.

"I am right. Did you see a fellow go out just before you came in?" I admitted that I had.

"He is a stockbroker," remarked Busby. "Ruthless, hard, cynical in speech. He was anxious for me to try to place a slim volume of poesy entitled *Silver Fragrance*. No, it had nothing to do with bimetallism. It was all hearts and moonbeams, and crooniness. Fact! I don't mind sentiment, I am just telling you."

We appeared to be getting away from the point. I worked back to it.

"So you can give me no hint about this play?" I asked.

"I have given you all the hint you want," replied Busby. "Mrs Hoe-Luss doesn't remember the name of the agent, because there was none. Obviously she could not have returned it to him, for the same reason. Miss Murphy does not know who the author was. But I bet she knew him. No contract can be found, because there was no contract."

"Is this the way you talked to the stockbroker?" I asked, laughing, "no wonder he looked discontented."

Busby put down his cigar, and regarded me quizzically. "You will never make a detective, Dr Soame. But perhaps you do not understand because you have not my experience of the budding, especially the blushing, author's mentality. Of course Hoe-Luss wrote that play himself."

I started. "He wrote it?"

"It leaps to the eye," replied Busby. "Here's a man with a French wife—and you know that the French and the Southern Irish are the most unromantic people alive—who has secretly written a play about roses and dew. He can't tell his wife. He can't expose this naked, fragile bantling to the merciless Gallic eye, at least under his own name."

"You have hit Marie off to a T," I told him.

He grinned. "Oh, the French are a standardised race, though they would hate to believe it—regimentation of the mind is their trouble. At any rate, this hard-faced, innocent-hearted financier is anxious to give his precious child a home. He sees an *ingénue* acting as he would have his heroine act; so simply, so naturally, with such an obvious absence of sophistication, that he realises he has met a twin soul. She will not laugh at his love scenes. The dread every young author has of exposing his sentiment to the hard light of the common eye will fade in her presence. He has money, the fag-end of a theatre lease, so he takes to himself a hermit, and an agent, and engages Miss Murphy for his star. I see it all."

"But why destroy the play?" I demanded, "for that was what must have happened to the script if it was not returned to an agent?"

"Gallic logic again," said Busby. "You may be sure his wife read it again, and decided that it was not worth five thousand pounds."

"And destroyed it?"

"I expect so."

I felt jubilant. If he was right, there was no longer any mystery about Jean's connection with William Hoe-Luss. But would Mattock accept what was merely a bit of intuition?

"But how shall I prove it?" I asked, as I thanked him, and got up.

Mr Busby smiled. "Tell her you wondered why her husband ever thought of writing *Springtide*, Dr Soame. For all she knows, he may have confided in you."

Chapter XIX
QUERYING THE PLAY

I WAS back in good time for dinner, and found Marie Hoe-Luss in the hall, smoking a cigarette, and (I should have said) watching the door. I took it that I could have ten minutes' talk before she went up to dress, so I sat down beside her, and asked where Jean Murphy was.

"With Geyle, I suppose," I added, smiling.

"He has not come back yet," she replied. "Your friend the Chief Inspector asked him to go to Winstone. He went after tea."

I wonder if that was why she was interested in the door. "I hope he will explain to him that Miss Murphy's connection with the affair—the tragedy at the château, I mean, was purely a matter of business," I said. "But, after all, you would be the best person to speak."

That startled her. She turned her face towards me, and gave me a questioning look. "What do you mean, Dr Soame? Speak to whom, and about what?"

"Oh, naturally, to Mattock about that play," I replied. "If your husband had never promised money to back her, she would not have been worried. Even now I don't see how they can connect her with his death, however remotely, but—"

She interrupted me anxiously. "You don't think they do?"

"Then why interrogate her now?" I asked. "I am sure the matter could be cleared up in a minute, if you told them that there was no longer any need to make a mystery about the authorship of the play."

I looked away as I said that, to enable her to make any facial readjustments she wished. She did not reply for a few moments, so I felt sure that Busby had put me on the right track.

"Does no one suspect it?" she asked presently.

"I cannot speak for others," I told her, "but, surely, your husband only intended to keep his authorship a mystery until the play had been put on, and tried out? If it flopped, he would not be anxious to claim it as his."

"But how clever of you to guess!" she cried.

I had to accept the misplaced laurels, for it would never do to tell her that I had consulted an outsider. "Oh, hardly. One didn't expect a clever and experienced business-man to finance an unknown play, unless he had some personal interest in it. The trouble is that the police are liable to mistake the nature of the personal interest."

She frowned. "You knew William too well for that."

"I did. But I am not in question here. Mattock is bound to investigate every line. If you can convince him that Miss Murphy's only connection with your husband was a professional one, it will eliminate her from the case, and make it easier for him to concentrate on other suspects."

She thought that over.

"Yes, I see. That might be the best plan," she murmured. "The fact is I read the play, but it did not strike me as a very good one. Was I to say so to William? Of course not. It was his secret hobby, his plaything. It would make him happy to have it played. I didn't grudge him that. And as you say, like most first dramatists, he was shy about acknowledging it."

I nodded. "A badge of the tribe."

She went on. "But it *was* a poor play. When the poor dear was dead, I read it again. He was brilliant in business; no one had a better head. But the play! Dr Soame, it was childish. It would be no memorial to poor William. You can make a play of roses and dew, but the roses must be wonderful, and the dew not mere water. I did not even debate the idea of putting it on. I knew it would be guyed by the critics, and I do want to keep my memories of William as he really was; so keen, and clever, and *intelligent*."

"So you burned the play?" I said.

"Yes. He was gone, and putting it on in the theatre would not give me the pleasure it would have given him. Then there was the five thousand pounds. So I had to keep up his fiction about the hermit and the agent. Now, of course, as you say, it may be dropped. I shall certainly tell the detective—so wise of you to suggest it."

She got up, smiling. I believe she told the truth. Had William lived, he would have insisted on launching his sentimental bantling; but, when he died, Marie's cold judgment, combined with her frugal instincts, made it quite certain that there would be to William no posthumous dramatic child.

"Jean is leaving the stage, or I should certainly have done something for her," she added, as she put her foot on the first stair. "But that play—no."

It seemed to me as I dressed, that we had got the number of suspects down to four: Geyle, Caley Burton, Joe, and Oliver. Mattock might suspect Marie too, for all I knew, but I did not.

Geyle came in just in time to scramble into his evening clothes and get down to dinner. Jean was very anxious to know what the police had said to him, but he smiled, unruffled, and remarked that Mattock had been very fair.

"No allegations of third degree from this quarter, darling," he said. "The man, reasonably enough, seems to think that the two deaths"—he looked rather apologetically at Marie as he said that—"are in some way linked. So he wished to know in what way my fortunes could be linked up with Mr Hoe-Luss's. It takes time to explain these things in the form of question and answer."

Jean looked relieved. If Geyle was acting, she was one to be easily deceived by it. "I shall be glad when it is all over," she sighed.

"So shall I," said Marie, rather sharply. "Let us drop it for the present."

Geyle nodded. "Much better. But Mattock asked me to say that he would be here to-morrow about eleven. He wants to know all about the château, and our movements on—er—that day."

"Very well," said Marie. "Did you get your business done in town?" she said, turning to me.

"Yes, thank you," I said. "I managed very well."

Mattock was alone when he called next morning. He asked Marie and Geyle to join him, and suggested that I should also be one of the party, to refer to in connection with any medical question that arose.

He did not open any intimidating note-book when the conference began, but sat at a table in the library, with Marie in an easy chair near the window, Geyle standing with his back to the fireplace, and myself seated between him and my hostess.

"This must be painful for you, Mrs Hoe-Luss," the detective began, "but it is very necessary if I am to get a grip of essentials. In the first place, I wish to know how the room in which your husband worked is situated. I mean, of course, in the château."

"It was in a little tourelle—round tower," she replied at once, "the château is a great rambling place, and at each corner on the first floor there is one of these towers—built out, if you know what I mean."

"Corbelled out—I know the kind of thing. In the portion of the house where the main bedrooms were?"

"No, we were mostly in the other half of the place. The tour—the tower was made into a little circular room, and there were eight steps from it—shallow steps, to a landing."

"On a passage?"

"Yes, they led on to a passage, that led to the main part of the house, but, at right angles, there was another passage that led to the stairs to the ground floor."

"Excuse me," said Geyle, "you will give the inspector the impression that these stairs gave access to the lower part of the château. They were actually," he told Mattock, "part of an outside, covered stair, that led to the grounds outside."

"So that anyone could have visited Mr Hoe-Luss from outside or inside."

"Yes, of course," said Geyle. "But I think we found that the door, for there is a door at the head of the second stairs, was locked on the inside."

Mattock smiled. "Possibly. But anyone who came up from outside could lock the door after him, and remain in the château. It did not occur to anyone that murder might have been done, so none of the usual precautions were taken, were they?"

"No," said Marie.

Mattock resumed. "Mr Hoe-Luss intended to make a prolonged study of some papers connected with a business transaction, and went to this isolated study to set to work. A meal of sorts was sent up to him, which he ate. Apart from Miss Hobert (who apparently did not know that he wished to be undisturbed), do you know if any of the other members of the party visited him?"

She shook her head. "No. None of them said he had."

"But there were some hours during which you could not keep your eye on every member of the party. Dr Geyle says he did not see Mr Hoe-Luss in his study, only when he was called by Miss Hobert, and found him on the floor of the passage."

Marie frowned. "Any one of the men might have visited him without my knowing. As I say, it is a great rambling place, and my guests did as they pleased. If they wanted to go out, or stay in, go to their rooms, or amuse themselves in company, they did so."

The detective turned to me. "You were Mr Hoe-Luss's doctor for some time, I think, Dr Soame. Would you say that he was a healthy man?"

"For his age, certainly," I said, "or was when I last overhauled him."

Mattock nodded, and looked at a paper in his hand. "It seems very strange," he said to Marie, "that your husband should die, even if he had eaten the more virulent fungi (which is doubtful), in so few hours. I don't think any case of the kind has been heard of."

"That is what struck me; but, of course, I had no communication with the French doctor," I said. "It seems to me sheer nonsense."

Mattock nodded again. "What did the doctor say to account for it, madam?"

Marie wrinkled her brows. "He said something about—would it be *status lymphaticus*?"

The detective gave me a glance. "What is that, Dr Soame?"

I explained as well as I could, and added that there were quite a few medical men who cynically remarked that the term was often used to account for a bodily condition for which the medical man was otherwise unable to account.

"Just as we read in the papers that Scotland Yard has certain unspecified clues from which in time something will be evolved," I told him.

He smiled faintly. "Then the doctor's theory was that this vague complaint left your husband in a state in which he was liable to succumb readily to poisoning?"

"That did seem to be his idea," she replied. "But really he was a timid little man, and not over confident. Then he said something about my husband's arteries being hardened, and so on, and a slight haemorrhage of the brain, I think."

"Cerebral haemorrhage," I said, staring at her, for I had not heard this before.

Mattock swung round on me. "What is your opinion, Dr Soame?"

"Mr Hoe-Luss was not young," I said. "The arteries do tend to lose their elasticity, to harden, and become rigid, as we grow older."

"Would that lead to a cerebral haemorrhage, doctor?"

"It does, in certain cases, lead to the development of aneurysm, which may cause a rupture of the arteries in the brain. But, in that case, I should expect to find signs of apoplexy—"

"A stroke?" he asked.

"Yes."

"Did Mr Hoe-Luss have a stroke?" he asked Marie, "or what did the doctor say about it?"

She looked rather helplessly at Geyle. Evidently she had been too upset to follow closely what the French doctor had said, or had failed to follow the drift of his technical explanation. Geyle asked might he reply for her.

"I don't pretend to be a doctor of medicine," he remarked, as Mattock nodded assent, "and it was not for me to contradict him. But I think he was an ignorant ass—"

"Maybe, sir; but what did he say; that is what I want to get at."

"Roughly, I understood him to say that Mr Hoe-Luss had been in a condition which rendered him more susceptible to the action of the poison in the fungi; that his arteries were hardened to such an extent that a violent bout of sickness had led to a rupture of one in the brain. He took it that Hoe-Luss got to the door, then fell down dead, and broke his neck in falling."

Prior to this, everyone had tried to fill my mind with more or less tendencious gossip; now I had a clearer idea of what had taken place. The detective also seemed satisfied, and asked what I thought of that.

"I do not say that it could not have happened," I replied. "*If* he had very rigid arteries, of which I found no sign when I overhauled him last; *if* he ate fungi, and was sick (violently so), he might get to the door, open it with a last effort, die of a stroke, fall downstairs, and dislocate his neck. But that seems to me to assume too much. Had I been confronted with a similar case, I should have accepted the theory of sickness, following the eating of the fungi, but decided that he had opened the door, and tried to go down the stairs to get help, then felt dizzy and stumbled forward, breaking his neck, and dying of that."

Marie gave a quick glance at Geyle, and seemed relieved. "I am sure that was it," she cried. "He was a stupid little man."

Mattock pursed his lips. "H'm, perhaps so. I think there was no attempt on the part of anyone to determine the exact nature of the poisoning?"

"Mrs Hoe-Luss tells me no organs were sent up for a pathological examination," I said.

"Very careless," said the detective. "However, that cannot be helped now. It is obvious that a good many people in the château could have visited Mr Hoe-Luss during the time that he was in the tower room, and equally obvious that no one admits it."

Geyle shrugged his shoulders. "That is true. Naturally we took the death to be the result of eating fungi."

Mattock got up. "Thank you for the information you have given me," he said. "It is not my business to determine the earlier matter, but it seems to me to have some bearing on the death of Mr Simcox, in so far as it supplies a motive."

"I do not see it, I'm afraid," said Marie.

"Perhaps not, but the information is useful, at all events, and I am obliged to you, madam. I needn't keep you any longer at present—You, doctor—" he turned to me, "might come with me for a few minutes. There is a point on which I should like your opinion."

Chapter XX
WHO BID ONE CLUB?

"I suppose you did not hear these additional details, doctor?" said Mattock, when I went out to the front door with him.

"No," I said. "I did not care to worry Mrs Hoe-Luss by asking for particulars of the symptoms, and so on. I was quite surprised to hear about the rupture of an artery in the brain, for example."

"I wonder," he began, as we strolled down the sunlit drive, "I wonder if there is any chance that this French doctor was got at? Mrs Hoe-Luss had a great deal of money, and there are other wealthy people possibly interested. I don't know that my Heads would stand for a trip to France, to interview the fellow, since the matter I am investigating is the death of Mr Simcox only."

It had already loomed as a possibility in my mind that some interested party might have bribed the medical man to give the verdict he did. But I could not believe it of Marie.

"I cannot say," I replied. "It may be so. One would have to know the man and his reputation to decide that."

"Quite," he returned. "I shall report on this fresh evidence, and see if anything can be done on the other side. If the two deaths are the work of one person, then the first death was not due to poisoning, or an accidental fall while dizzy."

"How would you read it then?"

He considered for a moment. "Suppose one of the interested parties went into the room, and found the man sick. It would be very easy for him to lend a helping hand to Hoe-Luss, open the door, get him to the head of the steep stairs, and push him suddenly down."

"Knowing that it might be assumed that the fall was due to nausea and vertigo?"

"Yes, that is what I mean. Look how that gives parallel for the death of Mr Simcox! If the first crime came off successfully, as it did, the criminal would be inclined to use a similar method to get rid of the young man. Murderers on a wholesale scale generally give themselves away by repeating themselves; and burglars are frequently caught because they tackle every job in the same way."

"Oh, I have often heard that," I observed. "It is certain that a man does not rupture an artery in the brain after death, too; so Hoe-Luss was alive when that happened, taking it to be correct that there was a rupture."

"Might not that be the result of the fall?"

"It might," I said.

Mattock suddenly dropped the subject. He said that Major Tobey was to pick him up at the park gates, and I suddenly decided that I would ask him to give me a lift home, too. I had just remembered that my *locum* had studied under Professor Weinforss, the Viennese authority on arterio sclerosis, and it struck me that he might be a useful adviser. At the same time,

I felt sure that I would have detected any incipient signs of the trouble in William Hoe-Luss when I last examined him.

Tobey was already waiting for us, and gave me a lift home. I sat in the back seat, while he and Mattock talked in low tones. When they dropped me at my own gate, and drove on, I went in, only to find that my *locum* had been called to a maternity case in a village ten miles away.

When my parlour-maid told me this, she directed my attention to a parcel which lay on the hall table. It had arrived that morning, and proved to have been posted in France. I took it into my surgery, and opened it eagerly, wondering what it could contain.

To my surprise, it contained a box, fairly large, but not heavy, and a note from Caley Burton, which I immediately opened and read.

Dear Dr Soame [it said],

On my way to Metz, it suddenly occurred to me that something should be done to decide the question brought up by young Simcox. I left for the château, and picked up en route a herbalist who is an expert in fungi.

We spent a long day searching in the park for various specimens; in particular, we made a search of the wood mentioned by Simcox. I am sending samples of the eleven kinds we discovered, labelled correctly by the herbalist. You will see that *Amanita phalloidis* is not among them. Perhaps you will be kind enough to pass this on to Major Tobey?

Yours,
Caley Burton

I left at once for Winstone with the box. I understood now why Burton had gone off the direct route. Here was as good proof as need be that Hoe-Luss had not died of eating *amanita*.

Mattock was not there when I reached the town, but Tobey took the box, and agreed that Burton's researches had helped to confirm our theory that a broken neck was the primary cause of Hoe-Luss's death.

"With this proviso," he said, when he volunteered to drive me back to the Chace, and we were getting into his car, "that there was no poisonous drug introduced into the stuff he ate. That is a possibility we cannot leave out of account; especially as the man's death left a large fortune at the widow's disposal."

When I saw Marie again, I told her of Burton's parcel, and saw her brighten up. "But how good of him," she cried. "I never thought of having a search made."

I nodded. If there was anything in Tobey's proviso about poison, and her culpability, I had the means to test it now.

"There is another thing that ought to have been done," I said, watching her face closely, "to decide if the local doctor was a knave or a fool. He may be a backwoods fellow, who has forgotten most of the little he learned, but he certainly acted and spoke most absurdly."

"But why should he?"

"If your husband met with foul play," I said gravely, "some interested party might have made it worth his while to give that rather absurd verdict. I repeat that, while your husband's arteries were not young, there was nothing to hint at excessive rigidity, or thickening."

She nodded. "I see what you mean. But how could one tell about the man. I do wish I had asked you to be a member of the party. If he made it all up, he would be afraid to repeat it to another doctor."

"I should certainly have talked it over with him," I said.

She looked at me earnestly. "It isn't too late, is it? Would you go over and see him for me? Do you think you could discover anything that way?"

I reflected that I could easily extend my holiday for a few days, and felt sure that a heart-to-heart talk with the doctor would give me a much clearer view of the facts than the muddled explanations I had heard from her, and Geyle, and others.

"I will pay your expenses, of course," she said. "Naturally."

I smiled. "Very well. I can run over there, and be back in four days at most. And when I see the man, I shall have a better idea of his character. I may be doing him a serious injustice in even suggesting that he would take a bribe."

She beamed on me so brightly, and expressed her gratitude so fervently, that any suspicions I may have harboured about her vanished at once.

I would telephone to my parlour-maid to have a bag packed for the morrow, go on to London, and cross to France next day. Marie was to give me a letter of introduction to Dr Leclerc, and I would return as soon as I conveniently could.

"I shouldn't tell him about Mr Simcox's death, though," said Marie. "You could just say that, as William's former medical man, you were anxious to know what had actually happened."

So it was settled, and I wrote that evening to Tobey, telling him of my decision, and suggesting that this might render it unnecessary for Mattock to make inquiries in France.

I may have flattered myself in saying that. I confess that I had formerly been rather scornful of those who read detective stories, or are interested in reports of crime. But already this affair had begun to get hold of me. Brought into close contact with a mystery, and even becoming a species of colleague to a man from Scotland Yard, I felt the thrill of the man-hunt.

I did not tell Geyle or Jean Murphy that I was going to Paris on this business. I excused it by saying that I was to meet once more a French surgeon of some eminence with whom I had worked during the war. That in itself gave me an idea. Dr Edmond Romères was now attached to one of the biggest hospitals in Paris, and might be able to tell me how best to get at the qualifications of the provincial medico who had attended the château.

"Lucky you!" said Jean, when I told her. "I have only been to Paris once, and that was when I went to the château last time."

Geyle cocked an eye at me. I could see that he did not believe my story. I had not mentioned this visit before, or suggested that I had any desire to renew an acquaintance begotten of the war.

"I must get back by Tuesday at latest," he told me. "But I hope to run back again in a fortnight. Jean and I are not going to let the grass grow under our feet."

He smiled at her, and she smiled back. "I am not returning to the stage, Dr Soame," she told me softly. "Never."

"Since no woman can serve two masters," grinned Geyle.

I left early next day, and crossed to France. On the Sunday morning, I looked up Romères, discovered that he lived in an apartment at Neuilly, and boasted a telephone number. I caught him before he went out, and received a cordial invitation to visit him in the afternoon.

"And you shall have tea, mon cher Soame," he added. "I was converted to it by you. But, at the moment, I have an appointment. If you are here at five, you will find me awaiting you."

He spoke excellent English, having been dowered as a child with one of those capable women known in wealthy French households as the 'Anglaise,' a governess, in short. So I renewed my acquaintance with the Luxembourg Gardens, lunched on the sunny terrasse of a café, and got down to Neuilly in time for the 'fif o'clock.'

Romères was as friendly as ever, but a trifle stouter about the waist-line. We exchanged views about postwar happenings, some reminiscences of our base hospital, and then, as we drank the rather weak and tepid tea, I asked him if he knew anything about the doctors in the French provinces.

He laughed heartily. "Ah, my dear Soame, alas, yes! But so do you. Shall I ever forget that bogy-man from Les Iles, who adventured on abdominal surgery with the technique of a woodman!"

"And certainly did not spare the trunk!" said I. "Yes, that was pretty horrible, and some of our colleagues may still be perpetrating war atrocities up and down the country. But a certain number are trained in Paris, are they not, even if they forget it in a few years?"

"I have, of course, a book in which their names and degrees are to be found," said Romères. "Is there any 'sawbones,' as your Dickens put it, whom you wish to meet again?"

I mentioned the doctor, and Romères threw back his head, and remained silent for a few moments, contemplating the ceiling. Then he smiled, nodded vigorously, and spoke.

"It is not an uncommon name, and I knew one—Christian name Albert. I have also heard of another. That other is the subject of one of Professor Aichard's best stories. That was a little man from the Midi, who came here to study some twenty years ago. His first professional job, my friend, was to remove a non-malignant tumour. Instead, he was remarkably successful in removing an organ which was not involved. He chose the more difficult task, says our dear Aichard, but unfortunately, it was not asked for, and the patient died."

I smiled. "What of Albert?"

"Oh, the other one, Albert, has done well. He runs a private clinic in Lyons, and is a coming man."

"Then it most be Aichard's dolt," I said. "Let me see. His Christian name was Telemaque."

"But what a name?" cried Romères. "Still, it is the same. It must be the same. Aichard, who is fond of the classics, always adds dryly that our friend was in sad need of a Mentor. I will look him up for you."

He turned to a book, after passing me the box of cigarettes, and looked up my man. It was the same. He shut the book, and laid it on his knee.

"Has his fame even reached to your foggy isle, Soame?"

It was not my business to expose the man to his compatriot, so I said that he had attended an English friend of mine some time before.

"Who is now dead?"

"As it happens, he is," I replied.

"I knew it," my friend laughed. "The jackanapes had to leave Paris in a hurry, and I heard that he had buried himself in the provinces."

"You must forgive and exonerate him this time, Romères," I told him. "My friend fell downstairs and broke his neck."

"So that he escaped Telemaque!" said Romères. "The fry-pan saved him from the fire."

I had to leave him soon after that, and travelled down to see the man, fully convinced that he was still the same muddle-minded footler who had given Professor Aichard a story to tell.

The hero of that story was certainly capable of deciding that William had died of eating fungi.

When I reached the little place, and had an interview with the doctor, he had all the appearance of a nervous bungler. Very small, and timid, and hesitating, he appeared to be afraid of me, of Marie, of the entire world. He had a scraggy little beard, adorned with snuff, rather dirty hands, and mourning nails. At a venture, and after a glance at his eyes, I should have said that he doped: in a sort of miserable, half-hearted way.

On the other hand, I felt sure that he was not a rogue, merely a fool. If his clothes, and his house, said anything, it was that he just made both ends meet rather raggedly. I did not judge by the cigarettes he offered me; for a Frenchman will enjoy tobacco that would poison an Englishman with a reasonable palate. But I felt sure that no bribes had come the way of Monsieur Telemaque.

He was not too pleased, when I told him that I had come to ask him about the affair at the château, but I took him to the local hotel, gave him lunch and a cigar, and so opened his mouth.

As I suspected, he promptly put his foot in it. He was one of those uncertain people who always act on first thoughts, and think second ones for the rest of their lives. When he heard that no *amanita* could be found in the park at the château, he was flabbergasted. He feared there might be a reinvestigation of the facts, and, having made one mistake in his life, dared not face the possibility that he had made another.

I reassured him. I said that it seemed very probable that William Hoe-Luss had suffered vertigo, as the result of eating *Russula emetica*, and broken his neck when trying to get help.

"You see," I added, "there was nothing you could do for him when you arrived, so nothing important hangs upon it. I happened to be travelling in this part, and desired the honour of making your acquaintance. As Mr Hoe-Luss's English physician, I had an interest in the case, and was anxious, too, to discover if there had been any degeneration of the arteries since I last examined him."

He rose to that at once, and made it clear to me that his diagnosis was not so much the result of an application of scientific observation or medical skill, as of a desire to fit the diagnosis to what he considered the facts. There was nothing in what he said to justify his statement that William had had hardened arteries, and sifter a little talk, he was quite ready to admit that the facts might be as I put them.

In other words, he was quite willing to admit a mistake, if that mistake did not lead to a public exposure of his inefficiency. It was obvious that he stood in awe of Marie, and had been willing to say anything that appeared to please her. A wicked old Englishwoman, said he, had hissed in his ear that someone had poisoned the poor gentleman. Since great ladies, like Madame, did not poison people, he had thought it right and wise to settle the question out of hand by telling her (this *méchante!*) that the fungi were undoubtedly the cause of death.

"There was, of course, no sign that the man had been poisoned intentionally?" I said.

He shook his head vigorously. "None at all, M'sieu! I have had the poisonings here, in the neighbourhood," he held up two fingers. "Two. But yes. One arsenic—a lover, you understand. The other: strychnine. There were none of the symptoms, no."

I never met a more confused little man, but he served my purpose. Incorruptible I am sure he was; and as incompetent as incorruptible.

Chapter XXI
FROM STRENGTH

When I returned, I found that both Jean and Dr Geyle had left; he to return to France; Jean to stay in town, and choose a trousseau, with the help of Fay Hobert.

I was rather surprised that the police let Geyle go, but, for all I knew, they might have a watch set upon him, even over there. Tobey told me that Mattock had got a colleague, who was mostly concerned with the investigation of city frauds, to go into the matter of the merger that Burton and William had been considering. The police always surprise me. They appear to be quiet, big men, who follow a sort of ponderous routine. Actually, they seem to have experts on most subjects, and the man who was getting to work in town eventually expounded financial matters as to the manner born.

Marie I found most flattering. I had lifted a great weight off her mind. She wrote at once to Geyle, and told him. I believe she also wrote to Joe, and Miss Green.

"But do you really believe that someone killed William?" she asked me, "or is it merely the view of the imaginative detective?"

"If no one did, why was Simcox killed?" I asked.

"Was he? Can we be sure?"

I told her that I certainly believed it, on the evidence, she frowned, then dropped the subject. I was leaving in the morning, having already prolonged my stay five days more than I had intended. After dinner I had a cigar, and strolled out alone to the flagged path.

But my new interest in detection did not help me to solve any of the mystery. I studied the windows, and the walls, I tried to deduce something from Mattock's doings on the ladder, and his measurements up and down. But I could make nothing of it. I had to fall back on the comfortably common-sense theory that someone had come behind the poor boy, and given him a 'leg up' out of the window.

It wasn't a bit of help to say that it was unlikely that anyone in the bedrooms further away could not have done the deed. No one had been seen going into Simcox's room, except Geyle, but undoubtedly people could have moved up and down the passage unobserved. The servants had all been downstairs, concerned with the cooking, or arranging, or serving of dinner. As for the guests, when you are dressing you do not open your door whenever you hear a footstep outside.

Joe could have done it. I did not trust or like Joe. So could Oliver, with a bit of luck; or Burton; or, of course, Geyle. Geyle would be an ass to do it after having been seen visiting Simcox, but he might have reasoned that we would say just that.

In a criminal case the ways of the innocent seem often to be as tortuous and inexplicable as those of the actual ill-doer.

A very short acquaintance with Chief Inspector Mattock had convinced me that the detective force is hampered by this fact, and also by the fact that they have to reckon with the double bluff. To a point, the subtle criminal is able to follow the official line of reasoning, and the conclusions to which it leads. By varying his own procedure, he may lead them sadly astray.

He has to choose between acting as a conventional evil-doer would do, and acting as his conventional prototype would not. He may leave clues through carelessness, or leave them because the detectives will reason that an experienced professional will not so readily give himself away. He may try to cover up, or he may appear to give the police every assistance, and expose himself ingenuously to create a false impression of his conduct and motives.

Joe, for example, might have dug up that fact about the uselessness of the pen-knife for Simcox's purpose, to suit his own ends. Burton might have sent the fungi to show that he was avid in pursuit of right and truth. Geyle might hope by his cheerful insouciance to escape detection; Oliver may have pointed out to me that he could have got indirect access to Simcox's room, arguing that I would expect him to keep the method dark, if he really had killed the young man.

But there was a factor which did not worry the detective, but hampered me in my innocent amateur efforts. I had not realised till then how much personal prejudices distort one's views. It was absurd to say that Joe was a potential criminal because I disliked his raffish ways, or Geyle because his smooth, slick type impressed me unfavourably. But it is easier to suspect those you do not care for, and there was something about Joe particularly that worried me.

That he was callous, greedy, and ambitious, showed itself in everything he said or did. He was undoubtedly angry with his aunt, and disgruntled about the will. I only failed to suspect him because I saw no possible reason why he should murder his uncle.

As I said, this was my last evening at the Chace. When I went in, I determined to have another talk with Marie. My *locum tenens* had been glad enough to carry on for another week, but I could hardly ask to stay on for the balance of it, nor did I see what good I could get from it. Personally, the visit had done me no harm. My hostess had mentioned me to a wealthy newcomer in the county, and I should probably keep my patients at the Chace. After all, I have got to live, like other people, and with so many squatters nowadays (and our being forbidden to advertise), you have to watch a country practice like a hawk.

Marie was in the small drawing-room, yawning over a book. I sat down by her, and smoked a cigarette for a few minutes in silence. She looked up presently, and asked me if it was true that Mattock had returned to town.

"I wonder whom he really suspects?" she added, when I told her that I had not heard.

"I was wondering whom *you* did," I said bluntly.

She frowned a little. "Frankly, no one. How can I? On the whole," she smiled grimly, "Aunt Green was right when she said I came out of it best—opportunity and motive are what they look for, it says in this book I have been reading."

I glanced at the detective yarn in her hand. "Yes, I believe so. There's no use beating about the bush, is there? Someone of your guests did it, and, whoever he is, he deserves to be hanged. Do you think it strange if I ask which of them seems to be capable of it, granting motive?"

She did not reply to the first part of my question. "Caley Burton or Joe," she replied, so promptly that I wondered if she had had them in her mind all along. "Burton has a ruthless reputation in business, and Joe has no heart at all."

I nodded. "Oliver?" I asked.

She shook her head. "Too queasy a stomach, Dr Soame. I am quite, quite sure of that. 'Gene's spirit might be willing, if it paid him, but the flesh is weak."

"Dr Geyle?" I said, and looked at her directly.

She did not disavow this as quickly or completely as I had expected.

"I could see him killing under certain circumstances," she said. "I know he has a certain hardness about him, and the kind of logic which ignores the sentimental trimming round facts. But I am equally certain that he liked William, and he is not the sort of man to hurt what he likes."

She knew more of Geyle than I did, and that might be a sufficiently correct estimate. "Joe," I said, "isn't loved by anyone, except Meriel, and I am not too sure of her. But what motive had he for killing his uncle? He was not a favourite; he did not, or wasn't entitled to, expect much from him. What possible motive could he have?"

She shrugged her shoulders. "I hate Joe!" she said, with unexpected warmth. "He's vulgar and aggressive. No sensitive man could have become engaged to that dreadful, calculating girl. But motive is another matter. I can't think of any."

"The whole business setting is so vague to me," I replied. "People like Oliver and Burton talk to me as if I was a financier in touch with every detail of commercial transactions; instead of a country doctor, who had his own job to do—there were two companies, I think; your husband's, which included the affiliated firm in Lorraine; and Burton's—the 'Solidaris,' I think he called it."

She nodded. "Yes. Oliver and Burton wanted a merger, William did not at first. But he was supplied with details, and was considering the matter more favourably, when he met with his death."

"Dr Geyle was the scientific man attached to the Lorraine company, and Joe the metallurgist here," I pursued. "But neither of them belonged to the 'Solidaris'?"

"No. They were both under my husband."

"Someone said to me that either Geyle or Joe would be chosen to be the scientific adviser, if the merger went through," I said. "Anything in that?"

"Yes, I think so. William told me that the French company was not doing too well. I have an idea that he meant to close down on it gradually, and concentrate on the company here. If the merger had come off, the 'Solidaris' company would have attended to the French side, and they have a man of their own."

"So that Joe, or Geyle would have had to go?"

"It would have come to that."

Like most Frenchwomen, Marie had a head for business. The wife over there generally knows a great deal more about her husband's affairs than her opposite number here.

I saw things clearer now, or thought I did. "The merger having fallen through, owing to your husband's death, who runs the English company?"

"The manager is taking charge for the moment," she said thoughtfully.

"And Joe?"

"Well, he has a little more responsibility, but he is certainly not in charge," she said. "Really, Dr Soame, I don't see it. And if I don't see it, when I dislike him so much—"

She stopped. I quite agreed. Burton was the next on our list We found no motive for him. Still, I wanted to make sure. Had he told me the truth? Was the Solidaris Company really doing as well as he had said? There could be no harm in ringing up my stockbroker next morning, and asking him if he knew anything about it.

I went to bed, late, and dissatisfied. Well; I was going, and my brief spell as assistant detective was over. If the professionals, Tobey and Mattock, could not do the job, what chance had I?

When I reached home, I had a talk with my *locum*. Things were quiet, and I thought I would leave him to do the barking for the last few days of his final week. I packed a bag, and went up to town, where I put up at a reasonable private hotel in the Cromwell Road.

When I reached town, and had luncheon, I went to see my broker, instead of telephoning to him.

Fawcus is quiet and shrewd, and a personal friend. I asked him if he knew anything of the 'Solidaris' company, and he nodded.

"Yes, a very promising concern, Soame," he told me. "There was a time, not so long ago, when its fate hung in the balance, but it is going ahead now like a house afire."

"How did that come about!" I asked him.

"Bit of a miracle," he replied. "Scientific, not supernatural, of course. An Alsatian fellow in their employ was set to work on research. I know for a fact that Caley Burton made rather a personal sacrifice to raise a fund for that. Unless the 'Solidaris' could discover a cheaper method of producing the stuff they manufacture, their name was mud."

"And did they?"

"They did. Valmuller—that is the chap's name—put in a year's intensive research and experiment. Then he hit it. His process immediately, and miraculously, as I told you, reduced costs by forty-five per cent. That enabled them to get at once on top of their rivals."

So far, I had confirmed from an independent source Caley Burton's statement to me. "Good," I said. "But wasn't there a question before that of a merger with Mr Hoe-Luss's company?"

Fawcus smiled. "I wonder what you are getting at, Soame? You never used to take any interest in any market other than the gilt-edged."

"Couldn't afford to!" I said, "but I thought you knew I was Hoe-Luss's medical man."

"I'd forgotten it," he said. "Let me see. Yes, I remember; though there was nothing very definite about it. But a rumour leaked out, and as a result, 'Solidaris' spurted for a fortnight. I could get you the figures, but I think the shares went from three hundred to about three-hundred-and-seventy francs. That was when Hoe-Luss died."

When I left him, I called on friends in town, and gave up worrying for the present over the case. Burton had been quite frank, and I was as far as ever from finding a motive for a murderer.

Chapter XXII
OLIVER TAKES ME OUT

LONDON is a marvellous place for losing people, and also for finding them. Vast as it is, it has such a definite centre, a circle of no great circumference in the West End, where gather not only those from the favoured residential districts, but also those who have come to see, or to be seen.

The shops attract some, and the clubs others. Bond Street, Piccadilly, round and about St James's, you may easily find your friends who have money, or leisure, or both.

On the Friday morning, I was strolling down Piccadilly, wondering how even dusty trees have an attraction when you are in London, and glancing through the railings at a fine red setter on a leash, when someone tapped me on the shoulder.

"Jolly good workers, Soame, though they look soft!" said a voice, and I turned round to find Oliver smiling at me. He had come out of his club, and been sharp enough to see me on the opposite pavement.

"Come and have a spot of lunch with me somewhere," he invited, when we had chatted for a few minutes. "I hope you aren't still in the clutches of the police?"

We lunched at a grill, and I asked him if he had had any polo since leaving the Chace.

"Just a practice game, yesterday," he told me. "We are playing the 90th Hussars to-morrow. Seen any polo?"

I told him that my experience of the game, even as a sightseer, was confined to watching a few regimental games in India during the war. I had nine months out there, towards the end of the struggle.

"Come and see us chew up the soldiers to-morrow," he said. "I'll give you a ticket for the Stand. But don't watch me. Our No 3 is the man; a holy terror, with wrists like elastic steel, if you know what I mean, and the best string of ponies in England at the moment."

I have always liked the speed and excitement of the game, though I know nothing of its finer points.

"I'll love to," I told him. "Where do you play, and at what time?"

He gave me the information, and added, "Did you know poor old William used to play? Bit on the heavy side, and no long hitter, but full of devil, and a dashed fine horseman."

"I heard he played," I agreed. "Very well. I'll be there."

Oliver looked down at the tablecloth. "That reminds me, Soame. I quite forgot to collect my legacy. Natural enough, of course, with all the fuss about that poor devil Simcox. I won't want to worry Marie, but perhaps, as you live near there, you could do something for me?"

"Of course," I said. "What is it?"

He laughed. "Well, strictly speaking, William didn't mention them in his will, but Marie said I could have 'em, and if you could collect 'em, and bung 'em along to me, I should be everlastingly obliged."

"Delighted, when I know what the mysterious 'ems are," I replied.

"Sorry," Oliver grinned. "Half a dozen polo-sticks, to be exact. He had some beauties that I always coveted. I said so often enough. The other day Marie reminded me, and said she would like me to have them. They were no use to her, and so on."

I nodded. "Of course I'll send them to you. Where are they kept?"

"Heaven knows," said he. "But if you ask Marie, or the butler, if she is out, you can get them. The butler used to be William's valet, you remember, and will know all about his polo kit."

I nodded. "Right," I said. "I'll pack them and send them by passenger train to your flat, shall I?"

"Do; and let me know the damage," said Oliver. We parted later. I was to meet him the next day at the entrance to the Stand, and he said with a twinkle that he hoped to put me in charge of a young woman, who wanted to know all about polo.

"You can fill her up with your Indian reminiscences," he added. "She is eager but ignorant."

I went to the ground next afternoon, and duly met Oliver near the Stand. He looked very smart in his well-cut breeches and silk shirt, his boots polished until they shone again, his muscular arms more visible than usual. He introduced me to his companion, a dark, eager little thing with fetching blue eyes, and a very engaging air of youthful vitality.

"Miss Vayne is going to marry a polo player," he told me. "So don't let her scandalise your neighbours with remarks about the way I swing my club!"

She grinned at me. "'Gene is a perfect pest, but I expect you know that, Dr Soame. I know they call it a stick."

"She's been looking it up in the encyclopaedia," said he. "Well, see you later in the tea-tent. Etta will bring you along, Soame."

I concluded that Oliver had put me in charge of his fiancée. She was certainly very bright and lively, adored him, and intended to learn something of the game in which he was an adept.

"When did all this happiness happen, Miss Vayne?" I asked her as we settled down in our seats. "Lately?"

"At half-past ten last night," said she. "Isn't he a darling?"

I concluded that it was going to be unpleasant for me, if I had to help put Oliver on the official spot. However, she chatted away till the two teams came on the ground, and then pointed out Oliver, whom I saw very well for myself, coming cantering up the ground on a bright bay.

"I don't call them ponies, do you?" she said. "I call them small horses."

"Except Oliver's bay mare, I hope," I replied. "No, I think polo ponies are changing, like the rest of us. Now I wonder which is the No 3 he told me to watch?"

She knew that: a thin man with ginger hair, on a chestnut. Then she wanted to know why they played with croquet ball painted white, and if they played thirty-five minutes each way.

I told her that the chukkers were of much shorter duration, and even then, they would have to change ponies frequently, some having quite big strings on the ground, in waiting.

"I wondered why 'Gene said he had four," little Miss Vayne replied. "Oh, are they going to start?"

She sat breathless as the game began, and indignant when a fierce-looking hussar rode Oliver off, and later another soldier kept knee to knee with him down the field.

"That's a foul," she cried. "He's bumping 'Gene's poor pony. Why doesn't the referee do something?"

I saw indignant looks to either side of us, and tried to explain. But now the girl was full of joy and delight. Oliver had got in a splendid backhander, and wheeling his pony about magically was galloping towards the flying ball.

A back saved the goal that time, but Oliver was soon at it again, and before the end of the chukker had scored the first goal with a drive from sixty yards out.

I must say that he looked twice the man he did in Chilean clothes, and his playing struck me, ignorant as I was, as magnificent. I hardly noticed No 3, who was the cynosure of our neighbours. When the second period began, the Hussars' No 2 came in for great censure from my little companion.

"That septic beast has just hooked 'Gene's club!" she protested. "I say, it is unfair. They have let him get away with the ball."

"Stick, stick, Miss Vayne," I said reproachfully. "It is all right. It was done in hitting the ball, not by way of obstruction."

"Well, that is a foul anyway!" cried she, a little later, when an over-zealous back crossed Oliver, who took a toss promptly. "It's the same beast, with the nasty dark face."

The indignant looks from our neighbours now changed to grins, and I felt more comfortable and began to enjoy thoroughly the fast game being played, the teams sweeping up and down and across the field like demons, the thunder of the ponies' hoofs, the swish of sticks handled by steely arms, the clack of the ball, the way it rose sometimes from the ground and hurtled head high towards one goal or the other.

The Red Polls were soon four up, to the two scored by their opponents. Oliver had accounted for half the score, inspired by the bright eyes watching him from my side, and I felt sure from the comments near us that he was regarded as a coming player.

What struck me most about all the play, almost forgotten in the years that had elapsed since the war, was the ease and certainty with which, even in a close mêlée, the players used their sticks. In a similar situation, I would undoubtedly have cracked the skulls of friends and enemies.

Listening again to the comments, I gathered that Oliver was not as well mounted as most of the others. Polo ponies are expensive, and I knew he was not rich.

"Get him a few tip-top—really tip-top—ponies," said a young man at my side, "and he'd make rings round 'em."

Yes, Oliver did put in some wonderful wrist work, which seemed to me not inferior to his admired No 3. Forehanded or backhanded, he was very sure in his hitting, and appeared hardly to look at the ball—a point so strictly enjoined on those who play golf. But then you don't play golf on miniature racehorses, with a lot of other centaurs jostling and charging you.

One backhanded save in particular drew thunders of applause from the spectators. A hussar (that pertinacious fellow, with the 'nasty dark face,' of course) had come dashing up the field in command of the ball, going like smoke. He slashed in a tremendous drive from fifty yards out, and Oliver swung an instantaneous backhander, stopped the ball, and whirled away up the ground, amid a roar that shook the Stand.

There were tears in Miss Vayne's eyes when I looked at her, and she thumped me on the back with her little fist.

Now indignant, now excited, as Oliver scored a triumph, or was, as she concluded, foully treated by the burr-like Hussar, my companion was in a state of wonderful happiness by the time the game came to an end, leaving the Red Polls the winners by a goal-three, said she, till I explained to her disgust that Oliver's team had a handicap.

"If they don't play as well, all the worse for them," she exclaimed, as we made our way to the tea-tent. "They ought to learn to play better, or only take on sides like themselves."

I discovered then that she played no games, not even tennis. She liked dancing, music, reading, and swimming. Oliver told me afterwards that she was as clever as a fish in the water. At any rate, he seemed proud of her, and after our afternoon together, I did hope that my suspicions of him were thoroughly unjustified.

"I expect you disgraced poor old Soame," he said to her, as we had tea. "Confess, Soame, that she openly wondered why I took up the two-eyed stance, or didn't put side on the ball!"

"Never," I said. "Her comments were so intelligent that they excited interest and pleasure to right and left of us."

"Hasn't our dear doctor a charming bedside manner!" she scoffed. "As for you, 'Gene, you did your best, I expect, but how could you hope to compete with that perfect darling soldier with the handsome dark face?"

When I had to go at last, 'Gene thanked me for taking care of her. "And now don't forget my other commission," he added. "Buzz those sticks along as soon as you can."

"I certainly shall," I said.

Which shows that coming events are occasionally Peter Schlemihls!

Chapter XXIII
A QUICK TRICK

My *locum* was going to another job at a town thirty miles away, and was not due until Monday. I asked him to stay the Sunday, and got home late on Saturday evening to find him just in from the last task of the day; attention on a labourer, who had cut his hand with a scythe.

His train left at five on Sunday, and I drove him and his traps to the station, and then, having the means of transport under me, decided to go on to the Chace to collect the polo-sticks for Oliver.

Marie was not at home. She had left to dine with Lady Bensham, the newcomer who had recently taken a place in the county. Porrit, the butler, opened to me, and hoped his mistress had not known that I was coming.

"No, I came back from town yesterday," I told him. "Saw a game of polo, by the way, and Sir Eugene Oliver playing."

Porrit brightened. "A very handy player, sir," he commented. "It was the master who put him up to it first. Always said he would make a player too, he did."

"Sir Eugene mentioned you—said you used to look after Mr Hoe-Luss's polo kit," I said. "He remembered that, you see."

Porrit nodded. "Indeed I did, sir."

"Now that is really the reason of my visit," I told him; "and there is no reason to bother your mistress about it. Do you know where Mr Hoe-Luss's things were kept since he died, his sticks and so on, I mean."

He nodded again. "Yes, sir, a bit of a shame I felt, though no one has any use for them now. They were put up in the lumber room at the top of the house, sir, and—"

"Wait a moment," I adjured him. "Mrs Hoe-Luss promised them to Sir Eugene; he had a fancy for them. He asked me to get them and send them on to him in town. I have my car outside, and if you will get them for me, I can take them now."

Porrit's face was a study. Until he spoke I wondered what emotion my suggestion had unaccountably awakened in his stolid breast.

"But they were taken away, sir, the day after you left," he said.

I started. "Taken away?"

"Yes, sir, that Major Tobey came with the man from London, and they went upstairs, and packed them up, and took them away."

This was extraordinarily quick work. "Did Mrs Hoe-Luss object?" I asked him.

"No, sir, she didn't say much."

"But why should the police want polo-sticks?"

"Perhaps Major Tobey is taking to polo," he said helpfully. "You know he hunts, sir."

"Ah, that may be so," I said quickly. I was really shocked and startled, but I did not wish to let Porrit see it. I knew now what my subconscious mind saw behind the neat stick-work of 'Gene Oliver, his steely wrists, and instantaneous physical reactions. Mattock and Tobey had kept me in the dark about that, confound them.

Almost in the same flash, I had a vision of little Etta Vayne, so adoring, so vivid and happy, with her polo player. Women are notoriously bad judges of character in men. But, of course, I said to myself hopefully, where was the motive?

Porrit obviously wondered why I hesitated. I took a sudden resolution. "I should like to see the lumber room if I may," I said.

His eyes glinted, then became again the respectful optics of the trained servant. "The police, sir, don't seem to have made much out of the business yet?"

I suppose he knew, like the rest of them, that the inquest had been official eye-wash.

"Perhaps not. I should like to have a look round."

He conducted me upstairs, by way of the first-floor passage. Perhaps he thought that I would resent being taken up the back stair from the domestic offices. We made our way into a wing, past the bathrooms, and so through a doorway to the back stairs, which gave access to the servant's bedrooms, and the lumber and cistern rooms on the top floor.

"This way, sir," said Porrit, as we reached the top, and turned left-handed into a passage.

Excitement grew on me. I knew we were in the wing where I had slept, and poor Hector Simcox. As we went on, I realised that the lumber room must be over one of those first-floor bedrooms nearer the front of the house.

Porrit opened a door, and showed me a large and quite orderly room. The floor was covered with a lino, and kept brushed and clean. No dust rested there, or on the piles of trunks, old furniture, or other odds and ends piled symmetrically.

It was about thirty by twenty feet in area, possibly extending over one of the lower rooms, and part of a second. There were two good windows, and the place was quite light.

"This is one of the few lumber rooms that look tidy," I said.

"Thank you, sir, we do our best," said Porrit modestly.

He stood in the doorway. I went over to one of the windows, opened it, and looked down. I admit that my flesh crept a little as I looked. The window at which I stood was above, though not in a line with, the side of the window at which poor Simcox had stood, previous to his fall.

Most of the rooms at the Chace were low-ceiled, and the upper floors were no exception to the rule.

I calculated roughly that not more than nine feet divided the sill of one window from the sill of that below.

I suddenly saw some method in Mattock's measurements. If he had made others since, I had not known of it, but he was too careful a man to neglect them.

My mind was working quickly now. The hints I had had were provoking. I wanted to know more, to see the wheels go round. Porrit was an amiable fellow, and I felt sure he would help me.

"I wonder, Porrit," I said, "if you would help me in a little experiment?"

His eyes glistened unprofessionally. Lives there a man with soul so dead that he will refuse to plunge into a criminal investigation, even in the most modest rôle. Porrit and the staff had, no doubt, canvassed the crime times without number. But he did not pretend even now to admit a crime.

"Certainly, sir," he said.

"Would you mind going to the room below," I said, not being explicit as to which room, "opening the window, and looking out—say at that sundial in the garden beyond?"

"Certainly, sir."

He turned quietly away, but I knew from his hurrying footsteps that his blood was stirred too. I lit a cigarette and waited, then leaned from the window, and looked down. Perhaps half a minute later, I saw Porrit's head and part of his shoulders emerge.

"Porrit!" I called, not too loudly.

He stared up at me. "Yes, sir?"

I could have touched his brow with a longish walking-stick. "Would you mind going into the room next door, and shut yourself in."

"Very well, sir."

"Let me know if you hear me calling, or speaking, Porrit."

I was quite proud of my idea. I waited, then called down three times for Porrit. I did not shout, of course.

With the window open Simcox could clearly have heard anyone calling to him in a clear voice.

The intelligent Porrit appeared at the window in a few minutes.

"I did not hear you, sir."

"I thought not. Now sit down in a chair where you are, and listen."

I spoke to him by name. He got up and popped his head out of the window.

"I heard that, sir."

It was obvious enough. "Good," I commended him. "Come up again, will you."

He was eager enough when he came back, and I had to tell him that I did not wish him to mention to anyone what we had done. This pleased him. He was flattered to be my confidential associate.

"No, sir, I won't," he said.

I mentioned a room in the other wing, and asked him if he could take me there by the quickest possible route.

I will say that Porrit did not try to discover what I was up to in this last experiment. I presume he knew.

"Come this way, sir," he said.

We went down the back stairs to the first floor, turned up the passage in the wing, down that parallel to the front of the house, and so to Oliver's bedroom at the far side.

"This," I said to myself, "will be a big feature in his defence. He would have to pass the occupied bedrooms both going and returning. He may have done so, of course, unobserved."

"I am presuming, sir," said Porrit, in a low voice, "that a guest would not—" He paused, and his gaze became fixed.

"Wouldn't what?" I asked.

"You asked for the most direct way, sir," he said. "But perhaps you meant this?"

I followed him down the passage on the wing in which we now were, and ascended a similar back stair to that in the other wing.

"You see, sir," he remarked, as we went up, "there used to be a bigger establishment kept up here, and there were some guest rooms on the top floor reached by this stair."

"Really?" I said.

"There was a sort of partition wall across the front passage up there, sir, now removed. Sort of separation, sir."

I saw what he meant. Guests and domestics had a protective partition between them. The planning of the upper floor was much the same as that of the one below, except that the rooms above were, on the whole, smaller. But there was a passage parallel to the front of the house, joined by a passage in either wing. If Oliver had gone down the wing from his bedroom, climbed the back stairs to the upper floor, he could have reached the lumber room in the other wing, by using two passages.

Was he heard moving overhead? I listened as Porrit and I walked along. No. The flooring was very sound if old, and there was a passage carpet of thick grey hair-cord.

I thanked Porrit, and tipped him, then I went home.

As I drove, I worried immensely over the matter of motive. Oliver was a director of companies, a director of the 'Solidaris.' But the merger he had supported had fallen through. It had come to nothing because William Hoe-Luss died. Was that support a bluff? If so, what had he gained either way?

It beat me, but of course Mattock was in a different position. The police would be pursuing inquiries, as the phrase goes. And how well they do it! Take any big case, consider the facts exposed in its hearing; the wealth of statements taken, and questions asked, the voluminous dossier, the acumen shown by experienced officers in investigating with skill every point that lies within their scope, and submitting to experts all that lies outside. We see most of the detective-sergeant, and hear most of his inspector, but there is the gifted hierarchy behind them, the Chief Inspector, the Superintendent, Chief Constable, Assistant Commissioner over the C.I.D. The criminal is up against a galaxy of brains.

I hadn't the least doubt that, since removing the polo-sticks, the indefatigable Mattock had men amassing every known fact about Oliver's career, domestic, financial, social, his relations with William, with the 'Solidaris,' the facts about the merger.

Of course, no one had expected it would come to that. Simcox was to have died 'accidentally' as William had done. An inquest and a funeral—adequate eye-wash.

But I was mostly sorry for little Etta Vayne.

Chapter XXIV
TOBEY LETS ME LOOK OVER HIS HAND

I was hardly settled down with a book and a pipe that evening, when Major Tobey came to see me. He came alone. Mattock was in town, he said.

I provided him with creature comforts, and gave him a long look.

"Now let us hear the latest instalments," I said. "The affair of the purloined polo-sticks."

He stared, then smiled a little. "You know that, do you. I wonder how? Seen Mrs Hoe-Luss?"

"Not since I returned, Tobey. The fact is I met Oliver in town, and he took me to see a game of polo. He mentioned the fact that he had been promised the reversion of Hoe-Luss's polo-sticks."

"Did he?" said Tobey. "Asked you—I mean told you—"

"First phrase was correct," I interrupted. "He asked me if I would get them and send them to him, without troubling Marie—Mrs Hoe-Luss."

He reflected. "Damn odd that. Did you promise?"

"Went over to fetch 'em this afternoon, and heard that you had already removed the loot," I observed.

Tobey pursed his lips, but spoke after a few moments. "Well, I expect you know how the wind blows now."

"I have an idea, Tobey. But is there a chance of a—conviction?"

"I don't think so," he said, rather to my surprise.

"I may be wrong, but I think it will end as other cases sometimes end. We know the man, but can't touch him. There is not, so far as I can see, the shadow of a motive."

"But I thought you need not prove motive?"

He laughed shortly. "That is the legal truth, Soame. But, though a coroner may sit without a jury, a judge does not. The Public Prosecutor will not move without a fair idea that he can get a conviction. Juries are about as appreciative of legal subtleties as earwigs of music. The judge may tell them that they need not worry about the motive, then they will retire and say to each other: 'No reason why he should have done it. We can't convict on that.'"

I saw his point. "If he is brought up," I said. "I can see a few medical experts brought in too to explain his aversion from blood and violence."

"'Skin for skin, what will a man give in exchange for his life?'" said Tobey. "Soame, a man in danger of being charged with murder may overcome his aversions for a moment, mayn't he? The instinct of self-preservation is very strong, eh?"

"Exceptionally so," I agreed.

"And this would be pretty quick, and, for an expert, not necessarily gory. I mean the blow that would stun Simcox, and send him out of the window?"

I agreed. Controlled strength is a factor in any game with a ball, from billiards to tennis, and I felt sure that Oliver could have killed Simcox with a backhander easily. Most of the fractured wounds were no doubt the result of the fall on the flags.

"Yes," I said, "and psychologically it is a fact that one very strong feeling will overpower another for the moment. But there will be a reaction."

"Not necessarily at once, Soame?"

"Often not. Hours after perhaps."

"And the beggar was pretty sick-looking."

I nodded. "And of course a man used to hitting with very little room to spare would do the job better than a novice."

"A swing parallel with a wall, say," Tobey observed. To his amusement I described the experiments in which Porrit had helped me.

"Good," he said. "Yes, I took it all along that someone attracted Simcox's attention by calling out, but it was difficult to say from what neighbouring window. The chap gave a call, Simcox stuck his head out, and got it in the neck."

"That would account for his not crying out," I said. "If Simcox had been conscious when he slipped over, he would have given a yell."

"Mattock said so from the first," Tobey replied. "A shout doesn't save you, but it's involuntary."

We looked at each other gravely.

"Of course you have examined the sticks," I said; "owing to the nature of the handles, though, you wouldn't find finger-prints."

"No, we tried it, of course, but nothing doing." He passed me the cigarettes, and added, "The fella who did it was determined there wouldn't be any. Mattock has eyes like a hawk. He found a tiny fibre of cloth stuck in the window fastening of the room—the lumber room. He has taken it up to Scotland Yard for analysis."

"Any stains on the head of the stick?" I asked.

"One was headless," said Tobey. "Five whole, one a shaft."

"Good heavens!" I cried. "I don't think the garden was searched very closely after we found Simcox. On the flagged path, of course, the thing would have showed up."

"Someone, if he had the nerve," he responded, "might have gone out and recovered it, but I don't think it flew off. I think it was broken off."

"Tell-tale then?"

"That is the theory, Soame," he replied. "Even a splash would be evidence. I don't believe Oliver forgot to take the sticks. He was going to play polo, and it would be in his mind. And why ask you to fetch 'em?"

"It does look fishy. Everything is fishy, but the motive, and that is invisible."

"The fella was in a quandary," Tobey mused. "You could see that. If he tried to stain or dirty the broken handle of the stick, he would know that analysis would show it. People are pretty familiar with our methods nowadays. He let it alone."

"We agreed that he didn't expect it to be a police matter at all," I dissented; "if it hadn't been for you now, I should have sent the sticks to him, and that would have been the end of it."

"Look here," said Tobey. "Mrs Hoe-Luss seems anxious enough for our success, but I don't think she is as frank as she might be. On the strength of my interviews, I would have put the crime on Joe Hoe-Luss. He's a nasty piece of work."

I smiled. One has always a warm corner in one's heart for the man who shares one's prejudices. "Absolutely. What do you want me to do?"

"There was some financial motive behind the affair at the château, Soame. Mattock and I agree on that. Could you get Mrs Hoe-Luss to tell you when the various guests arrived, women and all, especially Hoe-Luss, Oliver, Burton and Geyle?"

"I'll try," I said, "but what's the great idea?"

"I can't tell you. Mattock wants the information."

"Tobey," I said, "I am not a whale on Stock Exchange speculations, but I had a chat with my broker and it occurs to me that Oliver may have flown one banner, and fought under another, for his own hand of course. Or simply backed the merger to help a speculation of his own."

"Exactly how?"

I told him. "'Solidaris' were not very high previously, but when the merger was talked of, they rose sharply. Did Oliver buy a big block of shares, take his profit and sell out, before Hoe-Luss was killed?"

"Maybe, but surely if the merger was so useful the shares would have gone still higher if Hoe-Luss had lived to complete the merger?" said Tobey.

"It would seem so," I remarked, "but according to Mrs Hoe-Luss her husband's French company was not doing too well, and he thought of closing it down. He may have kept that from the Burton group till the thing was settled."

"It does provide a possible motive," he agreed, "but I must leave that to Mattock. He says that Inspector Hellyer, the man who carried all the investigations into the Wroth swindles on his own back, is busy following up the financial side. I thought I had got to know a bit about police work, but what Mattock told me of their industry in tracing sales and transfers of shares was a revelation. If Oliver was a 'bull' in the 'Solidaris' shares, prior to the murder, we shall soon hear."

I left him twenty minutes later, and went home. Things were getting too deep for me, and I was content to leave it to the Chief Inspector. I wondered, as I turned in that night, if Oliver had had the nerve to take the head of the polo-stick away with him. Or had he dumped it somewhere? It would be easy to hide.

Chapter XXV
HOW THE CARDS FELL

I FELT sure when I awoke that Porrit was discreet and a man of his word. He would not mention our experiments, but he would have to tell his mistress that I had called for the polo-sticks. Would she wonder, and, wondering, want me to explain?

I was just finishing breakfast when the telephone bell rang. She wished to see me, and would drive over at a quarter-past eleven. I looked at my diary. I should have to see a few patients in my surgery before eleven, at half-past twelve I had to visit a country patient.

Marie arrived in good time. "What is this about 'Gene wanting the polo-sticks?" she asked, when we had exchanged greetings. "Porrit told me."

"Didn't you promise them to him?"

She nodded. "Yes, I remember I did say something about it once. But that gentlemanly policeman of yours has taken them away. I want to know why. I didn't know it was anything to do with Oliver."

She was sharp enough. I fenced. "We cannot say that they have. I simply called because he asked me to send them to him."

"'Gene? I know. But, don't you see, if the police think they are a—" She regarded me thoughtfully and added, "A clue?"

"I never heard about that till I saw Porrit," I said. "No. Still, it's funny his asking you to send them."

"I would have sent them."

"He didn't wish to trouble you."

"Well, Dr Discretion," she said, smiling, "I don't believe you. I mean I don't believe that. 'Gene knows that I have much more free time on my hands than you. The thing is too utterly silly," she made an expansive gesture, "but I am sure the policeman suspects him. They don't know 'Gene."

"What you say may be true," I remarked. "I am only in this because I happen to be the police surgeon. I don't get all their secrets. Like you, I can hardly believe that Oliver was involved. Perhaps we can help to clear him."

"Are you setting up detective work as a side-line?"

I smiled. "It's a deep-laid instinct in most of us. I admit I have a theory, and it may be workable if I can get some information—about the party at the château, I mean."

"I thought you had met them all?"

"But not there," I said. "Tell me, if you will, who arrived first, and so on—the order of their coming."

"From which you will deduce—" she began, smiling.

"Heaven knows what, or of what value. But will you tell me?"

She thought it over. "Yes. Better write it down."

I felt quite official as I got pen and paper and prepared to take this voluntary statement.

These are the bones of it:

Aunt Green, Meriel, Joe, Mrs Graves, arrived at the château on the Tuesday.

Caley Burton and Oliver arrived next day, that is Wednesday.

Jean Murphy, with her friend Fay Hobert, arrived on the Thursday.

Late on Thursday afternoon, Hector Simcox turned up, was brought before William Hoe-Luss, and later asked to stay.

On Friday, Dr Geyle, who had not been able definitely to give the date of his arrival, turned up. She remembered that very well, because Geyle had gone to see her husband before his luggage was all out of the car, and been closeted with him for an hour before he went to pay his respects to his hostess.

"Now, I suppose you can tell me what that all signifies?" she ended amusedly.

I shook my head. "I require notice of that question," I replied. "By the way, Burton had a row with your husband, didn't he? When was that?"

She considered. "Saturday evening. They were both very hot about it for a while, but quite good friends after."

"I see," I said, and thanked her. I did not mention Oliver's possible interest in that, or I should have had to stand a fire of questions I could not, or did not wish to, answer.

She got up. "I am sorry if the police suspect Gene," she said. "As I said, it's too silly."

I looked at my notes after she had gone. It puzzled me to think what Mattock expected to discover from this fist of arrivals. I copied them out fairly, and sent them to Tobey by post.

The missing head of the polo-stick certainly appeared damning. It was not certain that it would be bloodstained, after a swing which had struck poor Simcox on the head, but it might be damaged in some way that made it advisable for the murderer to remove it.

I did not think we should ever see it again.

The fibre of cloth caught in the window fastener might be more useful as a clue. It is not only at Lyons that there are laboratories for the scientific investigation of unconsidered trifles picked up at the scene of a crime. Even country police nowadays perform miracles that would have astonished their London confrères fifty years ago.

That fibre would be classified, and if possible matched. It might be a bit of wool from the clothes of the murderer. There was the chance, of course, that it came from a suit worn by a servant, and had been torn off months or years before. But if they placed the fibre, there was a hope that it might be matched with the cloth worn by the killer of poor Hector. Tobey had not told me its colour, or quality, or kind.

I had a quarter of an hour to myself after lunch and sat down to write to Oliver. But what was I to say? If I mentioned the police action, I might give the show away prematurely. In this quandary I rang up Tobey. He told me not to write!

"He'll think you've forgotten," he said. "A busy doctor has more to do than act as Pickfords, what?"

So I didn't write. I wondered if it was quite fair to Oliver. I gave up that scruple. If he killed Hector, he didn't demand fair play. I felt too that Mattock was not one to take an unfair advantage. I know I am always irritated by books where the characters do their best to obstruct the police, and help the criminal because he seems a nice fellow.

Two days went by, and I saw nothing of Tobey. I believe he had gone up to town. My practice kept me busy just then, and it was the third day before I heard that Geyle had come back to England and spent an afternoon at the Yard, being interrogated. Curiously enough, he wrote and told me.

> DEAR SOAME [he said],
>
> The witches' pot, in which Aunt Green did most of the stirring, seems to have boiled over again. Someone seems to have been shadowing me lately, and this morning I was asked to go to the Yard for a chat.
>
> Scotland Yard's idea of a chat is apparently four hours' hard. Your friend Mattock was there, and old dog Tobey, and a genial stout ruffian who is, I believe, a Superintendent.
>
> No torture was applied, but from two till six, with a break for tea, I sat smoking and answering questions. They have resurrected poor old William, and want to know all about him, and the company, and me.
>
> For the financial part, I recommended Galey Burton. They wired him, and he volunteered to come at once. When he arrives, we are to have a second set-to. I can't make out what it is all about, but must see Marie to ask her a few questions on points not very clear to me.

So I shall run down to the Chace to-morrow morning, and if you would do me a kindness, would you come up after dinner. I'll make it all right with her.

Jean asks to be remembered to you. She is busy with the doings for the wedding.

Yours,
ARTHUR GEYLE

He did not seem at all put out, but he was that kind of man. I wondered if the police had begun to suspect him, not Oliver. Either way, it was a pity two such nice little women were involved in their fate. Four hours' questioning did not suggest that Geyle was regarded as an impossible choice as the murderer.

Of course, I went up to the Chace that evening, and was welcomed by Marie. I had a good look at Geyle who was as immaculate and as cheerfully imperturbable as ever.

We sat, and smoked with our coffee, and Geyle remarked that the Chief Inspector was an all-round man.

"I quite expected him to give me a lecture on physics," he smiled. "Finance was, of course, one of his best subjects."

"Better tell Dr Soame what he said," Marie remarked. "He may make some sense of it."

Geyle grinned. "Very well. The fact is, Soame, that Mattock began by asking me exactly what my job was. I told him. Then he wanted to know did I spend all my time at the company's laboratories, and where I had been the four weeks previous to William's death."

"Working as usual, I suppose?" I ventured.

"Working, but not as usual," he corrected me, with a smile. "It's fatal to try to string the police, Soame. You never know what they know. The matter had been confidential, but is so no longer. I told them what I had been doing during that month."

"And what was that?" I asked, as he paused.

"A little detective work," he said.

I started then. "You don't mean to tell me that you suspected something would happen?"

"To William? No. If you had any commercial experience, Soame, you would know that companies and commercial concerns have to keep a strict eye on what their friends and rivals are doing. Competition is so fierce, and prices cut so much nowadays, that you only get there by having the little something the others haven't got."

"I see what you mean."

"Unpleasant, but unavoidable," he went on. "Well, nothing dishonest was asked of me, but, as the chemical expert for my side, I was commissioned to discover why a certain Alsatian gentleman was hid away for twelve months or so—the more so because he was a man who was scientifically worthy of all the limelight they could throw on him."

An Alsatian? I remembered what I had been told now, and was anxious to hear more. "So you spent four weeks wondering?"

He nodded. "And working. I had some hints to go on; the general nature of the problem, and the bent, and methods, of the man tackling it. No, I did not employ ruffians to attack him, and secure the secret! I knew that he had one fault; he was careless with his materials after he had done with them, a fatal fault in a researcher. Personally, when I have made an important experiment, I destroy the debris, the materials. But the man I was after threw them away."

"You mean that he left them, to be found by anyone looking for them?"

"Yes. I am rather good at scientific synthesis, Soame. I collected the fragments, and set myself to think out the line on which he had been experimenting. His was a metallurgical problem, a problem that, if solved, would effect tremendous economies."

"Had you any luck?" I asked.

He nodded again. "I despaired for three whole weeks, and then I saw a little light. There was one chemical equation that seemed to be odd man out. To vary the metaphor, I had found a piece that was out of place in the jigsaw. It looked as inappropriate as the top of Nelson's cocked hat in a farmyard puzzle scene. And then, one day, I realised that my conventional prejudices had stood in my way. Instead of asking how he utilised this stuff, I had been saying that no metallurgist could use it as he had done."

"I thought you scientists had no prejudices," I said.

He grinned. "Few of us are as scientific as that, Soame. I had wasted a lot of time, but now I had to rush things. I worked continuously for thirty-six hours on the job, and, just when I was getting blind and blear-eyed, it stood out before me. I went to bed and slept for twelve hours off the reel, then got up, and made a blind dash for the château."

Marie laughed. "So blind that he did not see me till an hour after his arrival."

Geyle passed a hand over his smooth forehead. "But think of the news I had! Here was our Alsatian in possession of a secret, if I judged rightly. That would enable him to cut expenses for the 'solidaris' to the tune of forty or fifty per cent. I don't mind saying that I was pleased. I knew that our French company was not doing too well, I knew that I had secured my position with the company, even if the merger did come off. William had asked me to probe the secret, and I had done it."

Chemists, like doctors, have a struggle to keep their footing, I knew. No wonder Joe Hoe-Luss had hated the man who had pulled this off.

"Did the detective ask you why?" Marie demanded.

"The detective didn't need any hints," said he. "I told him all I had done, and he made no comments."

I was more in the dark than Mattock, it seemed, and did not hesitate to say so.

"Look here, Geyle," I observed. "I have lost my bearings to an extent. The 'Solidaris' had an expert, who discovered a way to cut overhead expenses considerably, I presume by manufacturing at a reduced cost."

"That's it. The process would be much cheaper."

"You very cleverly discovered what it was, rushed over to the Château de Luss, and told your employer. I see all that. But what use was it? Could you use the process yourselves? I had an idea that these things were patented, and so on."

"In any case, we should hardly use it," he replied. "We didn't make the same stuff, for one thing."

"Then why?" I asked.

He seemed surprised at my innocence. "My dear Soame, there was a question of the two companies being merged, wasn't there. The 'Solidaris' was not much better off than ourselves at the time I began work. Burton and Oliver were keen to push it through, but William was sitting on the fence. Naturally, as soon as I arrived with my news, he saw things in a different light."

"It meant new prosperity for the Solidaris Company?" I said.

"Of course. It is one thing to agree to merge with a company which has only fair prospects, quite another to come in when your opposite number has got a process that will make things hum for him. You would sooner take a partner who was a famous doctor than one who was just qualified, wouldn't you?"

I assented. "I am quite clear in my mind about your operations now," I said. "But not why the police drag them in—are you?"

"Thoroughly fogged," said Geyle, "and Marie has no ideas either. That is why I wanted to see you. I suppose your friend the Major didn't suggest that I might be—?"

"No," I said truthfully, "he didn't."

"I told you about the polo-sticks," Marie said to Geyle.

"And Oliver? Yes. But it's too silly."

"Do you know if he was speculating in the shares?" I asked.

Geyle considered that, and I felt sure that he had heard so. "I must say I believe he was," he replied slowly. "And I think he made a packet when they had a short boom."

Marie bit her lip. "Just chance coincidence."

Geyle looked at me. "I suppose Simcox could have been knocked out by one of those things, eh?"

"I have no doubt that he was."

"I knew the polo-sticks were up there," he said, eyeing me closely. "I heard Marie say to Porrit that the polo-sticks would be all right in the lumber room till they were wanted. I asked her who was to have them, and she said Oliver."

"Was Oliver there when she gave the instruction to Porrit?" I asked.

"No," said Geyle. "Only myself and Marie."

Was this the offensive-defensive? It is sometimes wise to anticipate an inevitable revelation. But Marie interrupted this train of thought.

"Let's go up and look at the room, Arthur," she said.

He nodded. "Good idea. Coming, Soame?"

Chapter XXVI
WHAT WAS IN ONE HAND

Geyle's 'detective' work over in France had been of a kind in which he specialised. I doubted if his knowledge would help him in this, more everyday, type of sleuth work. On the other hand, a man with a scientific mind, trained to study trifles, might see something that I had overlooked.

When we had gone upstairs, and switched on the light in the lumber room, he did not waste time surveying the tidy floor and neatly piled stacks of trunks and lumber, but went over at once to the window.

"It was on one of these window fastenings they found the fibre of cloth?" he asked. I had told him about that earlier, but he had not appeared to attach much importance to it.

"Yes," I said, while Marie looked eagerly at the inconspicuous little gadgets. "I take it that the policeman thought it was caught there when the man who killed Simcox opened the window."

He sneered. "I wish you could demonstrate to me, Soame, how a man with his arm up, opening that catch, could get his clothes entangled in it."

I had not thought of that.

"Perhaps a loose thread off his coat cuff?" I ventured.

"I don't think Oliver or any of us goes about with frayed cuffs," he retorted; "in any case, as you see, when I do it, my cuff falls back."

"Mattock is an experienced man," I protested. "Don't make the kind of mistake you confessed to in the last bit of detective work you did."

"*Touché!*" said Geyle, smiling suddenly. "You're quite right. Valmuller was working unconventionally but wisely, and Mattock may have been doing the same. Then where are we? In other words, what was the point in a fibre of cloth on the fastener?"

I suppose that contact with the police had sharpened my wits. "By Jove!" I cried. "There were no fingerprints on the fastener."

Marie did not seem to understand, but Geyle had it at once.

"One up to you—if you're right, I am too, for the fibre did not come from a cuff."

"When you two Vidoqs have quite finished congratulating each other, may I know what it means?" asked Marie.

He bowed ironically. "On the instant. If the fibre means anything at all, it is because Mattock suspected it came from a cloth held over the fingers of a man who had a wise objection to leaving his finger-prints here," he replied. "That's it, Soame?"

"Must be," I agreed.

We hunted about a little longer, then I had to leave, and drove off ten minutes later.

Geyle had put me on the right track, but I was still puzzled about him. I suddenly remembered that I had been indiscreet. If he was one of the suspects, I had provided him with some information on the line on which Mattock was working. Did he hope to create a good impression in my mind by his frank acceptance of the new evidence? I could not say. But I determined to be less forthcoming in future when any of the guests wanted my opinion on the case. They all knew that I was more or less in Tobey's confidence.

Oliver had told me that he did not know where the polo-sticks were. Geyle had taken pains to inform me that he did. Was the second bluff, and the first truth?

I must admit that I got a shock next day. I had a note from Tobey saying that the Home Office had given permission for an exhumation. It was to be carried out very secretly that night. I had not made the autopsy, but I was to attend the exhumation.

When the post-mortem was done, it was carried out with a view to deciding if the injuries made by a fall from a height, on to the flagged path below the window, could have caused death. There was no hint at that time of a polo-stick having been used. The theory, if there was a theory other than accident, was that someone had hoisted Simcox out, with a hand under the knee.

I saw my colleague after breakfast, and told him so. He agreed that he had not considered the possibility that a weapon had entered into the affair. The stick would not necessarily cause a fracture, but there might be some bruising, and signs on the muscular tissues in the neck. A blow sufficient to make the man lose his balance, as he leaned out, was all that had been necessary to kill Simcox.

"A polo-stick might be used crosswise," I told him. "It would be, in play. Or it might have been swung so that the end of the head struck the neck or skull. It was, I think, a square, not a cigar-shaped, head. At least, the other sticks were of that type."

"Anyway, I did not look for anything of that kind," he said, "and there were enough injuries to account for the death six times over, without thinking of any human intervention. You saw that for yourself."

Fortunately, the exhumation was kept such a secret that the melancholy business was over and done with in peace and quietness. It was a dreary job in that dark churchyard, and I was glad when the coffin was screwed up once more, and hidden out of sight.

My colleague and I accompanied Mattock and Tobey back to the latter's house, and settled down for an hour's discussion. None of us felt like sleeping that night, and the examination of the body had given us all food for thought.

There had been, we discovered, traces hinting that Simcox had been struck just under and behind the ear. No fracture (no osseous fracture, that is) was visible at that point, but there had been extensive bruising, and my colleague said he had drawn attention to it in his report.

"If you look it up," he remarked, and I saw that Mattock had it in his hand, "you will see that I put this down to contact with a corner of one of the flags, which was left rough."

"Well, it is really crazy paving," said Tobey.

Mattock found the reference, and read it. "Yes, doctor, you have it here."

"It couldn't have been made with the head of the stick parallel with the face in profile," I said.

He nodded. "No, used more like a pick."

Tobey addressed me next. "You told us you had a talk with Dr Geyle last night, Soame. I wonder if he knew where those sticks were kept?"

I explained what Geyle had told me, and they exchanged glances.

"You know, of course, that Geyle's account of things at the château is not in keeping with what we think took place," said Tobey.

I didn't, and Mattock shot an angry glance at Tobey, so I saw that I was not the only person guilty of an occasional indiscretion.

"All the people at the château give different accounts," the detective growled. "Did Geyle seem eager to explain this?"

"He volunteered the information about knowing where the sticks were."

Having said that, I decided to tell them that I had mentioned the fibre of cloth to Geyle.

They listened rather disapprovingly, and Mattock, when I ended, remarked dryly that he hoped I would not say too much to any of the guests.

"But, the cat being out of the bag, what did he say?" he added.

"We went up to look at the window," I told him, and explained our final conclusions with regard to the fibre.

Mattock pursed his lips, but did not deny that Geyle had hit on the solution. Nor did he comment on it.

"I see," he said. "Well to turn to another matter. Major Tobey and I have finally decided that Mr Hoe-Luss was murdered. Short of a confession, no one will ever know exactly what happened, but our theory about it is one that you knew something about before. Only now, we take it that it fits the facts as no other does."

I was glad that at least one point was settled definitely in his mind. Fix one factor in an equation and you can make a start.

"What is it?" I said.

"Simply that someone visited Mr Hoe-Luss, and found him feeling sick as the result of that meal he had. Had he found him in his normal health, and pushed him down the stairs, breaking his neck, he might have explained the accident, but it would have been difficult. It was not at all difficult to suggest, or let the circumstances suggest, that a man who was suffering from nausea might open his door, and fall downstairs, while going for help."

"You mean he saw an opportunity, and seized it?" I said.

"Exactly. Most likely, he did not know that Hoe-Luss had eaten poisonous fungi. But when the doctor came along and said so, and when he also assumed it to have been *Amanita phalloidis*, the murderer knew that he had an easy way out."

"And would naturally be anxious that this disclosure of Simcox's should not be repeated too often," remarked my colleague, who had heard some of the facts for the first time that night.

"Quite. Once heard it might be forgotten, but if Simcox was going to keep on about it, Mrs Hoe-Luss might make inquiries, and the fat would be in the fire."

"There is another thing too," said Tobey seriously. "The murderer may have wondered, when Simcox was so insistent about it, if Simcox suspected foul play. That was an additional reason for shutting his mouth. And Soame here inadvertently pointed out the way to do it, when he spoke of the lichen on the wall under the window, and Simcox's remark that he was going to get a specimen."

Tobey was right. I had by chance suggested how a faked accident could be arranged.

"When are you going to see Burton about the financial side of the affair?" I asked, after a pause, during which my colleague said good night, and was shown out by Tobey.

"To-morrow, we hope," replied Mattock. "He volunteered to come down here, and we shall be glad if you can turn up too. At three. Is that convenient?"

"I'll make it so."

"At the Chace," said Mattock. "Thank you."

Chapter XXVII
DUMMY

I WENT over in good time. I was beginning to be rather appalled at the developments of what had been ironically called Marie's 'Inquest.' An old woman's spiteful remarks, and some gossip, had been the spades to dig up one tragedy and produce another.

If it had not been for that, I should still have regarded that circle at the Chace as one of pleasant, indifferent, or unpleasant people, but not, as now, composed in some part of actual or potential criminals. The fact that Joe was not there this time had no significance. The inquiry itself acquired less by being surprisingly held in the small drawing-room. Was this to put us at our ease?

To my astonishment, Oliver was there when I turned up. He looked haggard and ill at ease. He spoke to me with undisguised alarm about the summons which had called him there, and asked me had I heard something about polo-sticks.

"You know I asked you to send them on to me, old man," he said, pathetically friendly.

I had been warned not to talk too much. "I expect we shall hear what Mattock has in his mind presently," I murmured.

We had met in the hall. Porrit came to us, and asked us to go into the drawing-room.

"Mattock receives!" said Oliver, with a rather ghastly smile.

Mattock was, however, quite informal. He stood with his back to the mantel, and looked quite at his ease.

"I think we are now all here, gentlemen," he said. "Very good of you to give me your assistance."

I looked round as I sat down. Caley Burton gave me a nod and a smile. He sat with his legs crossed, and a good cigar between his lips. Geyle lounged on a Chesterfield, puffing equably at a cigarette. Tobey sat bolt upright near a window. He was staring out when we came in, and stared out again when he had nodded to us. There was not a sight of a note-book, or a policeman of lower rank. Mattock had the air of a quiet man telling some story to a rather unappreciative audience at a club.

"Only too glad," said Burton, taking his cigar from his mouth. "I can't promise anything but the financial details; but those, I take it, are important."

I looked at Mattock. He rubbed his shoulders gently on the mantel behind him. "Yes, sir, that is so. Well, to be brief, it was generally assumed that Mr Simcox, who lately met with his death here, accidentally fell from his window."

"Yes," said Geyle.

We all looked at him. He resumed his cigarette, and piled a cushion behind his shoulders.

Mattock went on. "As the result of inquiries, there is some doubt if that was so. There is the grave possibility that Mr Simcox was murdered."

He studied our faces, and so did Tobey, who swung round suddenly.

"On what grounds?" asked Burton, frowning.

"We shall come to that, sir. The grounds for that belief are less obscure than the motive behind the murder. The fact is that there is no motive except one indirectly connected with finance."

"Spit it out!" cried Oliver, as if unable to contain himself longer. "Simcox and finance! I don't see the connection."

Mattock was not put out. His voice became gentle and conciliatory. "I quite understand, sir. But you may take it that the general lines of the investigation are in my hands. They seem to lead farther afield than I thought they would. I know you were all guests, except Dr Soame, at the Château de Luss, when Mr William Hoe-Luss met his death."

"Died?" said Burton.

"Met his death," said Mattock, his eyes on Oliver. "Any of you gentlemen is at liberty to refuse to answer any questions, or to make a statement, but to my mind there is a link, a connection between the two cases, and I am going to put a few questions. First as to the relations existing between the companies directed by Mr Hoe-Luss, and the Solidaris Company, directed by Mr Caley Burton, of which Sir Eugene Oliver was a director."

"Carry on," said Burton, who appeared perplexed, but calm. "We can tell you all about that."

"Thank you, sir. Then I want to know more about a merger of the two companies, which was mooted, but fell through owing to Mr Hoe-Luss's death."

"Come out into the open!" said Oliver, rather unexpectedly. "What's the link? We may all have our ideas, but why do your people think Simcox was killed?"

Mattock assented. "Very well. I will tell you what we assume to have been the facts with regard to Mr Simcox."

There was a tense silence while he briefly referred to William's death, and the absurd diagnosis of the provincial doctor, only pausing once, to ask me if I agreed with the last point.

"Yes," I said. "I interviewed the man myself. He admitted that it was probably an error of judgment."

"I wondered myself," said Burton. "I had heard Simcox was a skilled botanist, and it seemed unlikely that he would be mistaken. That is why I had a search made of the park. I took it that Simcox spoke the truth about the area he visited, so I only looked into the little wood."

"Would *Russula emetica* not kill?" asked Oliver.

"There might be cases," I said, "but not with normal healthy men. Sickness was about the worst of it, certainly if one allows only a comparatively limited period, as there."

Mattock went on. "Frankly, we take it that some interested party was glad of that wrong diagnosis, or verdict from the doctor. We take it"—and here he went on to explain the police theory of Hoe-Luss's death, winding up with the words, "So the dogmatic denials given to the fungus-poisoning theory, gentlemen, might obviously lead to a reconsideration of the earlier tragedy, especially as one or two malicious people were spreading hints that Mr Hoe-Luss's death had substantially profited one party."

"Which was absurd!" murmured Geyle.

"No one in his senses would believe it," observed Burton.

"That may be so, sir, but this party certainly was, and is, anxious to kill these rumours now and for all time. At any rate, if Mr Hoe-Luss met his death by violence, the man who killed him would be well aware of the effect Mr Simcox produced by his remarks."

"And shut his mouth, to put it briefly," said Burton. "Yes. That is the hypothesis. So we can't consider one case without considering the implications of the other, to which it throws back. If we find how Mr Hoe-Luss was killed, and the motive for it, we may discover who killed Mr Simcox. That is why I told you gentlemen that you can refuse to reply to my questions. Before I go any farther, may I ask if any one of you wishes to see me alone?"

"Let's keep it in committee," said Burton. "What do you say, Oliver?"

"Either way suits me," said the latter.

Geyle lit a fresh cigarette. "Content!" he said. "Seems as good a way as any other." He smoothed down his unruffled hair, and smiled.

Mattock turned to look at Oliver. "Thank you. I believe you are a director of companies, Sir Eugene?"

"Yes."

"Sit on a good many boards?"

"Five, I think."

"Including the 'Solidaris'?"

"Certainly."

"There are directors and directors," Mattock resumed; "some sign cheques and attend board meetings merely."

Oliver brightened a little at the ironic tone. "Yes, that is my kind of job. Vulgarly known as a 'guinea-pig.' But wait a moment. I actually do a little executive work for one company."

"Not the 'Solidaris'?"

"Sir Eugene has no say in the actual management, or administration, of that," said Burton.

"Thank you, sir. I have been informed, Sir Eugene, that you were speculating in the shares of that company a few weeks before Mr Hoe-Luss died?"

Oliver replied promptly. "I had a flutter. Yes. I took it that the projected merger with the other company would hoist the shares a bit."

"You were unaware that Mr Hoe-Luss's French company was not doing well?"

"Hoe-Luss did not tell us his weaknesses, of course," put in Burton. "Business is business."

"I never heard that," Oliver agreed. "But of course the negotiations were carried out between Mr Burton and Mr Hoe-Luss. I backed the project because I thought it would do us good, but I had no responsibility, and only roughly knew that Mr Hoe-Luss was not too willing at first."

Mattock nodded. "Mr Burton here admits that his company discovered a new process, which cut manufacturing costs forty or fifty per cent.," he said. "I don't think he made any secret of it."

"No," he told me that," I said, and looked at Burton for confirmation.

He smiled. "Yes, I did. It's quite true."

"I know now," remarked Oliver, "but I didn't know at the time I was at the château."

"Correct," said Burton. "I had had a report from our researcher, a man called Valmuller, but researchers' reports are like accounts of gold discoveries—they look very promising, but you can't tell at once whether the field contains high-grade ore."

"I understand. You waited to see if there was anything really worth while in the discovery. Then Mr Hoe-Luss died, and of course that upset things for a little."

"Exactly."

Mattock turned again to Oliver. "You play polo, Sir Eugene?"

Oliver began to sweat. Innocent or guilty, he recognised how those sticks might seem to tell against him.

"Yes. I play a good deal. You are going to ask me if Mrs Hoe-Luss promised me her late husband's sticks. She did. I asked Dr Soame here to send them on to me."

"Why not write the request to Mrs Hoe-Luss?"

"I didn't want to trouble her."

"Surely Dr Soame has plenty to fill up his time?"

"Yes, of course. It was inconsiderate of me. But," he glanced at me, "he was a friend. He'd been watching me play polo. It just came into my mind that he would do it for me."

"I didn't mind at all," I said.

Mattock disregarded me. "There were six sticks, square-headed—any broken?"

"None, when I saw them last. Mr Hoe-Luss thought of playing a little on the Riviera later. The sticks went to France."

"Did you know where they were stored in this house?"

"No. No idea."

Geyle gently raised himself on the Chesterfield. "May I second that? Only tell you what I know, of course. No soldier's evidence. I heard Mrs Hoe-Luss tell Oliver that he might have the sticks. Later on, the same day, I heard her tell Porrit to put them in the lumber room. I asked her who was to have them. It seemed to me that she must have changed her mind about giving them to Oliver. But she said no. He could fetch them away later."

"I certainly never knew," said Oliver, looking relieved.

Mattock accepted that. "To get back to these companies. You understood that Mr Hoe-Luss, either to make your side more eager, or because he was not sure of the benefit of the merger, was not at first anxious to sign an agreement?"

"Yes, Mr Burton told me so."

"Did you have any talk with Mr Hoe-Luss about it?"

"Once, at the château. I did my best to persuade him, and he said he appreciated my arguments. Otherwise the negotiations were not in my hands."

"Speaking from personal knowledge, then, you cannot say that Mr Hoe-Luss was actually persuaded to sign?"

"No. It is my own idea that he shied to the last, though I think he would have come in later, if we had been given time to explain the advantages."

"You never saw any agreement signed by him?"

"No."

"Not even a draft?"

"No."

Is it possible to be frightened or excited by quietness, because it is quiet when you do not expect it to be? I think it is. You can sit in court during a murder trial, and let the monotonous flow of evidence, the forensic exchanges of counsel, the apparent drowsiness of the judge, lull you into a serene but placid appreciation of indifferent matters well contested. Then you wake up, and realise that a man is being tried for his life, that the old man on the Bench may suddenly put on his black cap. It hits you like a blow.

I glanced at Oliver. His face gave me a cold shiver. Mattock suddenly nodded to him. "I see, sir. Thank you. You have been very clear."

Burton put the end of his cigar in an ash-tray, and crossed the other leg for a change. Geyle looked at the detective, and then, I thought pityingly, at Oliver, who was mopping his face with a handkerchief. It was a very hot day. The weather broke in the night, and there was a thunderstorm, followed by drizzle for a week. But that day it was blazing, and, even with all the windows open, the room was insufferable.

To all but Geyle, I should have said. He appeared quite comfortable. His face was cool and dry, his hair immaculate. He smoked on steadily, and had an Olympian calm.

"I wanted a word or two with Dr Geyle," said the detective. He shifted a foot, but otherwise seemed anchored to his supporting mantel. "To ask him about a certain process. I suppose, Dr Geyle, you have no objection to my mentioning this before the other gentlemen?"

"Prefer it," said Geyle, with a smile.

"So that we may check the evidence?" volunteered Burton.

There was a knock. Mattock called 'Come in!' and Porrit appeared.

"Tea is ready, sir," he said. "I was to ask if you would rather have it served in here."

Tobey got up. It was the first time he had spoken. "Fuggy here. I think we had better adjourn."

"I shall have my tea here," said Mattock.

Porrit bowed. We all went out, and towards the large drawing-room. Oliver and I were last. He was still sweating, and whispered in my ear.

"Pheugh! That was nasty."

"You passed with honours, I think," I said, as we went into the room where Marie awaited us.

Chapter XXVIII
THE LAST RUBBER

MARIE didn't say a word about the conference which had just taken place. Geyle came out wonderfully, the essence of coolness, and began to talk of the theatre, as if that was the subject nearest our hearts. Burton joined in. Oliver was the last to come to life again. My mind was very busy. It seized on something; a clue, or a hint? Had the whole thing been very irregular, and legally improper? But Chief Inspector Mattock was an experienced officer. I could hardly imagine him making that mistake. He had made it a talk rather than an examination. There was no stenographer present. We had been very vaguely warned that we could refuse to speak. But we had not been specifically or personally warned.

I knew there was a formula that was used, and very properly used. If a police officer suspects that the man he is questioning is guilty of the crime being investigated, he is bound to inform him that anything he says will be taken down, and may be used in evidence against him. And, thereafter, the officer is bound and restricted by very formal rules.

What could I deduce from Mattock's late procedure? Was it that he was unable so far to decide which of the three suspects was guilty? Could it be that he exonerated all, had someone else in his mind?

Joe? Joe was not there, but who was to say that he had come clear out of it? For all I knew, an inspector might have followed him to the north, to interrogate him.

I had heard most of the evidence Mattock was likely to get from the three present, and none of it to my mind suggested a motive for the death of William Hoe-Luss. The means? Yes. Oliver played polo. He could have done it. But so much of the Chief Inspector's interest was reserved for the financial relations of two public companies.

A large cigarette box was on a table by my side. After tea, Oliver found it an excuse, and came over to get a cigarette. He sat down by my side. I was rather apart. Geyle, with the utmost spirit, was contending against the others that realism in acting was a snare. He seemed to be a great student of the French drama, and had a fund of stories.

"What is Mattock up to, d'ye think?" Oliver asked me in a low voice.

"No notion," I said in the same tone; "but it just occurred to me that he hasn't warned any of you."

"Warned us?" Oliver raised his eyebrows. "Oh, I see. Good man! I see."

I heard him sigh faintly. I think he was relieved. He made a motion to take out his handkerchief, then stuffed it away again, as if he knew that the nervous action exposed his perturbation.

"He'll make it clear enough when he wants to," said I.

We found ourselves presently back in the little drawing-room, and I noticed that Mattock had sat down on a chair. He looked less hard like that, and we disposed ourselves more comfortably for the final round, as we hoped it would be.

"I won't keep you very long, gentlemen," said Mattock. "There was the question of this process—the 'Solidaris' process, a secret one, I take it?"

Burton looked across. "Meant to be," he said.

"Thank you, sir. I assumed it to be so. Well, Dr Geyle, the late Mr Hoe-Luss had an inkling that something of the kind was under way. Is that it?"

Geyle smiled. "Yes, that is so. Even the honest card player would like to know what his partner holds—would-be partner in this case."

"Yes. Quite. As you were his scientific adviser, he asked you to look into it?"

"To discover what it was, if I could."

"We are aware what he did, Chief Inspector," said Burton gently. "Any point in going over it again?"

"Oh, you knew later that Dr Geyle had discovered the secret, and informed Mr Hoe-Luss of the fact."

"We heard, of course, that he knew we had got a much more economical process, and we assumed that he had not investigated the matter on his own behalf."

"Then I think I need hardly ask Dr Geyle any more about it, sir."

I looked at my watch. Marie had asked us all to stay to dinner, but I had to see a patient at half-past six, then get back to change, and return. I got up.

"I suppose I am not wanted any longer, Mr Mattock?" I said.

"No, doctor, thank you. There are no further medical points I can refer to you."

I said good-bye to the rest, and drove off to my job.

I was cooler now too, and my mind had begun to simmer down. It seemed to me that Mattock had asked a great deal, and got nothing. I did not see how any man could make bricks with so little straw.

I was now quite obsessed with the idea of Joe. It looked so pointed that he had been left out, when Oliver had come from town, and Burton from Lorraine to talk. True, Joe did not play polo, but he was a champion fly-caster, and the wrists that can flick a fly thirty yards, with a ten-foot trout rod, are clever and steely enough to swing a polo-stick with aim and vigour.

I saw my patient, who was to my satisfaction much better than she believed, and managed to put in a visit to old Caper, who had sent a note down to my house, asking if I would have a look at his knee, which he had knocked on a stake while gardening. I had just time then to change, and drive over to the Chace, as dinner was announced.

Tobey and Mattock had gone. Everyone looked more cheerful, and even Oliver laughed at some of Geyle's witticisms. After dinner, Burton went to his room to write a couple of letters, and the rest of us smoked and talked.

Marie came presently, and sat down by me.

"How did things go?" she asked.

"I have no idea," I said. "The fact is the talk was over my head. I mean it was all business, and the points I missed. I suppose your husband didn't tell you all about his work?"

"Why should he?"

"I take it that French women generally know more than ours about that sort of thing," I said.

"But I am only half French," she smiled, "and that half isn't the business-like half. William was as close as an oyster on some points. And he was old-fashioned enough to think that women could never keep a secret."

"But wives are not women," I said.

She laughed. "William made no exceptions. I could never learn if he was refusing or accepting this merger business. He and Caley Burton were much alike in one thing. They relied on themselves. William had clever men on his board and his staff, but he did the important work himself. I don't think Caley let Oliver into his secrets, any more than William confided in Arthur."

"Geyle?" I asked.

"Yes. I asked William once if he believed that there was nothing to be gained by going in with the 'Solidaris.' Do you know what he said?"

"He thought not?"

She smiled. "No; he said 'You may be sure, darling, that there is nothing to be gained by talking about it!' Succinct, to say the least."

"Did it strike you," I began, when I had digested that, "that the detective seems to have left Joe out of his calculations. He would know at least as much as Geyle, if you are right, and he was the nephew, when all is said and done."

She nodded. "It did strike me. I wondered."

"I suppose," I said tentatively, "that the police haven't got at him privately?"

I had to explain to her then that there was the official formula, and when it was used, and why. She glanced at the clock, saw that it was not yet ten, and rose.

"Joe is still fishing in Northumberland," she said. "I'll ring him up. I expect I can get a trunk call. Don't tell any of the others."

She went out. Oliver and Geyle were so earnestly in talk that they hardly noticed her going, and did not even glance at me. I reached for another cigarette, and did not disturb them. I wanted to hear what Marie had heard, when she was on the telephone.

I was thinking of Jean Murphy, and Etta Vayne. Geyle could stick up for himself; but I was not so sure of Oliver, and his fate.

Marie was away twenty minutes. She came back, and sat down by me, to remark "Nothing doing," in a low, hurried voice.

"Couldn't get through?" I asked as hurriedly, for Geyle had got up and was looking our way.

"Yes, I did, but he has had no word from them," she replied. "Arthur, I've just been speaking over the telephone to Joe. He has had good sport."

"He should have been here for Mattock's fishing inquiry," said Geyle. "Dunno if he'd have called it sport, though."

"I wanted to know if he'd been troubled," she said, smiling, "by our friends, you know."

"Oh, Joe would only kill fish!" said Geyle.

"Any point in dancing that tango over again?" asked Oliver dully.

We dropped the subject, and tried to cheer him up. About twenty minutes later Porrit came in, and said that Chief Inspector Mattock wished to see Marie. She raised her eyebrows, and went out.

I made no comment, but very little was said till she came back again. She looked suddenly old, and very harassed.

"Too bad of the man to worry you so late, Marie," remarked Geyle sympathetically. "He kept you some time."

"Questions?" said Oliver eagerly. "Where's old Burton, by the way? Is he writing a report of the proceedings?"

Marie made a shocked movement of the hands. "He's gone with Chief Inspector Mattock and a sergeant," she said. "I don't know what is happening, but there it is."

We jumped to our feet; even the imperturbable Geyle looked flushed and excited.

"You don't mean they have arrested him?" he cried.

She shrugged her shoulders. "They did not tell me. The man apologised for coming so late, and asked if he could see Mr Burton. I saw them go out together later—to a car the man had outside."

"But, good heavens!" cried Oliver, then stopped.

Geyle's eyes were shining curiously. "That's it. By Jove! I got a notion this afternoon, when Mattock was grilling Oliver here about an agreement. It all seemed to tend one way."

"What way? Don't be cryptic!" I almost shouted in my excitement. "No one else saw it, I am sure."

Geyle looked scornful. "There wasn't any agreement found when William was discovered. If there ever was one, it had gone!"

Oliver stared, then turned to Marie. "But how did Burton know, if he did know, about those sticks, where they were?"

She caught her lip with her teeth, considered for a few moments, and replied, "I remember. Mr Burton was there when I promised them to you, 'Gene."

"Yes, but you didn't say anything to me about the lumber room."

"No, I didn't. But Arthur may have done. Did you, Arthur?"

Geyle nodded. "I think I did. It was after you had told me. Burton came down, and I said that another leaf in the book had been turned over. 'The last of poor William,' I said, or something like that; 'his cherished polo-sticks gone to the lumber room.' I suppose I was feeling sentimental."

"A crack polo player," I said suddenly, "wouldn't use the end of the head, I imagine."

Oliver asked what I meant, and I told him. He sat down suddenly, and put his head in his hands. I warned the others with a gesture to leave him alone.

Chapter XXIX
GRAND SLAM

Oliver suddenly raised his head again. The colour was flowing back into his face, but his eyes were still unnaturally bright.

"I had a look at those sticks, and then forgot to take them," he said.

We all stared at him. Marie found her tongue first.

"What *do* you mean?"

"The afternoon of the day Simcox was killed," said Oliver. "It's worried the life out of me ever since I heard Mattock had taken them away."

"Did anyone see you?" asked Geyle.

"That is what I didn't know. I was coming along the passage on the top floor when someone shut a bedroom door. I hadn't been looking that way. I wondered if one of the servants had seen me, and popped in again." He got suddenly to his feet. "I say, Marie, can I telephone at this time?"

She nodded, and he went out. I knew he was going to get through to Etta Vayne.

"So that's what put the wind up him this afternoon," Geyle said thoughtfully; "that, and the fact that he was a polo player, and in with Burton. I expect, though, that Mattock isn't used to seeing criminals giving themselves away like that, and would draw his own conclusions."

"I am sure of it," I said. "The man who killed Hoe-Luss and Simcox wouldn't sweat like a pig under questioning."

Marie had gone over to the bell, and rung it. Porrit came in.
"Madam?"

"Oh, Porrit. Mr Burton will not be here again to-night."

"Very good, madam."

"Do you remember, shortly after you came, Porrit," she went on, "Mr Burton came here to stay, and was shown over the house?"

The butler reflected. "Yes, madam, it was in the winter, I think."

"Yes, in November. Mr Hoe-Luss was thinking of selling," she said. "He had an idea of living permanently in France."

I remembered that too. When the income tax failed to go down, Hoe-Luss talked for a whole six months about leaving England for good.

Porrit went away. Marie raised her eyebrows. "He went into all the rooms. The lumber room then is the lumber room now."

"Didn't he say he was having a bath?" Geyle asked.

"When that poor boy was killed, yes."

Oliver came back, looking much better. I thought I might ask him a question before I went.

"I suppose the polo-sticks were all there, and unbroken, when you went up," I said.

He nodded.

"I was in the devil of a stew when Mattock hinted that one was broken. I was afraid to say that they were all right that afternoon. It would mean saying I had been up there."

I said good night, and went off home. I wanted to get through to Tobey, if I could, and make sure that Burton had really been arrested, not merely driven off to be examined. But when I tried to get him, I had no luck. He had not come home. So I went to bed, and slept.

I was surprised that I slept so soon, and so well. But I did not wake till eight, and then the whole thing flowed back on me. Patients might wait that day!

I bolted an early breakfast, and drove over to Tobey's house.

He had come in at three in the morning, and was still at his breakfast when I arrived. He poured himself another cup of coffee, and asked me to sit and have a cigarette while he finished.

"So Burton was arrested," I said. "It *was* arrest, I suppose?"

"Yes, he's in jail now, Soame," he replied, nodding. "The right place for the blighter."

"You gave us a tremendous surprise," said I.

"We gave him one!" said Tobey. "Callous and cool as he was, it did jar him. He is to come up before the magistrates to-morrow."

"I thought Mattock was making a dead-set at Oliver all the time," I observed. "Did he never suspect him, really?"

"Oh, he did. He says he thought they were both in it at first, and then he couldn't decide. You can take it from me that, when he stopped asking Oliver questions, he knew that the man was clear. Burton was so anxious to appear disinterested, and disposed to clear Oliver, that he overdid it—just like his display of zeal, when he got a mycologist to visit the park at the château, and send you a sample of all the fungi."

I told him what Oliver had told us last night, and he smiled. "Yes; one of the maids did see Oliver in the upper passage that afternoon. She was going to have a bath, and had just a wrapper on. She dodged back into her room. That's what first put us on the trail of those sticks. But, as Mattock said, the man wouldn't go tramping openly up there, if he intended to do in Simcox with one of the sticks from the lumber room. Still, since he was associated with the 'Solidaris,' Mattock had to watch him."

"The sticks were all right when Oliver saw them," I said, "and I am more and more certain that a polo player, who uses the end of the stick crosswise, wouldn't use it end on."

"Mattock agreed with you there," said Tobey. "It was a clumsy way."

"I suppose you really have a case against Burton?" I asked, as he left the table, and lit up. "I don't see it myself."

He laughed. "But then you didn't know that Scotland Yard had a man sent to Lorraine the day after Mattock came here. Well, they had, and one of their best workers at that."

I was not surprised in a way, though they had kept it dark from me. "I see one part clearly," I said.

"Burton could have made the pretence of taking a bath, and gone up the back stair in the west wing to the lumber room, with the servants all below."

"That is what we take it he did, Soame. He went up, called Simcox's name, and took a crack at his head with the polo stick when Simcox leaned out to look."

"Have you any proof that he killed Simcox at the time he was supposed to be in the bathroom?" I asked.

"Well, that is a convenient position for an alibi, but we had another pointer as well, the fibre of cloth that Mattock found on the window-catch of the lumber room."

"From his dressing-gown?" I asked eagerly.

"No. It was a fibre of pinkish cotton material, Soame. Mattock sent it to their analyst, and he put it through some tests. He said it was from a clean piece of cloth, and finally decided that it came from one of those face-cloths—you know the kind of thing, shaped like a fingerless glove, and made of stuff like towelling of a thin sort."

I admitted that I used one myself. Tobey smiled. "We saw yours, Soame. Geyle had one too, and Burton. Yours was all white, theirs were decorated with a little geometrical design in pink near the hand side."

"I wonder if Burton had any animus against Geyle?" I asked.

He nodded. "You'll see. It was Geyle caused the trouble; indirectly, of course. Mattock says it wouldn't have worried Burton overmuch if Geyle had got the credit for the two jobs."

"So Burton took his towel, and this face-cloth, went to the bathroom, and then hooked it upstairs," I said.

"He put the cloth over his hand to prevent any finger-prints getting on the catch?"

"So we assume."

"Even then you may find it difficult to fasten the job on Burton," I suggested.

"Not with our evidence from France," said he. "The trouble at first was that we were working from the wrong end—very nice logical conclusions from wrong premises. And we were misled by the evidence of people who thought they knew everything about the business side of the affair. We didn't catch them unconsciously tripping, because they told us what they thought was the truth."

I understood him now. "We doctors find the same thing sometimes, if we are in a hurry, and trust to the patient's account of the symptoms, Tobey. The pain they feel 'just here, doctor,' may be just anywhere else. Wrong diagnoses come as often from carelessness as fat-headedness. "

He grinned. "I expect so. At any rate, Mattock had interrogated Mrs Hoe-Luss, and Oliver, and Geyle, and Joe Hoe-Luss. He is not a bad judge of character, and he felt absolutely sure that they were telling the truth about the negotiations in France. He started working up his theory on that basis, and soon found that it was going to be the devil of a job joining his flats."

"He's intelligent enough to change his course, Tobey," I said.

"Absolutely. He came to me, and said he was up against it. We examined the evidence from all angles, and then he rather worried me by saying we must make a fresh start. The man over in Lorraine couldn't get anything. He had visited every typing bureau in the city of Metz, and some outside. He had pumped some of the employees of the 'Solidaris.' But there was nothing worth a snap."

"What did he expect to find?"

Tobey did not answer that, but went on: "So Mattock determined to turn his theories outside in, and had the man switched over to the Château de Luss, and round about. He discovered that Mr Hoe-Luss did not take a secretary with him there, and there was no typewriter in the place—that is to say in the château."

"But why a typewriter?" I asked.

"We took it that a business document would be in type," said he, "and if these negotiations were to be secret, there was a chance that the document would be typed by a French stenographer in a quiet place, who would be unlikely to understand the meaning or significance of the document."

"Did the man find one at last?" I asked.

Tobey lit a fresh cigarette. "Yes, or, rather, found that there had been one. Since there was no machine at the château, it was obvious that the work, if there was such work, had been put out. The inspector on the job went to Vaucol, a small town twenty miles from the château. He heard there that a middle-aged woman, a Mademoiselle Gauge, did typing. He had a talk with her, and she remembered having been commissioned to type a business document in quadruplicate no, that isn't right. She had two copies to make in English, and two in French. She did not know English, so was unable to say if the documents were a French original and an English translation, or separate documents."

"I suppose she was able to tell you what the French copy contained?" I said.

"Partially. It was just a job to her, and the details were muddled or forgotten, for the most part, but she did remember that it was an agreement to combine an English company and the 'Solidaris.' She was quite sure about that."

"Had she destroyed the original script from which she typed it, Tobey?"

He shook his head. "No. It was taken away with the finished copies."

"That explains Mattock's question to Oliver," I said. "He wanted to know if Burton had shown the agreement to him."

Tobey smiled faintly. "You are just where we were—on the wrong track. Here, you say, is Burton trying to force Hoe-Luss's hand, and anxious to get him to agree to the merger, while Hoe-Luss holds out. If that were so, ask yourself (as we had to do eventually) how it could profit Burton to murder Hoe-Luss, and so crash the merger?"

"I have wondered," I said.

"Because you are like a man trying to force a left-hand screw into a right-hand thread," he commented. "But if you were doing that really, you would soon chuck it, and try the other way. But I must say that Mattock and I had the advantage of you, for we knew from the inspector in France that the gentleman who had asked Mademoiselle Gauge to type the documents was William Hoe-Luss."

I stared. "Not Burton?"

"Certainly not Burton. He did not give his name, simply paid in advance for the job, and said he would call next day for the copies. He did call. Mademoiselle was shown his photograph, and recognised it at once. She did not recognise a similar photograph of Burton."

"No wonder you had to face about," I said.

"Mattock is quite an old hand, and pretty cool, but you should have seen him when we got that bit of news," Tobey observed. "He looked quite like a child with the threepenny bit from the Xmas pudding! All the bits of the puzzle now began to fit in."

"So Hoe-Luss was the wooer, not the wooed?" I said.

"They took turns, and Hoe-Luss finished up in that part," said my companion. "Let's call Hoe-Luss's companies *A*, and the 'Solidaris' *B*. *A* was doing pretty well in England, but not so well in France. But *B* was not at first aware of that, and was anxious to share in with *A*."

"Burton wooed Hoe-Luss?" I said.

"Yes, then the head of *B* had news, from a researcher he employed, that there was a chance of discovering a new process, which would be very profitable. His wooing began to lose vigour and heart."

"Then *A* set Dr Geyle to work to discover what was doing?" I exclaimed eagerly, "and he did!"

"So it seems," he replied. "Hoe-Luss concluded that Burton must be brought up to scratch at once, before the researcher could declare positively that he could deliver the goods. He still pretended to the hangers-on, like Oliver and Joe, that he was not anxious to complete the deal. But he asked Burton to the château, and also had a document prepared for his signature, in French and English. I take it that he had a conference with Burton, and told him bluntly he could take it or leave it."

"But would Burton sign like that?" I said.

"You must remember his position, and what he said yesterday about a potential gold-field, Soame. Unless the process was sure to be a success, the company could not go on without the backing of Hoe-Luss. He was afraid to gamble on it."

"But surely that is nonsense," I pleaded. "Geyle discovered that Valmuller had invented a process, therefore Valmuller must have told his employer of it *before* Geyle had the chance to report to Hoe-Luss."

Tobey smiled. "He didn't, and that is the irony of the thing. Geyle discovered the lines on which Valmuller was working, and suddenly saw how it could be done. He had jumped to it just a trifle more quickly than the other man on the research, and did not know it. He dashed over to the château as soon as he could. You were good enough to get the date of the arrival of the guests for us, so we know the time he got there, and informed his employer."

I had wondered why he wanted that schedule of arrivals. "You have proof, of course, that Valmuller only clocked in later?"

He nodded. "Yes. What happened was this. Hoe-Luss got the news, He saw that the 'Solidaris' would be an invaluable ally and partner. He faced Burton with the alternative, merge or not, at once. Burton had had no news from his man. He signed—"

"Can you be sure he signed?"

"If not, where is that document, and what of the four copies, French and English? They cannot be found, though there has been a most thorough search."

"Hoe-Luss may have found Burton obdurate and refusing to sign?"

"We thought of that. We interrogated Burton last night, after we had got him away from the Chace. He swore there was no agreement, that he had seen no document dealing with it. Now, I can imagine Burton refusing to sign, but I cannot imagine Hoe-Luss having these documents, and not showing them to him."

"True," I said. "Go on."

"We made inquiries about telephone messages to the château, during the days before Hoe-Luss's death. About midday, after Geyle's arrival, Burton had had a trunk-call from Metz. The inspector in France went to Metz. No one in the offices of the company had telephoned to Burton. He finally decided to interview Valmuller, who lived in the outskirts of the city. Valmuller, of course, did not understand the significance of the question, but was aware that the process was actually being worked, so made no secret of it. He noticed that he had telephoned on a certain date to Caley Burton. With the help of the local police, the date of that trunk call was confirmed. It was the day after Dr Geyle had arrived at the Château de Luss."

"That fixes it, of course," I agreed; "but isn't it strange that Geyle got ahead of the man who initiated the research?"

Tobey shook his head. "Not so odd as it looks, Soame. Haven't you seen a man at the covert-side keeping his eye on some old stager, who seems to know by instinct which line the fox will take? Of course you have. And the watcher may be better mounted. Once he sees his expert getting away in a certain direction, he overhauls him. I take it that Geyle has the better brain, and was the quicker worker. Once he saw how the thing could be tackled, he got ahead of Valmuller, and was able to tell Hoe-Luss, before Burton knew that the thing was a success."

I understood now. "I don't think it was exactly cricket," I said.

Tobey shrugged his shoulders. "Cricket? They don't play it in this kind of finance. It was what I would call a dirty job, but I expect Hoe-Luss was up against a crowd equally anxious to trump his tricks however they did it."

"You think that made up Hoe-Luss's mind for him?"

"I do," said Tobey. "I take it that he knew the 'Solidaris' was really on a good thing, and would be worth having in a combine. He put it to Burton that he must either sign the agreement he had had typed by Mademoiselle Gauge, or give up the idea. I am quite sure that Burton signed. Then, as I see it, Valmuller telephoned to say that he had solved the problem, and the company had a process at its hand that would mean great profits and lessened costs. It is on the cards that Burton went to Hoe-Luss and wanted to withdraw. At all events, they had a row. We know that. Possibly, Hoe-Luss triumphantly let it out that he knew of the process; possibly, Burton remembered how Geyle had suddenly turned up, and been closeted with Hoe-Luss. That's speculative, but I am sure that Burton was furious at the trick."

"That was natural enough, if it had gone no farther," I said.

"And justifiable enough. I don't even think that Burton went again to see Hoe-Luss, in that study in the tower room, intending to kill him. I think he wanted to argue about it again, to get the agreement torn up. No doubt there was another row. The document may have been before Hoe-Luss, among the papers he had been studying. He may have been feeling ill then, after that meal of fungi. Or he may have hastened the symptoms of sickness—which you agree are slow to appear—by getting excited. At any rate, we have evidence that he was sick. That gave Burton an opportunity. He opened the door; perhaps suggested that the other man ought to go and lie down, took him by the shoulder, ostensibly to help him, and then threw him head first down the stairs."

"In a fit of rage? Quite likely," I said.

"At the moment, yes; but he was quite cool enough afterwards to abstract the papers, for none of the copies has been found, as I said."

I am not much of a business-man, but one objection occurred to me. "I wonder if an agreement, signed without witnesses, would be valid?" I said. "Surely not?"

"Not legally; only as a gentleman's agreement of a kind." He smiled, and added, "I am afraid neither of them acted the conventional gentleman in this affair. It was Greek meeting Greek. Mattock and his inspector in France naturally thought of that. Hoe-Luss had driven Burton out one afternoon, only returning for dinner. If Mademoiselle Gauge and a friend had acted as witnesses, she would certainly have remembered it. It was only after Mattock and I left the Chace, yesterday, that a wire came from France, putting us on the track."

"That there were witnesses?"

"Exactly. Hoe-Luss was too foxy to go back to the little town where Mademoiselle lived. He drove Burton to a place forty miles away, and Burton signed the agreement in the office of a *notaire publique*. We can get witnesses over for the trial."

"I wonder why Burton agreed to such a hole-and-corner method?" I asked.

"I am not much of a business-man either," said Tobey, "but the Scotland Yard expert on such matters says Burton probably engineered a slump in 'Solidaris' before he disclosed the fact that the company had this new process; or it may have been because he thought the agreement with Hoe-Luss would cause a boom in the shares. There is, at any rate, evidence of a slump, and of Burton later buying in all the shares he could get, at bottom prices. He was on velvet when the rise came."

"He has the reputation of being ruthless," I said.

"And is!" replied Tobey. "When young Simcox got in the way later, he had to go too."

Chapter XXX
GAME AND RUBBER

I DID not see Dr Geyle again. I am not very sure that I wanted to renew the acquaintance either. It was all very well for him to say that Valmuller was careless in leaving the materials of his experiments about. He certainly did not carry them to Geyle's place, and dump them. Our imperturbable friend had obviously done a good deal of spying and, possibly, other things that are not to be approved in any system of ethics. Under orders, no doubt, but orders that he could have refused to obey, he had played what Tobey called a dirty trick, slyly picked another man's brains, and helped Hoe-Luss to cozen Burton into a merger that was more profitable to one side than the other.

The fact that Burton was ruthless and conscienceless does not affect the issue.

I felt sorry for Jean Murphy, but I think I have no cause to be. I hear they are ideally happy, and a reasonable knowledge of human psychology ought to have assured me from the first that a man may be untrustworthy in business matters, and a perfect husband to his wife.

Joe, of course, had had nothing to do with the affair. There I had failed again to judge character; prejudiced by his manners, his appearance, and his bitter grousing.

I felt happier about Oliver. I had not been so far out there; though I was at fault to a certain extent when I so easily accepted the polo-sticks as proof that the murder of young Simcox had been the work of a polo player.

The magistrates remanded Burton for trial. I went to town after that for a week end, and was invited by Oliver to lunch with him and Miss Vayne at his flat.

The sight of their obvious happiness took the bitter taste out of my mouth.

"I think I could almost have forgiven him the first job," said Oliver, as we sipped our coffee afterwards. "Hoe-Luss deserved it, or almost. But to do in that wretched boy was the limit. I earnestly hope he gets scragged."

"Don't be so bloodthirsty, 'Gene!" cried Etta. "You know you wouldn't hurt a fly."

"I don't propose to," said he, making a desperate sweep with his napkin at one that came buzzing overhead. "The usual official will do that for us."

"Bad shot!" she said, as the fly flew on. "Do you really think, Dr Soame, that he will be found guilty?"

I nodded. "I think he will."

"We're not going to take our honeymoon in France!" said Oliver.

The trial proper came on a month later, and justice was done?

Not exactly. The trial lasted five days. Countless experts, mycological, pathological, and financial, gave lengthy technical evidence, and counsel for the prosecution explained inevitably the steps which had led Caley Burton to kill Hoe-Luss, to recover an unprofitable agreement, and Hector Simcox, to cover up the former crime.

But he reckoned without a singularly unsubtle jury, which turned a deaf ear to law and logic, and was obviously inspired by the deepest distrust for circumstantial evidence. The foreman put several questions which showed (1) that he did not understand the financial side of the case, (2) that he still believed Hoe-Luss had been poisoned by eating fungi, (3) that he and his fellows were quite willing to return a verdict of murder, if someone would come forward to say that he saw Burton kill William, or, alternatively, throw Hector Simcox out of the window.

It has happened before. It will happen again. The police will look black, and talk bitterly of the jury system. The accused will leave the Court acquitted, and rejoicing.

And yet I do not know that Caley Burton rejoiced much when he was found not guilty. The company saw him no more, and his future as a director in England was at an end.

He went abroad, and presumably changed his name. He may be a prosperous financier once more over there. But I am quite sure his two successful murders will not have inclined him to try the charm of the third!

THE END

Lightning Source UK Ltd.
Milton Keynes UK
UKHW012017120122
397037UK00003B/812

9 781913 054892